AFTER
the
ASHES

DL GALLIE

Edited by **Karen Hrdlicka**, Barren Acres Editing

Proofread by **Lisa Edwards**, More Than Words Proofreading

Cover Designed by **Amanda Walker**, Amanda Walker Design & PA

Special edition cover designed by **Kate Farlow,** Y'All That Graphic.

Interior formatting by **DL Gallie**

I never pictured a life without Kip.

It was supposed to be me and him until the end, but the universe always has a way of screwing things up.

Moving on after losing him wasn't something I thought I was capable of, but when Penn Brookes comes into the picture, I realize I'm not so alone.

Suffering the same kind of loss as me and trying to be the best dad he can, I start to gravitate toward him.

We're one and the same, building our lives around broken pieces, and suddenly, something I never thought possible happens.

That spark I've only felt once before returns and lights something deep inside me.

Can we overcome our grief and build something great, or will the circumstances of the past stand in the way?

SPOTIFY PLAYLIST

Down Under - Men at Work
Wonderwall - Oasis
Never Tear Us Apart - INXS
Every Breath You Take - The Police
Down in Flames - Daughter Jack
I Will Return - Skylar Grey
With Arms Wide Open - Creed
Hello - Adele
Over You - Daughtry
Broken - Seether feat. Amy Lee
Zombie - Bad Wolves
Silence - Blindside
Something in the Way - Nirvana
Eye of the Storm - Blindside
Snuff - Slipknot
Comfortably Numb - Pink Floyd
Wake Me Up When September Ends - Green Day
Fix You - Coldplay
100 Years - Five for Fighting
All The Right Moves - OneRepublic
Two is Better Than One - Boys Like Girls feat. Taylor Swift
She's So High - Tae Bachman
These Days - Powderfinger
So Far Away - Avenged Sevenfold
The Flame - Cheap Trick
Here Without You (acoustic version) - 3 Doors Down
Ashes to Ashes - Faith No More
Lost It All - Black Veil Brides
Heart-Shaped Box - Nirvana
Fall to Pieces - Velvet Revolver
Fear on Fire - Ruelle
Wish You Were Here - Incubus

I See Fire - Janet Devlin
Whiskey in the Jar - Metallica
Far Away - Nickelback
Skinny Love - Bon Iver
Six Feet Under - Billie Eilish
Bluey Theme Tune - Bluey
See You Again - Wiz Khalifa feat. Charlie Puth
One More Light - Linken Park
Someone You Loved - Lewis Capaldi
Through Glass - Stone Sour
Right Left Wrong - Three Days Grace
In The End - Tommee Profitt, Fleurie, Jung Youth
Let Me Down Slowly - Alec Benjamin
Once Last Breath - Creed
Break In - Halestorm
I'll Make Love To You - Boyz II Men
This Layer - The Honorary Title
My Girl - The Temptations
Tennessee Whiskey - Chris Stapleton
I Will Wait - Mumford & Sons

This playlist can be found on Spotify.

"Sometimes you have to kind of die inside in order to rise from your own ashes and believe in yourself and love yourself to become a new person."

— Gerard Way

To all the firefighter superheroes on the front line, thank you!

PROLOGUE

ROMEO AND JULIET MAY HAVE BEEN ON TO SOMETHING, GOING together into the afterlife but there's one problem, I'm not like Juliet, I don't have the guts to take that final step.

You're gone and I'm still here.

My heart is irrevocably broken, and now, I have to live without you by my side, but how do you go on without that one person who was your everything? The person who loved you at your worst and adored you at your best. The person who made you a better human being. How do you go on?

I'm lost.

I'm alone.

I'm without you.

I miss you.

My soul is searching for you, but it will never find you because you're in another place now … and me? I'm still here, breathing. They say with time I'll be whole again but the me from before, that me is gone. That me died alongside you.

Life will never be the same again. I will never be the same again but for you and your memory, I will keep going. I will live for the both of us. I will love for the both of us. My love for you will never waver. You were my first true love and I will never forget you.

Ashes to ashes.

Dust to dust.

You were mine. I am yours. Always and forever.

1

MADDIE

TODAY HAS BEEN HECTIC BUT AT THE SAME TIME NOT. WORKING with Ginny Summers and her daughter on the annual firefighters' ball has been amazing, she sure knows how to throw a party. I kind of wish Penn and I weren't going away so we could attend, but it's our first wedding anniversary and I cannot wait to give him his present. It's not your traditional first anniversary present, but it's amazing nonetheless. As if he can sense I'm thinking about him, my phone begins to ring and when I glance at the screen, my grin widens. "I'm sorry, I need to get this, but if you need anything tonight, I'm just a phone call away."

Walking away from Ginny and her daughter, Tatum, I answer, "Hey, handsome, I was just thinking about you."

"I'm always thinking about you, Mads, always," he replies, causing my heart to skip a beat. How did I get so lucky to be married to a man as sweet as Penn Brookes?

"You are too sweet, husband of mine."

"I'll show you sweet later, wife of mine. I'm out front now."

"I've just finished up with Ginny. Give me five and I'll be out, I just need to run to the ladies. I know how you get about stopping along the way." My husband is not one for stopping when traveling somewhere and with my need to pee every five seconds at the moment, this is going to be one fun car trip. I really should have grabbed some adult diapers for the journey, but I'm sure a blowjob or two will appease Mr. 'we aren't stopping 'til we get there' along the way.

After using the facilities, I wash my hands quickly and before I exit the bathroom, I remove my panties and shove them into my handbag. I'm happy I had the forethought to wear a dress today, giving me another way to get extra points for the excessive pee stops that are bound to occur this afternoon. I'm going to use every sexy trick in the book this weekend.

Stepping outside, I wave at the concierge and climb into our car, making sure not to flash anyone as I do. Nothing worse than flashing your hoo-ha at work, well, for a stripper it would be okay but I'm not a stripper.

"Hi," he murmurs when I climb in. His gaze rakes over my body and leaves a burning trail of desire in its wake.

"Hi," I reply like a giddy schoolgirl whose crush just spoke to her.

"Fuck, babe," Penn hisses as I click my seatbelt into place, "your tits look fucking fantastic in that dress. I'm not sure I'll make it to Lake Collins before I need to fuck you and bury my face in them."

Looking over at my husband, I seductively smile. Reaching into my handbag, I grab my panties and drop them into his lap. "So you don't want to hear I'm not wearing any panties then?"

"You are a cocktease, Mrs. Brookes, and when we arrive, I'm going to fuck you all night long."

"Then hurry up and drive, Mr. Brookes."

He leans over and kisses me, but what was no doubt meant to be a quick kiss on the lips turns into a heated make-out session. Breaking the kiss, Penn winks at me and then takes off. He gets onto the highway and we make our way to Lake Collins.

Three hours, five pee stops, and a roadside blowjob later, we pull into the driveway of the quaint lakeside cabin we are staying in for the weekend. "Penn," I coo as I climb out and take in our home for the weekend, "this is beautiful. It's just like the one we stayed in when we first started dating."

"As soon as I found it, I knew it was the perfect place for our anniversary weekend away. Now, come over here so I can carry you over the threshold."

"Don't you only do that when you get married?"

"If it means I get to hold you in my arms, I'll do it every day." Holy swoon, Batman, and then he makes me swoon harder when he adds, "How did I get so lucky to marry a gal like you?"

"Because you fell, literally, into my lap while I was on a picnic date with Chad Dickton,"—yes, his last name was Dickton … totally matched his dick personality—"three years, two hundred and four days ago."

"You are such a nerd knowing that."

"You love me," I reply with a shrug. "Now, take me inside so I can have my wicked way with you."

"With pleasure."

Penn scoops me up into his arms and we enter the cabin, which is just as gorgeous on the inside as it is on the outside. As soon as the front door clicks closed, it's on. Penn places me on my feet, and the next thing I know, he's bending me over the back of the sofa, my dress is up, and he's sliding his dick into me from behind.

"Yes," I mewl. He reaches around to cup my boob, earning himself another moan. Slipping his hand inside the material, he pinches my nipple and I gasp at the sensation. Since becoming pregnant—FYI, that's my anniversary surprise for Penn—they have been so much more sensitive. The pressure sends an electrical current straight between my thighs and if it wasn't for the sofa beneath me, I'd be in a heap on the carpet. "I want to ride you," I pant.

Penn obviously likes the sound of that because he pulls out of me, spins me to face him, places his hands under my ass, and lifts me up. Wrapping my legs around his waist, he steps around the sofa and drops down with me in his lap.

Lifting to my knees, I lock my eyes on my husband's and slowly sink down on his cock. "Yesss," I hiss. I love fucking Penn in this position. He always hits that magical spot and I can watch the pleasure on his face up close and personal … plus he can play with my boobs.

As if he's in my head, he slides the straps of my dress off my shoulders and pushes the bodice down, exposing my tits to the cool, yet heated, cabin air. "Fuck, babe, your tits look huge today."

"Mmmhmpf," I moan. "Suck them," I demand.

Leaning forward, he cups my plump mounds, pushes them together, and then attacks them. Like a starved man, he licks and sucks them as I continue to ride him. It's sensation overload, and together we both tumble over the edge. He covers my mouth with his and we kiss our way through our climaxes.

Resting my forehead against his, I whisper, "I love you, Penn Brookes."

"I love you too, Maddie Brookes."

2

PENN

OUR ANNIVERSARY WEEKEND STARTED OFF WITH A BANG—PUN totally intended. If I thought the roadside blowjob was out of this world, that welcome fuck when we arrived was hot. H O double T hot. I have the best wife in the world. How did I get so lucky to snare a woman like Maddie? Truth be told, I was in lust from the moment I laid my eyes on her, she didn't know I existed until I fell, literally into her …

… *I was walking toward the coffee shop across from the park when from the corner of my eye, I spotted her. Stopping in my tracks, I watched her. She was sitting on a bench underneath the cherry tree in bloom, a textbook in her lap, and a pencil shoved into her hair that was up in a messy bun. She was wearing denim shorts and a navy-blue tank top. Understated but ohh so fucking sexy. I was in lust with her with that one glance, but then Chad 'I'm a fucking douche' Dickton arrived and kissed her on the cheek. Her face lit up at his arrival and mine, well, it crashed. It was no wonder a hottie like her was taken, but with him? Ugh, that was a prover-bial kick in the nuts.*

For weeks after that, I'd watch her from the coffee shop. She was always studying and he was always there, by her side, distracting her. I still remember the day as if it were yesterday when we spoke for the first time. She was sitting on a blanket with that dick, on another picnic date. She looked less than impressed and seeing that gave me hope that maybe one day, I'd get a chance to have a picnic in the park with her too.

With my iced coffee in hand, I decided to cut through the park to get to the train station, something I normally wouldn't do. My phone rang and I quickly answered it when I heard my mom's ringtone. I was distracted by Mom telling me something about the next-door neighbors and their trash cans or some crap when out of the corner of my eye, I see a random donkey running toward me. With my phone to my ear, and still mumbling "Mmmhmpf" to Mom, I turned to face the donkey and slowly, I began walking backward. With my eye locked on the lil' mofo, I continued to step backward. It was like that ass was a heat-seeking missile and I was his target. With my eyes locked on the donkey, I wasn't watching where I was going, and then it all went horribly wrong.

One minute, I was standing up, walking backward away from a stray ass, and the next, I was on my back in the middle of my dream girl and Chad Dickton's picnic. My head landed in her lap and I found myself staring up into the most amazing emerald green eyes I had ever seen. My iced coffee was all over Chad, whipped cream sliding down his face.

A growl from him snapped my attention away from her and when I looked at his coffee and cream-covered head, I began to laugh. This caused her to laugh as well. Our laughter increased when the crazy donkey joined us ... and started to lick the cream off of Chad.

My dream girl and I were laughing like hyenas meanwhile Chad was growling and swatting at the donkey to get it away from him. Seems the ass, liked the ass.

Chad jumped up and stormed away, grumbling, "This isn't fucking funny," leaving us cackling at his retreating form. He climbed into his truck and pulled out into traffic, cutting off someone in the process.

"Bye," she yelled out, "I'll pack all this up."

"Would you like a hand?" I asked her.

She turned her attention back to me. "Well, it's the least you and your donkey can do."

"It's not mine," I quickly informed her.

"I guessed that, since the tag around his collar says 'Property of Millerton Petting Zoo,' and if you ask me, you look more like a miniature pig kind of guy."

"And what does a donkey kind of guy look like?"

"Chad," she replied with a shrug. "Asses like asses."

That caused us both to start laughing again. "You have the most amazing green eyes," I told her.

"And you have an amazing smile," she threw back at me. "I'm Madeline, my friends, well everyone, calls me Maddie."

"I'm Penn, my friends call me Penn."

"I'd like to be your friend, Penn whose friends call him Penn."

"I'd like that, Maddie." A beautiful name for a beautiful girl, *I think as I continue to stare up at Maddie. She stared back at me and everything around me faded away. All I saw was Maddie, our new donkey friend, and a budding friendship ... or maybe more.*

"What are you grinning about?" Mads asks me, dropping onto the sofa next to me with a towel wrapped around her after her shower. She places her head in my lap, the reverse of the memory I was just thinking about.

"The day we met when that stray donkey tried to attack me."

"I still maintain that donkey knew Chad was an ass and that you were the one for me. He set the whole thing up."

"Yes, Donny the Donkey from the Millerton Petting Zoo played matchmaker that day."

"If he hadn't, you never would have grown a set of balls and come up to speak to me."

"I would have ... maybe."

"Let's agree to disagree, Penn, but whatever the case, I'm glad that ass ran off the other ass because I ended up falling in love with your ass."

"So, you only love me for my ass?"

"Among other things." She winks up at me.

Leaning down, I press my lips to hers. "I fucking love you, Madeline Brookes, and I cannot wait to grow old with you. And see your belly swell with a baby." Her eyes widen at my baby declaration. "What?"

"Give me a sec." She jumps up, her fluffy towel falls to the floor, leaving her naked as the day she was born. She races over to her handbag and pulls out a long narrow gift box.

"I thought we said no presents."

"YOU said no presents, but this is more of a gift for both of us so, really, it doesn't count."

She walks back over to me and straddles my lap. My cock twitches between us, knowing with one flick of my hips, I could be balls deep inside of her again. You know, nudists might be on to something. She shakes her head as if she can read my mind and hands me the gift box. "Happy anniversary, husband of mine."

"I really feel like an ass." I wriggle my eyebrows at the use of the word ass. "Because I really didn't get you anything."

"And we agreed not to, we're saving for a house but, Penn, this"—she nods to the box in my hands—"it didn't cost a lot. Trust me and I promise, it's something we can both use."

"Is it that new wee vibe thingy?"

"Yes, I bought us a dildo for our anniversary." She shakes her head. "Just open it, will you?" She squeezes my cock. "And then I can take care of that with my mouth again."

"You're such a blowjob whore," I tease her.

"I'm your blowjob whore."

"You can be my blowjob whore anytime you like."

"Well, hurry up and open our gift and then I can be your blowjob whore once again."

Placing a quick kiss on the tip of her nose, I shake the box. Whatever is inside rattles, but I have no idea what it could be. Lifting off the lid, I stare down at the stick and the first thing I notice is the two pink lines in the little window. My gaze flits from the test and up to Mads's eyes and back down again. "Is this? Are we? We're …"

Nodding, she smiles. "Yep, we're pregnant."

"Holy fucking shit, Mads. You've just made me the happiest man in the entire fucking world."

"Well, I'm about to make you even happier."

She slides off my lap, opens her mouth, and shows me just why she's a blowjob whore. My blowjob whore and the mother of my child. Life could not be more amazing than it is right now.

3

TATUM

... one year later

"You be sure to text me every day," Mom demands, pulling me in for another hug. She lets go of me and takes my hands, squeezing them tightly. "And we will do that FaceTime chat thing once a week, I don't care about the billion-hour time difference, I need to see my baby girl's face," Mom tearfully cries before dropping my hands and pulling me in for another hug outside the TSA checkpoint.

"I promise, Mom," I tell her, holding on a little tighter.

Today, Kip and I are flying to Australia. His stint in Lockhart Falls has come to an end, but I wasn't ready to say goodbye to him, or us. So, I reached out to the captain, Dave Sinclair, at the Bauckle Bay fire station—it's so weird calling it a fire station and not a firehouse, but after being with Kip for over a year now, I'm used to the weird Aussie language and the way they speak—and arranged an exchange similar to Kip's.

"She'll be fine, Ginny," Dad's rough voice says from next to Mom. Before I can blink, he's pulling me away from Mom and he's the one now enveloping me in a hug. "I'm going to miss you, Tater Tot, but I know you're going to do good things in Australia."

"Thanks, Dad," I whisper, swallowing back the lump forming in my throat.

Don't get me wrong, I love Mom, but Dad and I have this bond that I can't explain. Hugging him just now, I realize that I'm moving to the other side of the world, and this might be my last Dad hug for a long time.

"I'm going to miss you, Dad," I tearfully sniffle.

"You crying, Tater Tot?"

"No," I huff, "there's dust in my eyes."

"Mmmhmpf, sure ... but for what it's worth, there's dust in my eyes too."

Lifting my head, I see Dad's eyes all glassy and seeing him so emotional causes the dam to break. Tears are now cascading down my cheeks and my vision is blurry. "Damn dust," I blubber, pressing my face into his shoulder as I cry and cry. Dad holds me tighter, and Mom joins us, making me the meat in a Mom and Dad hug sandwich.

"We can stop at the liquor store and you can get me my bottle of Johnny Walker Blue," Dad brags to Mom, squeezing me tighter in his arms.

My head snaps up. "You guys bet, again?"

In unison, they reply, "What happens in Bet Club—"

"Stays in Bet Club," I finish and then the three of us laugh. Shaking my head, I reach behind to one-arm hug Mom. "I'm going to miss you guys so much."

"What about me?" Kain playfully whines from behind me. "Can I get in on this hug action?"

Looking over my shoulder, I grin at my brother. "Meh," I tell him with a shrug.

"I hope a drop bear eats you while you're in Australia," he throws back at me.

Rolling my eyes, I pull away from Mom and Dad and open my arms toward Kain. He opens his and beckons me forward in a come-hither move with his fingers. Shaking my head, I walk over to him and wrap my arms around his waist. "Gonna miss you, Brozart," I mumble into his chest.

"I'm not going to miss you," he teases and then I hear a sniffle. Looking up, I see Kain is trying to hold back tears.

"Looks like I'll be getting two bottles, Ginny. Kain was the first to cry."

Kain and I pull apart, we stare at our parents and shake our heads at them.

"Thanks, kids," Mom playfully drawls.

"You're welcome," Kain and I reply in sync and we both take a bow. I'm really going to miss my family but at the same time, I'm excited for the adventure ahead.

The overhead speaker crackles, reminding me that we need to go. We need to get through TSA so we don't miss our flight and this time, there are no hair clips in my hair to set off the machines, earning myself a pat down from Big Bertha, who I think enjoyed it a little too much. "We better go," I mutter but no one moves. The four of us, well, five, including Kip, just stand here, our gazes flicking from one to the other. "I'm … I'm going to miss you guys," I repeat, my eyes once again filling with tears.

"Come on, babe," Kip says, sliding his fingers through mine, giving me the lifeline I need right now.

"Mmmhmpf," I reply with a nod, but I still don't move. They call the flight again, "Guess I better go," I murmur but still, I don't move.

"Guess you better," Dad grumbles.

Kain urges, "Go on, git," in a weird accent.

And Mom, she just stands there with tears tracking down her cheeks, staring at me.

"Mooom," I cry, and I literally begin to sob now. Those tears I was holding back are now falling like the waterfall at Lockhart Falls. They continue to flow down my cheeks as the four of us step together for a group hug. Kip is behind me, but Dad reaches out and pulls him into the hug too. The five of us hug and cry at the TSA gate.

Finally, we break apart but none of us are in a rush. Sure, I'm excited to go to Australia but I'm going to miss my family like crazy. "You look after my baby," Dad warns Kip.

"With my life," he replies.

Dad nods and offers his hand to Kip. Kip takes it and then Dad pulls him in for a hug. Dad whispers something to Kip and he nods, looking back at me, and then turning his gaze back to Dad.

"He's a good one," Mom whispers, bumping my shoulder. "Go and have the adventure of a lifetime, Tatum."

Nodding, I swallow deeply and know that if we don't move now, we'll miss our flight. Hugging everyone once again, Kip and I join the line for screening.

Two hours later, we're sitting on the plane, all buckled in. The aircraft is taxiing out to the runway for takeoff. Looking over at Kip, my heart races in the way it always does when I look at him, and a sense of calm, of being home washes over me. He is the love of my life, and I cannot wait to embark on this journey with him.

4

KIP

… four years later

Flopping onto my back, I stare up at the ceiling, panting and completely spent. My heart is racing after making love to my fiancée, yep, Tate and I are engaged. I slapped a ring on her finger and soon she will be mine forever.

She snuggles into my side, throwing her leg over mine, and absentmindedly, she runs her fingertips through the smattering of hairs on my chest. Resting her hand over my heart she murmurs, "I love you, Kip Kitson."

"And I love you, Tatum Prudence Summers." Smiling, I place a kiss on her head and wait for it.

"Ugh, you had to middle name me?"

"Yep, sure did."

"You're lucky I love you, Kitson."

"Hell yeah, I am. The day you agreed to marry me was the happiest day of my life."

"I thought the happiest day was when you fought your first fire?"

"It was … until you said yes that is."

"Aww, you're too sweet."

"I know," I cockily reply.

"Modest too."

"Yet, you still love me." She digs me in the ribs. "Hey, that hurt."

"Aww, does the big bad firefighter want me to kiss it better?"

Placing my finger under her chin, I lift until her eyes are on mine. I stare into her hazel orbs and wink. "I know something else you can kiss." Raising my eyebrows suggestively, I gently run my palm down her side and across her stomach. With my eyes still locked on hers, I circle her navel before ever so slowly sliding my fingertip toward her pussy. Sure, we just finished making love but when I have a naked and wanting Tate in bed ... or the room ... or anywhere, I'm ready to go in the blink of an eye.

Rolling to her back, she widens her legs for easier access and raises her eyebrows suggestively back at me; minx. So I turn the path of my fingers around and head back up her stomach toward her tits. Her glorious tits. She growls, causing me to laugh.

She opens her mouth to speak but before she can utter a word, I cup her breast with my palm and gently squeeze. Leaning forward, I take her nipple into my mouth and suck. A pleasurable moan slips through her lips and while she's focused on my mouth on her boobs, I slide my other hand down the path from before and apply some pressure to her clit. "Yessssss," she mewls, wriggling beneath me at the pleasure being laved on her breasts and clit.

Slipping my middle finger through her wet folds, I plunge it deep inside her, again earning myself another moan. I'm not sure if she's turned on by this or if it's remnants from our lovemaking only moments ago, but whatever the case, my fiancée's pussy is soaked.

Lifting my head, with my eyes locked on hers, I pump my finger in and out. Adding a second digit, I slow down my ministrations as I lean forward and press my lips to hers. My tongue slides in and out in sync with my fingers in her pussy. Breaking the kiss, I stare down at Tate. Her eyes are closed, her cheeks are stained pink, and she's lost to the pleasure currently building inside of her.

"I'm close," she murmurs and I know she is, her walls are clenching around my fingers. Leaning down, I suck and bite on her nipple and she screams her release into our bedroom. I continue to thrust my fingers in and out until she collapses into the mattress below.

She's still coming down from her orgasmic high when I lift her up onto my lap. My rock-hard shaft slides through her lips and without me saying anything, she lifts to her knees and lowers herself down onto my cock. When she's fully seated, she begins to rock her hips in circles, grinding her clit on my pelvis.

Lifting her hands, she fondles her breasts. Not wanting to miss out, I lift my hands and slide my fingers through hers. Together we massage her tits and tug on her nipples until they're stiff peaks. We repeat the action over and over as she continues to ride me.

Sitting up, I hold her to my chest, and she wraps her legs around my waist. I piston my hips up as she thrusts down. I bury my face in her tits and lick her skin. Taking a nipple into my mouth, I gently bite down on the tip. She moans and the sound resonates in my balls and they begin to tingle. Tate reaches behind her and squeezes them. "Babe, if you do that again, I'm going to explode before you do."

"That's okay," she breathlessly pants, "I'm already an orgasm up on you."

"No, it's not okay, besides you should always be at least two up on me," I growl through clenched teeth as I thrust up harder into her.

"Mmmhmpf," she moans, not hearing a word I just said because she's in the zone, the orgasm zone. Leaning forward,

I suck her nipple harder, garnering a guttural growl from her. Sliding my hand down between us, I pinch her clit. She hisses and drops her head back. Another deep throaty moan slips from her lips and her walls clench my cock. She grunts, "I'm coming" just as her body locks up and she tumbles over the edge. Moaning in that 'ohhh fuck. ohhh fuck. ohhh fuck' kind of way.

The sounds coming from her set me off and together we ride out our climaxes.

Tatum lifts her head and gazes into my eyes, both of us panting and completely spent. The love we feel for each other radiates between us with that one look. Our moment is interrupted when my phone pings with the station's alert tone. Soon after Tatum's beeps too. We look quizzically at each other.

Reaching over, I grab my beeping phone and read the message. "Shit," I mumble. "This is bad, epically bad."

5

PENN

"Happy birthday to you, hip hip. Hooray," everyone sings to our lil' man.

Fletcher stares at the flickering candle, mesmerized by the flame. He's always been obsessed with fire trucks and fire, hence his fire truck-themed fifth birthday party.

"You need to blow, baby," Mads encourages Fletcher.

"That's what she said," I mumble under my breath, earning myself a glare from my irresistible wife. However, underneath said glare is also her 'I'll be happy to 'blow' you once Fletcher is down for a nap and all our guests have left' look. My first thought is, *let's kick all these fuckers out right now, no one needs cake*. Then I look to our son and know that my blowjob will have to wait. I'm such a good dad, putting my son's birthday party ahead of myself getting a blowjob.

"I can't believe Fletcher is five already," my mom says, joining me as we watch Mads and Fletcher distribute the cake.

"He'll be off to college before we know it," Teri, Maddie's mom adds. "It only feels like yesterday we were celebrating Madeline's fifth birthday."

Mads rolls her eyes at the conversation and shakes her head. "Mom, I'm twenty-eight now—"

"And you'll always be my baby girl," Teri interrupts. "Just like Fletcher will always be your baby boy." She looks to Mom. "Am I right, Samantha?"

Mom nods. "Yep, Penn may be thirty, but he'll always be my baby."

"You two need to lay off the chardonnay," I tease them.

"We're having margaritas, thank you very much." The two of them clink their glasses and take a sip. My mom and Teri are like Thelma and Louise, and it makes me so happy my mom and dad get along with my in-laws. Actually, I love that both our families get along so well together. I couldn't imagine not getting along with my in-laws. I really won the jackpot when it comes to the Hollyfields.

"Do I need to separate you two? Again?"

"Noooo," they both singsong and adding more fuel to the fire, Dad walks in with the pitcher of margaritas and fills up their glasses.

"It's a shame your sister couldn't make it here today," Mom states, a sadness washing over her. "But she just started that new job with Life's Too Sport and couldn't get away."

"How's Wren liking it?" I ask, feeling a little bad because I haven't had a chance to call and catch up with her lately, but life has been crazy recently.

"She loves the job but her newest client is some hockey person. She says he's a doucheman or something or other."

"Are you referring to Stefan Däuchmen?"

"That's the one." She nods.

As she says this, she gets this look on her face. I have a feeling I know why but I ask anyway, "What's with the face?"

"I think she found her future husband."

"You said that about the guy at the grocery store too, Mom."

"I know I did. I was certain he was the one for her, just

turned out I was certain she'd found her best friend, not her husband, but this time, Penn, I feel it in my bones. Wren and this douacheman are meant to be. It's just like I was with you and Maddie and look how you two turned out?"

"You and your feelings," I reply, still shaking my head and grinning. When Samantha Brookes gets one of her 'feelings' she's not often wrong, well, except for the grocery store guy. "Looks like I'm going to have to give my baby sister a call, check out this Stefan guy." And if what I've read online is anything to go by, she needs to steer clear of Stefan Däuchmen because he apparently lives up to his moniker of Doucheman.

"Leave your sister alone," Mom admonishes me. "You might be thirty, Penn Brookes Jr., but I will tan your ass if you torment her."

"Ohhhhh, you just got juniored," Mads teases me, sliding her arm around my waist. "What did you do?"

"Nothing," I defensively reply, while Mom says, "He's gearing up to taunt his sister."

"About what?"

"Her new client," I inform my sexy-as-hell wife.

"Stefan? Why?"

"How do you know about him?" I question her.

"We spoke on the phone the other day. She was telling me how he's been riding her ass since she started, and he's the first client she's wanted to physically strangle."

"I'm sure she'll be riding him soon … according to Mom."

"Penn," all the women surrounding me growl, earning myself another slap in the stomach from Mads.

"What?" I hiss. "If Mom's feeling crap is true, that'll happen or it already is happening."

"That might be the case, Penn, but do you have to be so crass about it?" Mom replies, shaking her head at me.

"Okay, is this better …" I drift off because I can't think of a nicer way to say that my sister is fucking her hockey player.

"You can't think of a nice way to say it, can you?" Mads teases me, poking me in the ribs.

"Yes, I can, I'm just …"

"Full of shit," she teases me, "but that's okay 'cause I love you, regardless of that." She lifts to her tippy-toes and presses her lips to mine. The kiss starts off PG but when she pushes her tongue into my mouth and makes that little moan sound that I love, it becomes X-rated. The spell surrounding us is broken when someone clears their throat, my bet is on Dad. He's not one for public displays of affection and when Mads and I pull apart, I was right. Dad is looking at us. Shocking me, he nods toward the hallway and our bedroom, and lifts his hands, flashing them in a 'you've got ten' kind of way.

Nodding at him, I take Mads's hand in mine and tug her down the hallway, into our bedroom—making sure to lock the door—and into our en suite, where I also close and lock the door. Spinning my sexy-as-hell wife around, I press her into the door and cover her mouth with mine. One hand cups her boob, again earning me another throaty sexy moan. My other hand skates down her body, bunching the hem of her sundress in my hand. I push it up until I can slide my hand into her panties. "You're already wet," I whisper against her lips.

"I'm always wet around you, dear husband of mine."

Running my fingertip over the top of her panties through her slit, she thrusts herself forward into my hand. "Please," she begs, and hearing her beg like that causes me to smile.

Dropping to my knees, I pull her panties down and she kicks them off. Leaning forward, I breathe in and I'm assaulted with her scent. My cock hardens but right now, this is all about her. Nuzzling my nose against her cleft, my tongue darts out and I lick up her slit. Circling her clit, I gently nip the bundle of nerves before I slide my tongue back down through her folds. Her arousal coats my tongue. "Fuck, babe, you taste like heaven."

"Less talking, more licking," she demands.

I can't help but chuckle, but I want the same thing, so I give her exactly what she wants. Plunging my tongue into her slit, I look up and watch the pleasure wash over her. Her head drops back and hits the door, her eyes are closed, and she focuses on my tongue thrusting in and out of her. She opens her eyes and stares down at me, the look she gives me is sexy as hell. Freeing myself from my pants, I grip my cock and squeeze as I continue to suckle on her pussy.

Surprising me, she pushes on my head, pushing me away from her. "I ... I need to ride you."

I'm not going to pass up the opportunity to fuck my wife, so I quickly pull my pants and briefs down and drop to my ass. My cock stands up straight, hard and proud, the veins on the side throbbing with the need to be inside her. She lifts her dress up and over her head, leaving her naked before me. "No bra?"

"Nope, you know I hate those death contraptions."

Once again I chuckle, but that chuckle soon disappears when she steps over to me and lowers herself down onto my shaft. There is no better feeling in this world than when my cock slides into her. We both moan at the intrusion, when she's fully seated, she rests her hands on my shoulders and begins to ride me. My dick slips in and out of her hot, wet channel. Our eyes are locked on one another, nothing exists in this moment except for the two of us.

She leans forward and covers my mouth with hers. She pushes her tongue into my mouth, thrusting it in and out in sync with my dick thrusting in and out of her pussy. Lifting my hand between us, I cup and massage her boob. She leans back, resting her hands on my thighs, giving me free access to her tits, her gorgeous perfect tits. Cupping both of her plump mounds in my hands, I massage. She moans in that way that has my already hard cock, hardening further. "Suck them," she whispers, and she doesn't have to ask me twice.

Leaning forward, I lick the tip of her nipple before wrapping my lips around the stiff peak and sucking, gently biting down. She likes that because I feel her pussy walls clench around me. Biting again, she once again clenches. "You keep clenching like that and I'm going to come."

"Do it," she pants.

"Not before you, you know the rules."

"Me before you," she breathlessly whispers.

"Yep, you before me," I repeat.

"Then you better fuck me harder, Penn."

"That's such a hardship but I guess I can comply."

"Shut up and fuck me, Penn."

"Yes, ma'am." I slide my arms around her shoulders, holding on to her and I begin to fuck her harder. My hips thrust up when hers thrust down. We fall into a punishing rhythm that has my whole body tingling, and soon I feel that buzz in my balls. I'm not going to be able to hold out much longer, but she needs to come and she needs to come now. Slipping my hand between us, I find her clit and circle the pad of my finger around it.

"Penn," she growls my name. Digging her fingers into my back, if I was shirtless, she would draw blood. Her eyes roll into the back of her head. Her head drops back. Her body stiffens and I feel the moment she shatters. I feel the moment her walls tighten around my cock and she showers me with her release. Seeing her let go sets me off and I follow her into an orgasmic blissed-out state. We milk every last ounce of our release from one another.

Resting my forehead against hers, we stare at each other panting. Our hearts racing. "I love you, Penn Brookes Jr."

"And I love you, Madeline "Mads" Brookes nee Hollyfield."

She giggles and the sound is music to my ears. "What's so funny?"

"I can't believe we just snuck away from our son's

birthday party to have a quickie in the bathroom. We're parents now, we're supposed to be responsible."

"We are responsible, it would have been irresponsible of us to do this in the middle of the living room, even if in the middle of that room is where he was conceived."

"Penn," she hisses, slapping my chest.

"What?" I defensively ask.

She shakes her head at me but she's trying to school that gorgeous smile of hers—so I know I'm not in any trouble—and if I was, well, I'd just push her to her back and fuck her again. I could fuck her all day, every day. I lucked out the day she said yes to marrying me. I'm one lucky son of a bitch. I have the perfect wife, an amazing son, and an auto repair shop that is thriving. Nothing, and I mean nothing, can bring me down.

6

KIP

WHEN OUR PAGERS WENT OFF SEVENTY-TWO HOURS AGO, WE HAD an idea of what we were walking into, but we were wrong. Absolutely wrong. This fire is catastrophic, in all my years as a firefighter, I've never seen a blaze firsthand like this. You see reports of wildfires in California or the horrific fire that ravaged the Amazon jungle a few years ago but this? Here? In Australia? Never have I ever seen anything like it. This fire is currently ravaging my home state of New South Wales. Most of the state is ablaze right now. There's fire from the Queensland border, down to the Victorian border, and across to the South Australian/Northern Territory borders. Hell, there are fires in every other state too, but the one in New South Wales is the deadliest of them all.

Some smaller towns in the outback have been wiped out and farther down the coast at Thrifton, fifteen people were trapped on a small island off the coast. They left it too late to evacuate and became trapped. Thanks to the efforts of a fishing trawler and an old guy in a tinny, they were rescued … and issued with hefty fines for their stupidity.

With the whole of New South Wales literally on fire right now, we need all the help we can get. When Tate's little brother, Kain, heard about it, he jumped on the first flight from the US to come and help us out. He's due to arrive later today. Mr. Summers wanted to help but I learned that he's scared of flying. There's no way he could handle the flight, hence why in the last three years we have always flown back to the States to visit. Mrs. S. has convinced him to cruise both ways, so later this year they are going to come out for a visit, and Tate and I are considering getting married while they are here.

We've decided to have a ceremony here and another back in Lockhart Falls. That way all our friends can be with us to celebrate our special day. I still remember the day I took both Mr. S. and Kain to the bar at The James Hotel to ask them permission to marry Tate. They gave me their blessing without an ounce of hesitation, but not before Kain gave me the "You hurt my sister, I'll kill you" speech. That day with them was the scariest of my life and I run into burning buildings for a living, so that's saying how ferocious he was about Tatum, but I get it. When Tatum and I have a daughter, I'm pretty sure I'll react the same way the first time she brings home a boy.

"You look like shit," Tatum declares when she steps into the break room and sees me. She walks toward me and my eyes rake over her body. Even though she's covered in soot and is all sweaty and gross, she's still the most beautiful woman I've ever seen.

"And you look gorgeous," I throw back at her, standing up to kiss her hello.

"Sweet talker," she coos, walking into my open arms. She slides hers around my waist and gazes into my eyes. "I love you."

"I love you too." And I mean it, I love her to the moon and back. She lifts up and presses her lips to mine. What starts out as a sweet kiss, quickly turns heated. She pushes me back onto the couch and straddles my lap. "Think we have time to head home for a quickie before we have to pick up Kain?"

"Yes, the answer is always yes when it comes to sex, but it will have to be a super quick one 'cause we both need to shower and freshen up. I don't think airport security would like us being there all covered in soot and sweat and sex."

"I have the perfect suggestion for that."

"And what might that be, oh wise one?"

She grins at me and suggestively waggles her eyebrows. "Two words, shower sex."

"You clearly have the looks and the brains in this relationship."

"You have the looks too." She leans in and whispers, "And the best dick." She circles her hips as she says this and my cock instantly hardens. She jumps up and nods toward the door. "Let's go."

Groaning, I stand up and readjust myself. Tatum laughs and when I look at her, I shake my head and roll my eyes. She beckons me forward with her finger and as I do when it comes to her, like a moth to a flame I walk toward her. Lacing my fingers with hers, we say our goodbyes to the crew and head out to my ute, or as Tate calls it an SUV. We race home for a quickie and a shower before heading to the airport to meet Kain.

Stepping through the front door, we immediately strip off our clothes, leaving a breadcrumb trail of garments as we make our way to the shower. By the time we make it to the bathroom, we are as naked as the day we were born, and my cock is rock-hard and weeping for Tate. She reaches into the shower and turns the taps on, as much as she likes to tell me it's a faucet, we're in Australia now and it's a tap.

While we wait for the water to heat up because we have a

hot water system that's old and crap, Tate pushes me against the vanity and covers my mouth with hers. Her tongue pushes past my lips, caressing and tangling with mine while her hands explore my body. My skin tingles under her touch and when she wraps her dainty hand around my shaft, I hiss at the contact. She grips the base and flicks her wrist, up and down she tugs on my shaft, giving me the most amazing hand job.

The room fills with steam and what was meant to be a quickie is anything but a quickie. Before we make it to the shower, I come just from her playing with my dick. Wanting to return the favor, I drop to my knees and bring her to her knees—metaphorically speaking—with my tongue and fingers.

Licking my lips after she drenches my face with her release, I lift her into my arms and before I step into the shower, my once again hard dick slides inside her. Pressing her against the shower wall, the water beats down on us as I fuck her hard and fast, finally we get to the quickie part. We both scream out each other's name when we come.

Placing her back on her feet, she gives me one last kiss before we begin to wash ourselves. Being the gentleman that I am, I soap up my hands and begin to wash Tate. My soapy hands wash her back before sliding around to her front to soap up her breasts. Her soapy hands slide behind her and she cleans my cock. Gripping it tightly in her palm, she spins around in my arms and my eyes drop to her soapy chest. She's gloriously wet and naked. Even though we've both just come twice, the want and desire in her eyes reflecting back at me has me lifting her up and fucking her again. This time it's hard and fast, the epitome of a quickie.

After orgasm number three, our sexual urges have been satisfied and we get washed. Climbing out, we re-dress and then head out to my ute and make our way to the airport to collect Kain.

7

MADDIE

THE LAST FEW DAYS HAVE BEEN SUPER QUIET AT WORK, AND IT'S days like this I wish I was at home being a mom and wife again and not working part-time back at The James Hotel. Those first twelve months of being home with Fletcher twenty-four-seven were amazing but to be honest, I was ready to get back to work so I could have a little more adult conversation. Plus, there are only so many times a day you can listen to the *Bluey* theme song without wanting to stab yourself in the ears with a pencil. Maybe it's time for Penn and me to give Fletch a baby brother or sister. That way I can be a stay-at-home mom again. We always said we wanted two kids, but life kind of got in the way and we fell into a routine. Fletcher is five now, that's bigger than the age gap between Penn and Wren. They have such a great brother/sister bond and I want that for Fletch and baby number two but is five, well possibly six, by the time I get pregnant and carry a baby for the nine months, too much of an age gap? One thing for sure though, baby number two will NOT have a name matching Fletcher in any way whatsoever. Penn's family all have matching almost similar names, Penn

Sr. and Samantha are amazing parents but to name their kids Penn and Wren, that's a bit much. Yep, my in-laws named their kids Penn and Wren. I remember when I first started dating Penn, I referred to him as PJ—Penn Jr.—and the look he gave me, you would think I called him a C U Next Thursday or something. He growled, "It's Penn" and I have not made that mistake since.

Names aside, I lean back in my chair and decide that tonight over a bottle of wine on the back deck, I will approach the subject of another baby with Penn.

"What's got you thinking so hard over there, Mrs. Brookes?" Penn asks, walking into my office with a brown paper bag in one hand and a drink tray in the other. Jumping in fright, I cover my chest with my hand.

"Shit, Penn, you scared me," I tell him.

"You were a million miles away. What's got you thinking so hard over there?"

He places our lunch down on my desk and leans over to give me a kiss. It's more than just a quick peck hello and it causes my blood to begin to simmer and my clit to throb. I wonder if this is my body's way of telling me that it's ready for a baby. It's ready to have some fun making a baby, and why not start with a quickie in the office?

"Feel free to kiss me hello like that anytime, dear husband of mine."

"Duly noted, sexy wife of mine. But seriously, what were you thinking so hard about?"

"Ummm, well, I, ummm …"

"That serious, huh?"

Staring up at my husband, I reach out and take his hand. Threading my fingers through his, I decide to just go for it. Closing my eyes, I quickly spit it out, "IWantUsToHaveAnotherBaby?" The words all blur into one and when I open my eyes and look up at Penn, his expression is blank. I'm not sure if it's because he didn't understand me or if I shocked him.

"You ... you wanna have another baby?" Nodding, I offer him a small smile. "You wanna give Fletcher a baby brother or sister?" Nodding again, I bite my lip as I wait for him to answer me. He starts nodding and I find myself nodding along with him. He still hasn't answered my question and I have no clue right now as to what he's thinking. He leans against my desk next to me and stares at the wall across from us, now it's his turn to think hard.

"Penn?" I say his name like a question. "Are you okay?" He nods again, but still doesn't utter a word. I think I broke him with my baby request. Standing up, I move in front of him and cup his cheeks in my palms. He flicks his gaze to mine. "We don't have to if—" Before I can finish, he grips my cheeks in his palms and presses his lips to mine.

"Yes," he mumbles against my mouth before he licks across my lips and pushes his tongue into mine. Closing my eyes, I give myself over to Penn and the kiss. Kissing Penn has always been amazing, and this kiss is no different. He pulls back and rests his forehead against mine. "I wasn't sure you wanted another after the rough way Fletcher entered this world." After a thirty-five-hour labor, my blood pressure dropped drastically and they had to do an emergency C-section and then after Fletcher was safely out, I began to hemorrhage and they were considering an emergency hysterectomy when suddenly I stopped bleeding. The doctors were puzzled, but thankfully everything down there is still intact and I have a healthy womb ready and waiting to grow a baby brother or sister for Fletcher.

"I've always wanted another baby, Penn, but the time just didn't feel right, but now ... now I'm ready to expand our family, if you are?"

"I'm more than ready, Mads, but if you want it to remain just the three of us, I'll be happy, but most of all, I want you to be happy."

"And I want you to be happy too, but I think it's time. We

always said we didn't want Fletch to be an only child. I hated not having a sibling to play with growing up and I don't want that for him."

"Then it looks like we're trying for another baby."

"Looks like it." I nod in agreement, smiling like Ronald McDonald because I'm so freakin' McHappy right now.

"Shall we start now?" Penn suggests, waggling his eyebrows at me.

"I am not having sex with you in my office," I hiss and slap his chest. Even if a few moments ago I wondered the same thing but when push comes to shove—his penis into my vagina—I can't do office sex.

"We've had sex in my office," he protests.

"Yes, but you're the only employee at your office, no one will come in wanting something."

"A customer could walk in," he throws back at me. "Besides, your office door has a lock and right now, all I can think about is sinking my cock deep inside that sweet pussy of yours and planting my seed in there and having one of your eggs yell 'come and get me, boys' and we make baby Brookes number two."

"This isn't a scene from *Look Who's Talking*, my eggs and your swimmers don't talk."

"How do you know what goes on in your vagina and womb?"

Shaking my head, I try and hold back a smirk. "You are something else, Penn Brookes."

"Why thank you, Maddie Brookes. So how 'bout it? A lunchtime quickie?"

"How about we eat first 'cause this momma-to-be is starving and she's going to need energy if we're going to have an office quickie."

"You drive a hard bargain, but there's a Philly cheesesteak in there with my name on it and as much as I want to put a baby in your belly, that sandwich is calling my name right this second."

"You have yourself a deal, Mr. Brookes."

Penn and I devour our sandwiches and then he devours me quickly, with the promise of more devouring later when I get home after tonight's function.

8

TATUM

KIP AND I ARE WAITING IN ARRIVALS FOR KAIN TO EXIT CUSTOMS. I have my "Welcome Home from Prison!" sign ready to go and as soon as I see him, I lift it up and shake it around. When he spots me, he shakes his head, starts laughing his head off, and the bastard that he is turns and pretends to walk away from me.

"Kain Abner Alaric Summers," I shout, garnering his attention, "do not turn your back on me."

He spins around to face me and slowly begins to walk toward me. "Tatum Prudence Summers, get your ass over here and give your baby brother a hug." When he's close to me, without warning I launch myself through the air at him. With his quick reflexes, he drops his duffel and catches me. We hug the shit out of each other, causing people to grumble and step around us. The last time we saw each other was almost a year ago.

"Good to see you, sis," Kain greets, dropping me to my feet and pulling me into his side.

"You too, little bro. You too." I pull him in for another hug.

"Thanks for the welcome sign."

"You're welcome."

He pulls back and gives me a grin, the grin that won over many girls back in junior high. "You realize this means war now?"

"Bring it," I reply, digging him in the ribs.

He looks over my shoulder and smiles. Turning my head, I see Kip walking toward us. "Good to see you, man," Kip greets my brother, offering his hand to shake.

Pushing me to the side, Kain steps toward Kip and they do that manly handshake, one-armed hug thing that guys do. "Good flight?" Kip asks Kain as I slide my arm around my brother's waist. I didn't realize how much I missed him until just now.

"Long. Freakin' long. Why do you guys live so far away?"

"Ohh, poor baby," I tease, "is the big bad firefighter exhausted after sitting on his ass for fifteen hours?" He sticks his tongue out at me and being the responsible older sister that I'm not, I reach out and pinch his tongue.

"Ouch, you bitch."

"You love me," I reply with a sweet and innocent smile. "Will this make up for it?" From my pocket I pull out a miniature bottle of Fireball whiskey.

"You are definitely my favorite sister," Kain says with a smile as he takes the bottle from me. He immediately twists off the cap and shoots it back. "Ahhhhhhhh," he croons, licking his lips.

Then his words register in my brain. "Hey," I scoff, smacking him in the arm, "I'm your only sister."

"Hence my favorite," he cheekily replies.

We begin to bicker like we usually do and when we are finished razzing each other, I find myself grinning. I'm so happy to have my brother here … even if he can be an annoying jerkface at times, he's my brother and I love him unconditionally. Then I look over to Kip and see him sadly staring at us, I know he's wishing he had a family like we do. As a kid, he bounced from foster home to foster home and it wasn't until he became a firefighter that he found his 'family,' and through that family, he met me—well us. He instantly became a member of the Summers family and finally, he found his forever family. Mom and Dad took him in as if he was one of their own. Kain loves him like a brother, and me, well, I love him more than I love coffee and that's a bloody lot. Oh My God, I sounded so Australian saying bloody. The day I met Kip Kitson, I found the love of my life and I cannot wait to marry him so we can start a family of our own. Kip is going to make a wonderful father one day, and I can't wait to see him shine.

"Come on, guys," I say, not dwelling on the sad moments, "let's head home for a few more of those," I point to the empty bottle in Kain's hand. "Because tomorrow is going to be another big one."

"You had me at those," Kain says, shaking the empty bottle at us.

He bends down, picks up his duffel, and throws his arm around my shoulders. I slink mine around his waist and the three of us head out to Kip's Hilux ute. "Nice wheels," Kain declares as he throws his duffel into the back.

"Thanks, she's my second love." Kip winks at me over the back of the ute.

"Love you too, babe." I blow him a kiss and climb into the back seat, leaving the front for Kain since he's a good foot taller than me and needs the extra legroom, but the doofus opens the driver's door. "Other side, dickwad," I tease.

"Fuck off, I'm jet-lagged," he snaps.

"Nice excuse," I reply with a laugh. Flipping me the bird, he slams the driver's door shut, walks around, and jumps in the passenger side.

Kip shakes his head at the banter between my brother and me. When he climbs behind the wheel, I lean forward and press a kiss to his cheek and cuddle his neck. "I love you."

"Ugh, please, I don't need to see this lovey-dovey shit. I

did NOT miss that between you two. I don't know how many times I've seen your lily-white ass, Kip."

"At least it's not my ass," I inform him.

"Yes, thank fuck for that," he replies, clipping his belt in.

"I think you love my ass, Kain, you always seem to be looking at it."

"Like his older sister, he appreciates a fine ass and you, Kip Kitson, have the finest ass there is."

"Ugh, I'm gonna be sick. Remind me again why I came down here?"

"To help fight the fire of all fires," I quietly murmur.

Leaning back in my seat, a feeling of unease washes over me. This is a fire like we have never seen before. I'm used to building fires and maybe the occasional back-burn that gets out of hand, but this, this is a fire for the history books.

Once the three of us are buckled in, Kain cranks the tunes. "Sweet Home Alabama" by Lynyrd Skynyrd comes on and the three of us sing along. Just as we pull up at home, "Wonderwall" by Oasis starts to play. We stay in the car singing our hearts out until the song's finished.

Climbing out, Kain grabs his bag, and we head inside. Kip shows him to the guest room and I grab three beers and the bottle of Fireball—we always have one on hand—and head into the living room to wait for them.

Taking a seat on the couch, I look up to see Kip and Kain enter the room. The two of them are thick as thieves, I can see why they get along so well. I'm so glad that Kip came over on the exchange, that trip changed my life. I fell hard and fast for him, and it was a no-brainer for me to come back to Australia with him. I'm just lucky my dad is the captain and was able to help me arrange the exchange, which turned into me applying for citizenship and staying on. Kip and I haven't decided where we are going to settle yet, but having options is always a good thing.

The sound of Kip's voice saying my name snaps me back to the present.

"Yeah?"

"You were a million miles away. You okay, babe?" He pulls me into his side and places a kiss on my temple.

Nodding my head, I smile. "Yeah, I'm good. Glad to have a night off."

"How bad is it?" Kain asks as he takes a sip of his beer.

"It's bad, dude," Kip replies, "real fuckin' bad." His tone gives emphasis as to just how bad it really is out there.

"I've never seen one like this before and the weather isn't helping," I add.

"How so?" Kain questions.

"Where do we start?" Kip replies. "The temperatures are soaring. The winds are crazy. Every time we seem to get something under control, it all changes and screws us over again and the fires are creating their own fire-fueled thunderstorms, which produce their own dry lightning, violent winds, black hail, and even fire tornados."

"Fuck me. I thought the Cali wildfires were bad, this sounds ten times worse," Kain shakes his head and squeezes the back of his neck like he does when he's anxious.

"Not sure you can compare the two, little bro. Fire is fire. And this one is destructive as hell. We need to be on point so we can put this bitch out."

We all go silent and take in my words, not realizing that in the coming days, things were about to take a turn no one ever saw coming.

9

KIP

Waking before the alarm, I roll to my side and gaze over at Tatum. Even when she's sleeping, she's gorgeous. It was her smile that I was first drawn to, but the more I got to know Tatum Summers, the more I fell for this amazing woman.

"Watching me sleep is creepy," she sleepily mumbles. Opening her gorgeous green eyes, she looks over at me and smiles.

"It's not creepy when I do it."

She shakes her head and whispers, "Still creepy, Kip, but I love you anyway."

"And I love you too."

Leaning toward me, she presses her lips to mine. "Good morning, Creeper McCreeperson," she murmurs after kissing me good morning.

"Good morning, sexy o sexy one," I reply against her lips. Snaking one hand into her hair, I rest the other on her hip. We continue to kiss one another. With each caress of our tongues, our bodies inch closer and closer together. My cock is rock-hard. Rolling her to her back, I cocoon her underneath me and stare down at her. We silently gaze lovingly at one another. She spreads her legs wide and that's all the encouragement I need to take this further. I shuffle between her thighs and with my eyes locked on hers, I slide my cock into her wet channel. This is why sleeping naked is the best way to sleep, easy access at any time. No clothing in the way, the moment isn't broken with the need to remove clothes.

A moan slips through her lips as I slowly thrust in and out of her. She closes her eyes and lets the pleasure coursing through her body envelop her. Covering her mouth with mine, I swallow each and every moan, not wanting to wake Kain, but at the same time not giving a rat's ass about him.

Tatum opens her eyes again and we stare at one another. Our bodies slide together languidly, the friction gaining with each thrust. Her eyes widen. Her body tenses and she lets out a throaty growl, confirming she is indeed tumbling over the edge. Seeing her come undone like that sets me off, and I come with a guttural growl just as a banging on our door occurs, followed by Kain's voice. "Time to go, lovers."

Tatum and I giggle. "Give us five!" I shout back.

"Only five? I thought you were better than that, Kitson," comes his reply with a laugh.

"Asshole!" I yell back as I climb off Tatum and offer her my hand. Helping her up, we walk into the en suite. She jumps into the shower and I grab our toothbrushes. Once they each have toothpaste on them, I step into the shower and hand Tatum hers.

We stare at one another and clean our teeth. Placing the brushes on the shelf, I grab the loofah, squeeze on some coconut lime body wash, and soap up her body. When she's all clean, she repeats the process using my body wash.

Climbing out, we dry off and get dressed.

Stepping into the main living area, I smile when I see Kain in our kitchen making three to-go coffees in our travel mugs. "Look at you being all domesticated," Tatum teases her brother as she twists her hair up into a messy bun.

"Coffee is lifeblood, you of all people should know that.

Tate is your soon-to-be wife."

"Hey," she protests but it's moot because Tatum and coffee go together like peanut butter and honey.

Watching Kain flit around the kitchen feels different, it's surreal having him here for this. Normally he's here and we'd be heading to the beach or to a bar, but this time he's here to help us fight the fire of all fires. He hands me my mug and I take a sip; a moan breaks free. "Dude, this is the best coffee I have ever had."

"It's my secret ingredient," he hands Tatum hers, leans over, and kisses her on the cheek. "Morning, sis."

"Morning," she says back, taking a sip from her mug. She moans and smiles as the caffeine infuses her soul.

"And what's your secret ingredient?" I inquire.

"If I tell you, then I'd have to kill you and that would make Tater Tot sad, and I don't want to do that to my big sis."

"You're so full of shit, Kain," Tatum jokes. She turns to me. "Babe, the secret ingredient is cinnamon."

"How did you know?"

"Der, you twit," she quips, "your granny is my granny."

I see the moment that comment registers on Kain's face. Tatum and I both laugh at him. He flips us the bird and helps Tatum grab some snacks for today. The two of them bicker like they always do, and I smile when I see how happy Tatum is to have her brother here. It still amazes me that she packed up and moved so far away to be with me, when in reality, apart from the guys at the station, there's nothing keeping me here. Maybe when this is all over, I'll broach the topic of us moving to the US to be closer to her family.

Kain recently moved to Castaway Grove with his best friend, Burton. Momma and Papa Summers are going to be traveling the world soon. Papa Summers is going to retire later this year, so really, Tatum and I could go anywhere. I'm snapped back to the present when Kain states, "Let's go show this fire who's boss."

10

PENN

A LOUD KNOCKING ON THE FRONT DOOR STARTLES ME AWAKE. Blinking rapidly, I sit up on the sofa and realize all the lights in the house are still on and Mads isn't here. The knocking continues. Shaking my head, I sleepily shuffle over to the front door and when I open it, I see two police officers. My eyes widen and before they even speak, I know it's not good news. "Can I help you, officers?"

"Mr. Brookes?" he questions and I nod. "Is your wife, Madeline Brookes?"

"Yes, is … is she okay? What's going on? Why are you here?" I fire the questions at the officers. My heart races and my mind conjures every possible scenario as to why they are here, and I don't like any of the pictures currently in my mind.

"I'm sorry to inform you but your wife has been in an accident." Double blinking, I stare at the officer. I see his lips moving but I don't hear or register a word he utters.

They just stare at me, and I realize he has finished speaking. "I … I'm sorry," I finally mutter, "can you, umm, repeat that?"

"Your wife was involved in a car accident earlier this evening. She's been rushed to Lockhart Falls Memorial Hospital in critical condition."

Once again, I stare at the officer, blinking. My mouth opens and closes and as if sensing something is wrong, Fletcher walks into the room. "Daddy." At the sound of his voice, all three of us turn to look at him as he makes his way over to us. "Where's Mommy?" he asks in a sleep-addled voice.

Dropping to my knees, I stare at our son and swallow deeply. How do I explain this to a five-year-old? I'm barely comprehending it. "Hey, buddy." I reach out to him and hold onto his little hand. "What are you doing out of bed?"

"Mommy didn't kiss me night-night and I wanted a Mommy kiss so I came to find Mommy for my kiss." He looks around me at the officers and then he grips my cheeks in his little palms. "Where's Mommy, Daddy?"

"I … umm … shit," I stammer. Pulling Fletch into my arms, I drop to my ass in the doorway with two police officers standing above me, and I ignore them as I sit here holding on to my son. The longer I hold him, the more I realize that I don't feel her anymore. My heart is beating differently and I just know, I know she's gone. The urge to see her slams into me, I need to get to the hospital. I need to see her with my own two eyes to confirm my worst fear, but what if I'm wrong? What if she's okay and I'm overreacting? Yes, I'm overreacting, I have to be. Mads isn't gone.

Jumping up with Fletcher in my arms, I turn and look to the officers who are still loitering in the doorway. "Can … can you take us to her?"

They nod and from the blank pensive looks on their faces, I just know this isn't good. The longer we stand here, the more I need to see Mads and I need to see her now. Grabbing my keys and wallet from the hall table, I follow the officers out to the police cruiser. Fletcher and I climb into the back and we silently make the trip to Lockhart Falls Memorial. The last time I was here was when Fletcher was born. It was such a happy moment walking through these doors, but today, I don't know how I feel as I enter the building.

The officers walk up to the front desk and moments later, Fletcher and I are taken back to see Mads. The nurse stops outside a curtain. "She's in there." She sadly smiles at me and I hate that look, it's patronizing and not helpful at all. Nodding my head, I reach up, pull the curtain aside, and stare at the bed. My eyes well with tears as I take in Mads lying there but before I step into the room, alarms start blaring from the machines she's attached to. Nurses and doctors rush to Mads's bedside, pushing me aside so they can work on her.

It's bedlam but it's organized bedlam. Standing here with a sleeping Fletcher in my arms, I watch as they work on my wife. In a blur, she's whisked past me and taken farther into the hospital. Someone says something about OR two but I'm too shocked to really understand anything.

Standing here, I watch them wheel her away from us. The same nurse escorts Fletcher and me to a private waiting room. Sitting down, I hold tightly onto our son. Praying with everything I have that Mads pulls through this.

"Mr. Brookes?" a feminine voice asks. Looking up, I see a doctor standing before me. I was so lost in thought I didn't even hear the door open.

"That's me," I reply, not sure what else to say.

"I'm Dr. René, I was the one operating on your wife ..." She continues to talk but all I can focus on is the word 'was' and then my fear is confirmed when I hear the words I was dreading pass through her lips. "I'm sorry, Mr. Brookes, she didn't make it."

Choking back the sob wanting to break free, I stare at the doctor. "She's gone," I whisper and she nods. She becomes blurry as tears well in my eyes.

My.

Wife.

Is.

Gone.

Wiping at my eyes, I nod my head. "What … what happens now?"

"Do you know if your wife was a donor?"

Nodding, I sniff and hold on to Fletcher tighter. He's all I have left of Mads now. "Yes, she is, yes. I'll sign whatever you need, she'd want that." The first tear falls, followed by an avalanche of them. When I look up again, it's just Fletch and me in the room. For a few moments, I just sit here and sob, hugging my son and missing my life. "I need to see her," I whisper to the room. Standing up, I walk to the door and step out into the hallway.

"Can I help you?" a nurse walking past asks, sensing my need for assistance.

"I … I need to see my wife."

"And who is your wife?"

"Umm … Madeline Brookes, she … she …" Then I mouth the word "died" to her because I'm not ready to implode Fletcher's world. He's only five. He's an intuitive five-year-old, but he's just lost his mom. I want to keep him innocent for as long as I can. This is going to hit him hard. He and Mads had the most beautiful bond, their relationship reminds me of the one I have with my mom. He's going to be lost without Mads and as his father, I need to protect him. I need to be strong for him.

"Ohh, you're Mr. Brookes?" she asks and I nod. "I can take you to her."

"Thank you."

She turns the way she came and I follow her. We come to a stop outside a door. "She's in this room."

"Thank you," I whisper.

"I'm so sorry for your loss."

Turning to face her, I stare expecting to see pity but all I see is grief. This strange woman is mourning the death of my wife and seeing her so upset over Mads is somehow comforting. Nodding at me, I look through the door and see Mads in the bed. My hand hovers over the door handle but I freeze because as soon as I push this door open, it becomes real. As soon as I step into this room, my wife will be gone.

Taking a deep breath, I shake my head from side to side. I can't do it. I can't go into that room. I'm not ready. Stepping backward, I hit the wall across from her room and with my eyes locked on the door to her room, I slide down to the floor. Shuffling Fletcher around in my arms, I hug him tightly to me and I cry again, letting the tears fall. I know men are supposed to be tough but right now, I'm the least tough man there is. How do I say goodbye to the mother of my son? How do I let go of the one who loves me unconditionally? Why is this happening to us? We were supposed to be trying for baby number two.

A shadow appears above me and when I look up, I see my mom and dad standing above me. It's dark in the corridor and makes them look like ominous shadows, but seeing them here causes my eyes to water again. "She … she's gone," I tearfully whisper, a lone tear slides down my cheek and splashes onto Fletcher's face.

"Ohhhh, Penn," Mom tearfully mumbles. "What happened? Were you hurt too? Is Fletcher okay? What can I do?" For a moment, I briefly smile due to Mom and her fifty million questions. Questions are Mom's go-to in a situation, and this is one situation I never want to be in again. Not needing answers, she just crouches down and envelops Fletcher and me in her arms.

Lifting one arm from Fletcher, I hug her tightly back and I cry into her shoulder until I have no more tears left to cry. I haven't cried on my mom's shoulder like this since I was seven years old and our dog, Samboy, ran away.

Mom drops back to her haunches and begins to rub Fetcher's back, "Nanna?" he mumbles when he looks over his shoulder and sees his nanna here.

"Hey, buddy, would you like to come get some ice cream with Nanna?" With one question, not fifty million, Mom gets Fletcher preoccupied so I can face what's behind the door across from me. I need time to process this before I tell him that his mom is gone.

"In the middle of the night?" he excitedly asks, his eyes as wide as saucers. Ice cream isn't going to ease his hurt and I hate that, but what can I do? His mom is gone.

"Yep." She nods, trying to hold back her own tears.

"Can I, Dad?" he asks me and when I see his little face light up with excitement, a lump forms in the back of my throat, not allowing me to speak, so I just nod. Swallowing down the lump, I find my voice. "You sure can, bud, it can be our secret."

He pushes off my chest, stands up, and offers his little hand to Mom. She clears her throat and stands up before taking his hand in hers. Hand in hand, the two of them walk down the hallway. Looking up at my dad, I see nothing but grief reflecting back at me. Standing up, I stare at him. "Dad, I can't do this. I can't go into that room and say goodbye. How do I tell my son that his mom isn't coming home? I can't do this, Dad, I just can't."

"You can, Penn. You're stronger than you think." He reaches over and squeezes my shoulder in that reassuring Dad way. "You need to go in there and you need to say goodbye. You'll regret it if you don't, Son. I'll be right by your side, anything you need, I'm here."

Staring at the man who raised me, I nod. I know he's right, but this is the hardest thing I've ever had to do. Stepping across the corridor, I put my hand on the door handle, and this time I push down, opening the door.

11

TATUM

THE THREE OF US ARE BACK HOME, SITTING ON THE COUCH absolutely exhausted. Today was full-on but Lady Luck was on our side and we got a little reprieve when it started to rain. It was only about an inch of liquid gold but that little rain shower made a major difference. The fire near us is no longer out of control, but it's still massive and we aren't out of the woods yet.

"What a day," Kain exclaims, collapsing onto the couch across from me. Like me, he's covered in soot, dirt, sweat, and is totally spent.

"Yep," I offer as I flop down into my seat and lift my feet up, resting them on the coffee table. A grin forms because if Mom was here, she'd be slapping my feet to get them off the table.

Kip joins us and places two beers on the coffee table next to my feet, and gives me a look that would rival Mom's. I chuckle to myself as he sits in 'his' armchair, leaning back like the sexy man he is. He rests his foot on his knee, drops his head back, and closes his eyes. He takes a sip of his beer and lets out a sigh. He's just as dirty as Kain and I have no doubt that I look just like the two of them.

Sitting up, I kick off my shoes, and snuggle back in 'my' corner of the couch, pulling my legs under my butt. Reaching up, I tug at my hairband, pulling my hair free. My blonde locks cascade down my back and when I run my fingers through it, all I smell is smoke. "Ugh, I'm never going to get this smoke smell out of my hair."

"You and me both, babe," Kip offers but Kain ignores us. He's focused on his phone when a grin appears on his face. "What you grinning at, Brozart?" I ask, leaning forward to grab the beers from the coffee table. I slide one across to Kain before grabbing mine and bringing it to my lips. The yeasty goodness slides down my throat, leaving me feeling some-what refreshed. I don't know what it is about an ice-cold beer after a hard day's work, it just hits differently to other beers.

"Nothing," he defensively snaps but amongst the ash and soot on his face, I notice his cheeks are stained pink.

"Bullshit, your cheeks are rosy and you've got that look in your eyes you get when you're in lust." I say lust because I don't think my brother has ever been in love. Kip starts making kissing sounds, and I can't help but chuckle. "Are you in lust, maybe even love, little brother?" His eyes pop open at my question.

He lifts his gaze from his phone and from the look on his face, I think I'm right. "Maybe," he sheepishly admits, shrug-ging his shoulders before reaching for his beer and taking a sip. "This is a great beer," he states, trying to change the subject.

"It is. It's from a brewery up in Queensland called Malt Me," I tell him but I don't let him off the hook that easily. "Now, who's the girl?"

He sighs. "It's early days. She drives me fucking crazy but I can't stop thinking about her."

"Is it serious?" I question my brother.

"It could be … if she'd stop pissing me off."

Looking to my brother, I smile and shake my head. I've

never seen him like this over a girl, and glancing to Kip, I can see he's itching to tease him too. "How is she pissing you off?"

"She lit a fire on the beach during summer," he snarls, hatred in his eyes over her lighting a beach fire.

"Annnd?" I press, surely that's not what has his panties in a twist.

"It was a fire," he spits back at me.

"Pretty sure fires are allowed on the beach, unless there's a fire ban."

"Not the point. She left it unattended to get more drinks. Plus, she could have safely used the firepit in her backyard."

"What a bitch," I tease with an exaggerated eye roll for good measure. "How dare she have fun. On the beach. In summer." I place emphasis on those three statements, earning myself a bird flip from him. "What else has she done to get under your skin?"

"Stuff," he defensively snaps with a shrug before crossing his arms across his chest like a petulant child.

Kip and I both laugh. "Ohh, this is priceless," I say through my laughter. "Seriously, get over it and get the girl. Does she make you happy?" Kain nods and gets a goofy loved-up look on his face. "Then pull your head out of your ass and go for it. When you get back to the States, wine and dine her. I want a sis-in-law and if she's getting to you like this, then she's perfect for you."

"I agree with Tatum," Kip says, looking over to him. I blow a kiss and he pretends to catch it and pop it into his pocket.

"Traitor," Kain teases. "Okay, ohh wise sister of mine, how do I win her over?"

"For starters, stop being a fire Nazi. What does she like?"

"Stuff."

"Stuff, wow, you seem really into this one."

"Shut up. I th—" Before he can finish both my and Kip's

phones vibrate across the coffee table. Kip looks at me apprehensively because the tone is the station's one. We each pick the devices up and as I read the text that just came in, my eyes widen. This is bad, epically bad.

"Shit," Kip and I both say at the same time.

Jumping up, we both head toward the front door and without saying a word, Kain follows. The three of us race out to Kip's ute. Silently we climb in and head back to the RFS—Rural Fire Service—headquarters. So much for a quiet beer and shower, it's all-hands-on-deck because the winds have changed and it's not good, not good at all.

12

MADDIE

MY BODY HURTS BUT AT THE SAME TIME, IT'S NUMB. MY MIND IS active and I hear every word the doctors are saying, and I feel each and every word. I wish they were wrong, but they aren't. I'm dying. I'm not going to make it home tonight. I'm not going to get to see my little boy grow up. Or fall in love and get married. Make me a nanna. And Penn, my beautiful, beautiful Penn. I'll never get another forehead kiss or a cheeky butt squeeze, and there won't be any more quickies at an event or in my office. I can't even remember if I said I love you after lunch today, surely I did, right?

He's here. I can feel him. I wish I could open my eyes and see him one last time. He presses a kiss to my knuckles and I feel his kiss everywhere. "I'm here, baby," he cries, "I'll be here until I can't. I won't leave your side. You don't have to do this alone."

"Penn," I murmur but the sound of my voice echoes in my mind. He can't hear me, but I can hear him. "I'm so scared, Penn," I confide, even though he can't hear me. "I don't want to leave you but it hurts. My body is broken and my heart is shattering at the thought of leaving you and Fletch, but I have to. The pain is too much. I'm sorry I let you down. I'm sorry we won't grow old together. I'm sorry, so fucking sorry. And yes, I just swore, that's how sorry I am. I will always love you, Penn, but you have to move on. You are still young and sexy and have so much love to give. Fletcher needs a mom and you need someone to love and be loved by. I give you my blessing to love again, Penn. I wish you could hear this because I know your stubborn ass will refuse, and it's your stubbornness I fell in love with. I love you, Penn Brookes Jr., now and forever."

My body is cold and I don't feel anything anymore. My body is empty, my heart. My lungs. I can still feel them but they're fading away from me and then I realize what's happening. He remembered, he's donated my organs and now someone else is going to get a second chance. I wish I could have gotten a second chance, but now it's time for me to go. It's time for me to go into the light and watch over them. I'll still get to see Fletcher grow up but it will be from above and not by his side. I'll always be watching. My body and soul may be gone but my love, it will always remain.

13

PENN

Stepping into Maddie's room, my breath hitches in my throat when I see my wife up close. Her beautiful face is bruised and covered in abrasions. Her auburn hair is dull and lifeless. Tubes are everywhere and the machines by her bed are doing their thing to keep her alive right now; without them, she'd be gone. We were supposed to grow old together. Give Fletch a baby brother or sister. We were going to travel the world too. Instead, I have to fill out papers to allow the doctors to harvest her organs, and then I need to arrange a funeral and not the trip of a lifetime.

Putting one foot in front of the other, I cross the room to her bedside. Picking up her tiny hand in mine, I press a kiss to her knuckles and drop down into the shit-green chair by her bed. "I'm here, baby," I cry. "I'll be here until I can't. I won't leave your side. You don't have to do this alone."

Alone.

That's exactly what I will be when I leave this hospital. Never in a million years did I think this would happen. This morning we were so happy, if I'd known this was going to be how the day ended, I would have kissed her longer. Given her a stronger hug. Turned our lunchtime quickie into something more. I can't even remember if I told her I loved her as she raced out of her office and into her meeting.

"I love you, Mads," I murmur, "so fucking much. Why, baby? Why are you leaving me?" Tears once again stream down my cheeks. Standing up, I lean over and hug her. Resting my head on her chest, I let it all out and sob. My shoulders shake as grief pours out of me. "Why, Mads, why?" I keep repeating over and over.

A hand touches my back and without looking up, I know it's Mom. Turning around, I wipe at the tears on my face and see both my parents. "Where's Fletch?"

"With the nurses. He has them all wrapped around his little finger. They're being introduced to *Bluey*." I laugh because that little blue heeler will keep him occupied for hours, and I'm so grateful for that right now. This is hard enough as it is, but with an inquisitive five-year-old, it's going to be even harder. As it stands now, he asks a million and one questions before breakfast, and no doubt, he will have a million and one questions about this too. I just hope I can answer them for him. "Mom, how do I tell him that his mom is not coming home?" My voice breaks at the end.

Mom steps over to me and reaches up to cup my cheek. "You be honest with him, Penn. You let him cry. You let him scream, and you love him with everything you have. But most of all, you never let him forget his mom."

Nodding, I swallow deeply and process her words, wondering if I can cry and scream too. "Mom," I cry, "she's gone. My Mads is gone."

"Ohhh, Penn." She wraps her arms around me tightly and once again I fall apart. I know men are regarded as tough and they shouldn't cry or show emotion, but I have no control. My emotions aren't mine right now. I'm just existing ... in a pit of grief and disbelief. I keep hoping I will wake up any minute now, and I'll find myself in bed at home with Mads sleeping soundly next to me. "I'm so, so sorry, baby."

Our moment is interrupted when Teri and Sandy arrive. Their eyes are locked on their daughter in the bed, hooked up to so many different machines. Then they see me in Mom's arms and immediately know she's gone.

"No," Teri wails as she walks toward me, shaking her head from side to side. Her eyes fill with tears. "Please, Penn, please tell me I'm wrong and she's just sleeping. Please don't tell me my baby is gone. Please, Penn, please."

Sniffling, I shake my head and close my eyes. "Ssss … she's gone, Teri," I whisper. Opening my eyes, I look up at my mother-in-law and repeat, "She's gone."

Teri falls to her knees in the middle of the room and breaks down. Sandy drops down next to her and wraps his arms around his wife. I was so selfish in my turmoil, I never stopped to think what it would be like for them. They're about to say goodbye to their daughter, their one and only daughter.

Leaning against the wall, I look to the ceiling. The bright glow from the fluorescent light blinds me, but I just stare up into it and wonder if this is what Mads will see when she crosses over. Will she be scared? Will her body repair itself, so she can live in the afterlife unbroken? Or will she forever bear the scars of the accident?

The accident? My head snaps up, I need answers. Walking out of Mads's room, I march toward the nurses' station. Someone calls out my name, but I need to speak to the officer. I need to know exactly what happened.

"Mr. Brookes, how can I help you?" Dr. René asks.

"I need to speak with the officer who came to my house. I need to know what happened."

"I'm sorry, Mr. Brookes, only family is allowed on this ward."

"I need to speak with him now," I demand, slamming my fist on the counter at the nurses' station.

"Sir, you need to calm down. As I said—"

"I don't fucking care, I need to speak to the officer now. I need to know what happened. I need answers, God dammit." I slap the counter again. "No, what I fucking need is for my wife to be alive. I need to hug her and hold her and kiss her. I just need her, but that can't happen, so I'll take the next best thing, answers. Now get me the fucking person I need to speak with."

"Penn Brookes Jr.," my dad snaps my name and I look over my shoulder at him walking toward Dr. René and me. "I know you're hurting right now, Son, but you need to calm down." Spinning around to face him, I'm ready to explode on him, but my dad knows me too well because he lifts his index finger in the way that used to scare the ever-loving shit out of me when I was little. "The doctor said she can't help you, but let's go find someone who can. Okay?"

Staring at him, I start nodding, knowing he's right. Turning back to the doctor I sadly look at her. "I'm sorry for that, Dr. René, I'm … I'm sorry."

She nods. "I understand, Mr. Brookes, and for what it's worth, I *do* know what you're going through." I stare at her in the 'yeah, sure' kind of way and roll my eyes in a conde-scending way. "I was in my last year of med school and my wife was killed. She was crossing the road with our daughter on the way to dance practice when a drunk driver slammed into them. She sacrificed herself to save our baby girl, according to witnesses' accounts. So, when I tell you I know what it's like to have your person ripped from your life, I know because I've experienced it firsthand. I'm living it every day."

"Will the pain ever go away?"

"Not entirely, but it does ease. Some days are better than others, but then there are some days that it crushes you and the pain you're feeling right now comes crashing back."

"How do I go on?"

"You do it for your son, just like I do it for our daughter."

"You have a daughter?"

She nods. "Yep, we had two girls. Katherine will be fifteen this year and, boy oh boy, she's so much like her mother it isn't funny. She's what keeps me going, and your son will be what keeps you going too. If your wife was like mine, when we meet up again in the afterlife, she's going to point out all the things I did wrong raising Kat, but also tell me I did an amazing job. Then we are going to drink heavenly margaritas and wake up with no hangover because there's no pain in heaven. It's just happiness and margaritas."

A laugh slips out because I can picture Mads berating me for letting Mom take Fletch for ice cream earlier and then I see us, sitting on the porch steps sharing a bottle of red between us and eating cheese and crackers.

"From that smile on your face, I'm guessing you're picturing a happy reunion with your wife?"

"Yeah, but before that, she was yelling at me for letting Fletch get ice cream in the middle of the night with his grandma."

"She sounds like a wonderful woman, but I'm pretty sure she'd give you a free pass on tonight's ice cream. Emotions are high and we do things we usually wouldn't."

Yeah, like yell at a doctor. "Yeah, I guess," I dejectedly reply. "I really am sorry for snapping at you."

"It's your free pass," she tells me, "but next time, I'll call security and they'll haul your ass out of here."

Nodding again, I turn toward Dad and walk over to him. When I reach him, he lifts his hand up and squeezes my shoulder. "I'm proud of you, Son."

"Proud that I just yelled at a health care professional?"

"No, I'm proud that you owned your mistake. As much as it feels like your world is crumbling right now, you will get through this. Your mother and I and your sister will be here every step of the way. Teri and Sandy will too and just like you, they're grieving. Family sticks together, Penn, through the good times and the bad."

"Thanks, Dad."

A lady from the transplant team arrives and pulls me into an office. It's all a blur of paperwork and words I don't fully understand. All I know is that Mads death won't be in vain. She will be giving multiple people a second chance and I will do everything in my power to honor the amazing woman my wife is ... was.

14

KIP

TATE, KAIN, AND I RACE BACK TO THE RFS HEADQUARTERS, WE are working out of their base at the moment rather than the Bauckle Bay station. After the briefing, we climb into our allocated truck and wait for clearance to head to our designated area.

Looking out the window, I see a mum and her two young kids walking toward the truck. Opening the door, I climb down and Tate follows. When they reach us, the mum speaks first, "Hey, you mind if the kids get a pic in front of the truck?"

"How about they climb in the back?"

"Really? Can we?" the little boy eagerly shouts, jumping up and down with excitement.

"Sure, come on over and climb up."

Before he does, he looks to his mum. "Please, Mum, can we?"

She nods and he races to the truck and eagerly climbs in. His sister hesitantly climbs in behind him. Kain hands his hat to the little boy and he pops it on his head, his little face beaming with excitement. "Go on, Mum, you hop in too," I encourage her.

Mum nods and climbs up. She sits next to her daughter, and this seems to ease the daughter's nerves, and she too starts to get excited. The captain hands his captain's hat to her and she pops it on her head. The mum smiles brightly at her daughter who is wearing Tate's. The three of them are delighted to be in the back of the rig and wear our safety hats.

"Give me your camera and I'll take a photo," I offer.

She hands her iPhone over to me and I snap a few pics for her. They climb down and I hand the phone back to her. The little boy asks us questions about the truck and firefighting. His sister has come out of her shell and is firing questions of her own at us while their mum chats with Cap, Kain, and Tatum.

Cap's phone rings and all conversations halt. He hangs up and his gaze flits between the three of us. "It's go time."

Our visitors step back and watch as we climb in. The kids wave us off and we head back into the danger zone. "Man, I love seeing little kids like that get so excited to see us. Makes me feel like a superhero," Kain says as the sky above fills with dense smoke.

Everyone in the truck is silent as we drive down the road, the atmosphere full of apprehension and nerves with each kilometre we drive. The sky changes from sunny and bright to dark and dismal in a matter of seconds. Everything around us is scorched and black from the fire we extinguished earlier. The air is filled with thick smoke, it's so thick it's blocking out the sun; turning daytime into nighttime. Thunder is cracking above from the storm the fire has created. I really hope there's no lightning as that can start new fires and we have enough to deal with at the moment.

"Fuck me," Kain utters as we drive through the area. Cap is in the driver's seat, and he's focused on the road ahead, well, what's left of it.

"This looks like something from an apocalyptic movie," I state as I take in the scene before me. The darkness surrounding us has taken on a copperish-red hue now and it's ominously silent.

"In all my thirty-three years, I've never seen anything like this before," Cap morosely utters, shaking his head at the devastation but he keeps driving. We see the other crews ahead and pull up behind them. Cap climbs out while we wait in the truck for our orders. It's eerily quiet and I don't like it at all. A feeling of unease washes over me but before I can process anything, Cap is back, and we head farther up the road to assist another crew.

We are not even fifty meters down the road when it all goes to shit. Things go from fine to disastrous in two point five seconds flat. One minute we're driving along through smoke and the next, the truck is surrounded by flames. We hold fire blankets to the windows to help with the heat. It's hotter than Hades in the truck right now but as quickly as the flames flare up, they die down just as fast.

We reach a clearing and Cap pulls over. "Everyone good?"

A chorus of "yeahs" echoes through the cab. Seems my gut was correct, and let's hope I don't feel that again. Reaching over, I take Tate's hand in mine, I know we're at work, but I need to hold her close to me.

We head farther down the road and finally, we meet up with the other crew. We all climb out and wait by the truck for our orders while Cap heads over to speak to the lieutenant. Before we get our orders, everything around us erupts in flames. Another firestorm has formed and this time, we're trapped outside of the truck.

We're effectively screwed and not in the naked fun way. All I can think about is getting the fuck out of here, but how?

15

TATUM

HOLY SHIT, I THINK AS FIRE ENGULFS THE AREA AROUND US. IF I thought it was hot in the truck, being out amongst it must be what it's like in a kiln. Flames soar high into the sky. Embers blow in the vicious wind that's kicked up and lightning flickers around us. I can't hear anything except for the roar of the burning blaze.

Pressing myself against the rig for protection, my eyes dart around looking for an escape, but I don't see a way out.

We're trapped.

There's no escape.

We're in the middle of a firestorm and there's nowhere to go.

It's hotter than Hades right now and bright, so blindingly bright. I've never seen a fire like this before or flames this color. They're almost violet and mixed with yellows, reds, and oranges. In a way it's beautiful, dangerously beautiful, but beautiful, nonetheless.

Turning my head into my shoulder, I shield my face, we hadn't had a chance to pop our masks on yet. One minute we were standing around, discussing getting the gear out and the next, we're crouched down next to the vehicle, using it as protection.

Closing my eyes fear starts to seep in and I drop to the ground and scrunch myself into a ball. With panic kicking in, I'm frozen. Everything I ever learned has left my brain. My body remains still but my mind is yelling at me to do something. To move. To do anything, but my limbs refuse to move. I'm hunkering down by the fire truck, acting like a fool and not the firefighter I know I can be. It isn't until someone grabs my arm and pulls, that I'm snapped back to the present.

Lifting my head, I open my eyes and see Kip. He's just as scared as I am but seeing him, having him close, kicks my senses and body into action. I take a moment to look him over, physically he looks fine, but his eyes are full of panic, fear, and unease. No doubt, exactly what mine look like.

He takes my hand in his and drags me toward the front of the truck and around to the safety of the other side of the vehicle. Kip rounds the hood and I've only taken two steps when tragedy strikes again. A tree crashes down nearby and it causes a domino effect. Tree after tree falls to the ground, causing the ground to shake.

A tree directly in front of us begins to fall and I just stand here and watch it coming toward me, at the last minute, Kip pulls on my hand and flings us away from the falling tree, which somehow landed on the front of the truck and not us.

From the unexpected force of his movements, I lose my footing in the ash-laced ground and begin to fall. Our hands are clasped together, and I take him down with me. We land on the ground with a thud and then there's another almighty crash, the tree bounces off the hood of the truck and onto Kip and me.

I'm knocked out for a few seconds and when I open my eyes again, I realize we are trapped and unable to move. I can hear the pained cries from the teams nearby. Their pleas echo through the air. My vision is dotty and I can't see clearly or move. I'm unable to do anything but lie here and await rescue.

Something large is crushing me but due to my spotty vision and the smoke around us, I can't see what is trapping me. I try to blink my vision clear, but my eyes are gritty with ash, dirt, and soot. They are stinging so I close them to protect my eyes.

Someone yells, "Lift" but then an intense heat engulfs me just as I feel pressure on my hand. It's a feeling I recognize and I smile. Somehow through all of this, Kips and my hands stay joined. Opening my eyes, I turn my head and realize that the pressure on me is Kip. My eyes rake over him but he's not moving, "Kip," I screech, but he doesn't move.

His eyes pop open and when our gazes meet, he mouths, "I love you" just as a whooshing sound echoes through my head again. The last thing I remember before darkness drags me under is a feeling of absolute dread slamming into me.

16

KIP

SOMEHOW, I STILL HAVE TATE'S HAND IN MINE, IT'S THE ONLY thing I can sense at this moment. It feels like time is standing still. My heart is beating but it's slow, very slow. Breathing is difficult. Everything is fuzzy but when I open my eyes, everything is bright and colorful. With each blink it gets brighter and brighter.

My body is cold and considering the immense heat emanating from the flames nearby, it's odd. How can I be cold and burning at the same time? With each breath and blink, everything is becoming blurry and hazy. It's getting harder and harder to breathe and my eyelids are heavy. My eyes close and this time, I leave them closed as the life inside of me begins to slip away.

Tatum squeezes my hand, well, I think she does. I try to squeeze back but my body won't respond. With all my might, I manage to turn my head and open my eyes one last time. My gaze lands on her and when I see her body wriggling next to me, I sigh in relief. She's alive, that's all that matters. She's trying to sit up but each time, she flops back to the earth below. I think she's yelling my name, but everything is muffled by the ringing in my ears.

Closing my eyes again, I feel my body relax. It's now freezing, it's ohh so cold. My body is numb but at the same time, there's an unbelievable pressure pressing down on me. Everything hurts and I know I'm not going to make it.

Forcing my eyes open, our gaze locks and I mouth, "I love you." My heart skips a beat, just like it did the day we met and the day I asked her to marry me. I will always love you, Tatum Prudence Summers, always and forever. With a smile on my face, my lids droop closed, and I close my eyes for the very last time.

17

TATUM

OPENING MY EYES, EVERYTHING IS BLURRY. BLINKING A FEW times, the ceiling comes into focus, and I sigh, relaxing into the mattress beneath me. It's soft but the sheet covering my body is scratchy against my skin. There's a charred scent in the air and a constant loud beeping is coming from next to me. Turning my head, I see that the irritating noise is coming from the heart rate monitor I'm hooked up to. *That's strange*, I think, *why am I hooked up to that?* But then I feel my heart erratically beating in my chest and realize why the machine is beeping away.

Closing my eyes, I try to remember why I'm here but it's all blank right now. Opening my eyes again, I look around the room, hoping for a clue, but it's bare and sheds no light on what's happened to me.

Fear begins to creep in that something terrible has occurred. Have I been kidnapped? Been in an accident? Am I dead and stuck in purgatory with that machine incessantly beeping for the rest of eternity? The annoying machine starts to beep faster and faster. Louder and louder. And then an alarm blares from the machine. Closing my eyes again, I take a few deep breaths in hopes of calming myself down and settling the screeching sound and, thankfully, it works. A few moments later, the noise dulls and once again the only sound is the beeping machine and my hurried breaths.

My throat is dry and burning. *Burning*, that word resonates within me, but I can't remember why. I try and swallow but my mouth is drier than the Mojave Desert right now. Licking my lips, I notice they're cracked and in need of some lip balm.

The door to my room opens and then I see Kain step in. He's covered in soot and looks like shit. His eyes connect with mine and relief flashes in them when he sees me staring back at him.

"Hey, big sis," he says, his voice quiet and very un-Kain like.

"Hey," I croak. I want to say more but it hurts. "Water," I manage to squeak out while pointing to the cup on the wheeled table at the end of my bed.

Kain walks toward me, grabs the cup, pops a straw in, and brings it to my lips. Lifting my head to take a drink, I drop back to the mattress wincing, as a searing pain tears through my upper chest. "Easy there, Tater Tot," Kain coos. This time, he brings the cup closer and guides the straw to my lips. Wrapping them around it, I take a sip, followed by another and another. I swallow down the water as if I'm shooting Fireball while playing higher or lower with Kain and Kip. This water is the best liquid I've ever drunk. The coolness of the water instantly soothes my throat, but it gurgles in my empty stomach and I realize I'm hungry.

"Thanks," I mumble, wiping my mouth with the back of my hand, being careful to not knock the drip in my hand. "Where's Kip?"

Kain's eyes pop wide open and his face pales. Underneath the sooty mess on his face, I see my question has shocked him to the core. A shiver runs through my body at his reaction and a feeling of unease develops low in my stomach, the water I just drank close to coming back up.

Swallowing down the lump forming in the back of my throat, I stare at my brother. "Kain," I plead. "Where is he? Where's Kip?"

He does that double-blink thing he does when he has bad news. "Tater Tot, we got caught." I nod, closing my eyes as I try to remember. "We were engulfed—" Opening my eyes, I raise my hand to stop him because it's all coming back to me. The memories crash into my mind and in vivid high-definition Technicolor, I see the events that led to me being here.

"No-no-no," I cry, shaking my head from side to side. Tears pour down my cheeks like an avalanche as the scene continues to play on repeat, over and over in my mind.

The deafening roar of the fire as it engulfed everything around us.

The flames licking high into the sky.

The heat building around me.

The cries of our team and the other firefighters and volunteers.

The devastation of the scorched earth, the burned trees.

Something heavy pressing down on me.

A pressure on my hand squeezing tightly.

Kip mouthing, "I love you," and then it rewinds to the beginning and starts to play again.

My heart hurts as I remember everything.

My head throbs as the memories take form in my mind.

The pressure in my head increases with each replay.

And, my heart, my heart aches, not from the pain of the fire, but from what I remember. From what I know deep down I've lost.

Looking to my brother for confirmation, when he nods, I cover my mouth as realization sets in. Kip's gone and it's why he's not here. Kain comes closer to me, and there's a whoosh of air when he drops down into the chair beside my bed. He lowers his head to the mattress and his shoulders shake, he's crying.

Swiping at my eyes, I sniffle. Reaching out, I touch his head and he lifts his up and sadly looks at me. I hate the look on his face reflecting back at me.

"Please, no, Kain," I cry, my eyes refilling with tears, making the room and Kain blurry. "Please tell me it was just a dream. A really vivid, horrible, shitty nightmare and that you're just fucking with me." I pause waiting for my brother to confess it's not true, but he remains mute. "Please, Kain," I beg. "Please tell me it was just a really bad nightmare."

"I'm sorry, Tater Tot, I can't. He's … he's gone." I hear the two words I was dreading, and hearing the brokenness in his voice, combined with the tears in his eyes, confirms that he's not tricking me. It's real, Kip is gone. "I'm so, so sorry."

"Noooooooo," I wail, shaking my head from side to side. Slamming my fists into the bed, I repeat, "No. No. No," over and over. My shrill cries echo through the room as the grief hits me with the force of a category-five tornado.

The machine beside me begins to beep erratically again. My heart beats faster and faster, faster than when I first woke up, as my soul shatters at the realization of what's happened.

My life from this point forward has irrevocably changed.

It will never be the same again.

I will never be the same again.

Kip is dead.

18

PENN

"Where's Mommy?" A little voice speaks up from beside me. I've been sitting on the floor in the waiting room, waiting for the doctors to run one final test before I have to say goodbye to Mads. I hope they take forever because I can't do it, I can't say goodbye. I am so lost in my grief; I hadn't even realized that Mom and Dad returned with Fletcher, and he is sitting next to me. Teri and Sandy are sitting across from me, both of them just as broken as me.

"Daddy?" my lil' man asks again.

"Climb up here, buddy." I lower my legs and beckon Fletcher to me by tapping my thigh. "Come snuggle with Daddy." He shuffles over and climbs onto my lap. He sits sideways and I hold him to my chest. A lump forms in the back of my throat. How do I tell him? He's only five and his mom is gone. "Buddy, Mommy ... Mommy had an accident." Somehow, I find the strength to continue, "She hit her head and she's gone to sleep."

"So we have to be quiet 'til she wakes up?"

"No, buddy." I shake my head. "She ... she's like Sleeping Beauty and will never wake up."

"Buts you can kiss her, and she'll wake up like Beauty did."

"Not this time, buddy. If I could kiss Mommy to wake her up, I'd do it forever."

"Is she in heaven with Woofey?"

"Yeah, buddy, she is."

"That's good." He nods. "Woofey won't be alone anymore."

"He won't, Mommy will take good care of him now."

"Who will be my mommy now then? Can it be the lady at the food place? She gave me two scoops of ice cream AAAAND chocolate sprinkles." His little eyes widen and he covers his mouth as he looks over to Mom with wide eyes. "Sorry, Nanna, I told Daddy."

"It's okay, buddy, I have a sneaking suspicion he knows since your face is covered in chocolate."

"Nanna's right, I did know, but guess what?"

"What?"

"Middle of the night ice cream is ALWAYS a good idea. Maybe you and I can sneak some together one time."

"Mom won't like that at all," Fletcher says, playing with the buttons on my shirt. And he's right, Mads would have gotten mad at us, but then she would have helped herself to a bowl and joined us. "Will she get to have middle-of-the-night ice cream in Heaven, Dad?"

"I'm sure she will, Fletch."

"Heaven sounds nice, I wish we could visit her there."

"Me too, buddy, me too."

The transplant lady, whose name I cannot remember right now, returns. "Mr. Brookes." I look up at her. "It's time."

Nodding, I hold on to Fletcher in my arms that little bit tighter. Fletch climbs off my lap and waits for me to stand up. He reaches for my hand and with my son's hand in mine, we walk out of the waiting room. The six of us head down the corridor to Mads's room to say our final goodbyes. Putting one foot in front of the other, I hold on to our son tightly. Wishing with everything I have that when we walk back into the room, she'll be sitting up in bed and yell "Tricked ya!" but I know, that's not going to happen. This will be our final goodbye.

Like earlier, my hand hovers over the door handle. Dad steps beside me and squeezes my shoulder in that parents' way. "You can do this, Penn."

Nodding, I push down on the handle and we all enter her room. My eyes immediately drift to her, she just looks like she's sleeping.

"She's sleeping," Fletcher whispers.

"Yeah, buddy, she is. We ..." I swallow back the lump. "We need to say goodbye so she can go be with Woofey."

"But I'll miss her, like I miss Woofey."

"I'll miss her too, buddy."

"Can I hug her?"

"Yeah, you can." Placing him onto the bed, he climbs on top of her and snuggles into her side like he does when he comes into our room on a Sunday morning for snuggles. "I love you, Mommy, give Woofey a hug for me."

Seeing him lying on her like that breaks my heart. I choke back a sob and slide onto the bed, beside them. Resting my head on her shoulder, I drape my arm over Fletcher and the three of us lie here for the last time together.

Sniffles sound from behind me and when I look over my shoulder, I see her mom and my mom tearfully hugging one another. Why is the world so cruel to take her away from so many people who love her? Why couldn't it be some criminal? Some pedophile who doesn't deserve to live? Why did it have to be the love of my life and the mother of my son?

"I miss you already, Mads," I whisper.

"You've still got me, Daddy," a little voice says, and his words tear me open a little more.

"I know, buddy, I know." Running my fingers through his

hair, he stares at me. He has tears in his little eyes, eyes that look so much like his mother's. "You have her eyes," I murmur.

"No, I don't, see?" He proceeds to lift up Maddie's eyelids showing me her eyes. This causes me to chuckle, but that chuckle turns into a sob when I see that her eyes are lifeless. Mads has, had, the most amazing green eyes. I've never seen a shade like it before, well, not until Fletcher came along. He's the spitting image of his mother, temperament and all. She will live on through him and I'll make sure he never forgets her because there's no chance of me forgetting her.

Mads will live on in our memories. In our hearts and due to her generosity, up to seven people will get a second chance because of her. Madeline "Maddie" Brookes nee Hollyfield will never be forgotten, not as long as I'm breathing.

19

TATUM

THE OVERWHELMING URGE TO PEE AWAKENS ME AND WHEN I open my eyes again, I see my mom sitting in the chair next to my bed. "Mom?" I say her name like a question because I'm confused over seeing her here. Last time I was awake, it was Kain in that chair. Speaking of my brother, I look around the room for him, but I don't see him.

"Hi, baby," she coos. She shuffles forward in her seat and brushes a tendril of hair off my forehead and tucks it behind my ear. Kip used to do that too, he loved playing with my hair, twirling it around his finger ... or wrapping my long locks around his fist as he'd fuck me from behind.

"He's gone, Mom," I whisper, "he'll never ..." I don't finish that thought because my mom doesn't need to know that specific memory.

"I know, baby, I'm so sorry."

"I ... I think he saved me, Mom. My memory is fuzzy, but I remember him taking my hand and pulling me, and then I'm sure he shielded me with his body. He sacrificed himself for me, Mom. How do I live with that? He died saving me."

"He died saving you because he loved you unconditionally and it's because of that that you're alive, Tatum. Don't let his death be in vain. You live for the two of you."

Nodding at her, I sniffle and wipe my eyes. When I open them again, I smile when I see Dad and Kain enter my room. "Dad, you're here," I voice.

"Of course, I put on my big girl panties, downed a couple of Valium, and fifteen hours, four minutes, and thirty-five seconds later, I landed safely in Australia." The fact my dad did that means the world to me, and then I can't help but laugh when he adds, "Your mother and I are taking a cruise to get home."

Shaking my head, my gaze flicks between my family members. I can't believe they are all here. I'm grateful they are because I don't think I would get through this alone. Kain shuffles on his feet and that's when I notice he has a large coffee from Kupz in his hand. "Is that for me?" I ask him.

"Ummm, no, it's for me."

"Kain," Dad warns him, "give the coffee to your sister. Told you the smell of caffeine would wake her up."

"Actually, it was the need to pee that woke me up but once I empty my bladder, I would love that cup of coffee."

"Lucky I love you, Tater Tot, and lucky for you, I also have a triple chocolate muffin to go with your coffee."

"You are the best brother I have."

"I'm the only brother you have … unless Mom and Dad are hiding something?"

"Kain," Dad berates him again and smacks him up the side of the head, "there's a time for jokes and now isn't it." Dad berating him causes me to laugh and that reminds me I need to pee.

"Can you help me up, Mom? I'm gonna pee myself otherwise."

"Of course." She stands and helps me sit up. She fusses with the IV and once it's attached to the wheelie thing, she steps back and I stand. Gripping the pole, I shuffle into the adjoining bathroom.

"Ugh, Tate, put your ass away," Kain complains and fake vomits. "I don't need to see that."

Seems my hospital gown just did a Britney and I flashed my ass—not my hoo-ha—to my parents and brother. Flipping him the bird, I continue over to the bathroom and finally make it to the toilet. Sitting down, I relieve my bladder and I swear, that's the best pee of my life. My bladder was so full, damn fluids. Flushing the toilet, I walk to the sink to wash my hands and when I look at my reflection in the mirror, my eyes widen.

Apart from a scratch on my cheek, I have no other visible injuries. I rip the gown off and spin around to look at my back but again, I see nothing. How is it that I have one teeny tiny scratch, but Kip died? It doesn't make sense and it certainly isn't fair.

Covering my mouth, I shriek out a sob and fall to the floor. Naked, I sit here and cry. Mom comes rushing in. "Ohhh, Tatum." She drops down in front of me and pulls me into her arms. "Let it all out, baby, I've got you."

"Why, Mom, why? Why do I only have a scratch and Kip's gone? It's not fair, it should have been me who died, not him. It should have been me." Wrapping my arms around Mom, I cry into her shoulder. My body heaves as grief pours out of me and I repeatedly mumble, "It should have been me."

Mom and I sit huddled on the bathroom floor until I have no more tears left to cry. "Come up, Tatum, let's get you dressed and back into bed."

Nodding in reply, Mom helps me up and re-dresses me in pajamas that magically appeared. Mom must see my confusion. "Kain went and packed you a bag."

"He's a good brother."

"I heard that," he shouts from my room, "and there were witnesses, you can't dispute that you said it."

"I didn't hear anything," Dad says as Mom and I reenter my room. "Did you, Ginny?"

"Hear what?" Mom asks with a shrug as she helps me back into bed.

"You two both suck." Kain huffs.

"We still love you, Son," Dad tells him. Then he looks to me. "How you doing, sweetheart?"

"I don't know, Dad. I'm just numb."

"That's to be expected. Dave and a few of the guys came around while you were in the bathroom just now but I told them today isn't a good day, said maybe tomorrow."

"Thanks, Dad. I'm not really up for visitors so I appreciate that."

"We'll get out of your hair then," Mom says, fluffing my blanket.

"You guys are fine. I don't want to be alone, but I also don't want people here either. Does that make sense?"

"Oddly, yes," Mom agrees, brushing a tendril of hair off my face and tucking it behind my ear in that soothing Mom kind of way. "I remember when Nanna passed, I felt the same way so I completely understand."

"Thanks, Mom."

"Can we get you anything?"

"You just being here is enough." But really, I want to say *get me Kip* but that's never going to happen. Besides, I've seen *Pet Cemetery*, the dead never come back the same and I don't want to remember him like that. I want to remember him as the sexy Australian firefighter, who is the genetically beautiful baby of Chris Hemsworth, Hugh Jackman, Heath Ledger— may he Rest in Peace and now be drinking Fireball with Kip —and Margot Robbie. That's the Kip I want to live on in my memory. That's the Kip I'll love forever.

20

PENN

IT'S BEEN THREE DAYS SINCE MY WORLD IMPLODED ON ITSELF AND if it wasn't for my mom, Wren, and Teri, Fletcher and I would have starved by now. Lying in our bed, I run my finger over her pillow absentmindedly. I can still smell her; I never want to wash these sheets again. I don't know how I'm going to carry on without her. Mads was my everything, my reason for breathing. When she died, a piece of me died too.

"Daaaaaad," Fletcher's little voice sings from the doorway.

Looking up from her pillow, I see our son standing in the doorway. "What's up, buddy?"

"I miss Mommy."

"Me too, buddy, me too."

Tapping the mattress next to me, he walks over and climbs up. He has a grape juice box in his hands. Just as I reach out to take it from him, he squeezes on it as he climbs up and purple juice covers Mads's pillow. "Look what you've done," I growl at him as I jump off the bed. Fletcher stands next to me wide-eyed. "You've ruined her smell," I hiss. "Why would you do that?" I snap at my son and his bottom lip wobbles and he begins to cry. "Crying isn't going to turn back time and stop the spill. Hell, it won't even fucking go back four days. If it could, I'd go back and offer to drive her to work. If only I'd fucking driven her that day, she'd still be a-fucking-live." Bringing the pillow to my nose, I sniff but all I can smell is grape juice. "You've ruined it," I shout, throwing the pillow away from me. It lands at Dad's feet, and he bends down and picks it up.

"Penn Brookes Jr., you need to rein it in," he growls, glaring daggers at me.

"Or what, Dad?" I snarl back at him. "You going to spank me?"

"The way you're acting right now, you deserve one."

"He spilled his fucking juice box, Dad."

"So, you wash the pillow, it's not the end of the world."

"It was her fucking pillow, Dad. Her. Fucking. Pillow." He nods at me like I've lost my mind and right now, I think I have. "I … I could still smell her on it and now, now, all I can fucking smell is grape juice." Snatching the pillow from him, I sniff it again and again, trying to find a spot that smells like her. That doesn't smell like juice, but that's all I can smell.

"Fletcher, buddy," Mom says from the doorway as I continue to sniff the pillow. "Come with Nanna. Daddy needs a moment." Fletcher pushes past me and races over to Mom. He's sobbing right now and seeing him so upset has no effect on me.

Dropping to the floor, I hug the ruined pillow to my chest when I find a spot that smells like her. Bringing it to my face, I bury my head into it. Closing my eyes, I smile as I breathe her in. The door clicks closed and I feel Dad towering above me. I can't look at him right now. I know I'm going to see disappointment reflecting back at me because I'm disappointed in myself too.

"Penn," my dad finally speaks, the silence stretching much longer than I thought it would.

Pulling the pillow away from my face, I sheepishly look

up at my dad. I feel like a little kid who's about to get a talking to. "I'm broken, Dad, I'm not strong enough to go on. I don't wanna be here anymore. I can't do this without her."

"You can and you will, Penn. That little boy needs you." Then he says something that cuts me to my core, "Maddie would be so ashamed of you right now."

Staring up at my dad, I blink and process his words, *Maddie would be so ashamed of you right now.* "Fuck," I hiss because he's right.

"What have I done, Dad? He's going to hate me."

"He won't hate you, Penn. He's just as upset as you are but he's only five, he's processing this differently than you. You need to remember that you're the adult. You need to find a way to grieve and be there for him at the same time. Be the dad I know you can be."

"Dad, I'm the dad who's currently getting a lecture from his dad for losing his shit over a juice box. I'm a douchedad."

This causes him to chuckle. "Some things never change. Remember when you were seven and you spilled your juice box on Mom's new beige rug?"

"I got in so much trouble that day."

"Because you tried to blame it on your sister."

"I still maintain it was her fault, she should have just given me hers and then I wouldn't have reached out to snatch it from her."

"Ergo, your fault."

"Potato. Vodka," I reply with a shrug.

"You good now?" he asks, dropping down next to me, resting his back against the bed.

"I honestly don't fucking know, Dad."

"I should kick your ass for swearing, even if you are a grown man. I'll give you a pass today but from tomorrow, Penn, you need to start thinking about someone other than yourself. Your mother and I will be here every step of the way, but you need to let go of this anger. You need to not yell at your son for making a mistake."

"I know, Dad, I know but … how do I do this without her?"

"I wish I had the answers but all I can suggest is, take one day at a time. Focus on the good times, don't let go of those memories, and you be a dad to that little boy out there. He needs you more than ever right now. You have to remember; he just lost his mom—"

"I lost my wife too," I throw back at him, anger lacing my tone but for the life of me, I don't know why I'm so angry at him pointing out that Fletcher lost his mom.

"I know that. What I'm getting at, Penn, is that it's not just about you. Fletcher and you are a team. Sure, your team's a woman down but you still have each other, the game isn't over yet. You need to be there for one another, and you as the adult, first and foremost, need to be there for your son. No more losing your shit over a juice box. You want to lose your shit over a juice box, you grab me. I can take it."

"Thanks, Dad," I tell him. "I guess I better go apologize to my son."

"Sounds like a plan. You've got this, Penn, and just know, I'm here for you."

Nodding, I stare over at Dad. He's right, we are Team Brookes and we will get through this.

21

TATUM

They've just discharged me from the hospital and I'm waiting for Kain to bring the car around. The rumble of a truck's engine catches my attention and when I look up, I see Kip's truck coming toward me. It's like a punch to the vagina, he loved that truck almost as much as he loved me.

"I fucking love this thing," Kain proudly declares as he jumps out and comes over to me. Offering me his hand, he pulls me up from the wheelchair I waited for him in. I wince when I stand up straight, my bruised ribs are still twingey and every now and then, it pulls and hurts like a bitch. Dropping back to the seat, I lower my head and begin to cry.

Lifting my head, I look up at my brother. "I'm broken, Kain, I'm not strong enough. I can't go on. I don't wanna be here anymore."

"You bite your tongue, Tatum Prudence Summers." He drops to his knees before me and takes my hand in his. "You are the strongest person I know, Tater Tot. You will get through this, I bet my left nut on it."

"Please don't bet your nuts, that's just gross. At least bet something good like Mom and Dad do."

"Whatevs," he says, shaking his head at me. "Look, your life is one big shit sandwich right now but with time, that will change into a Vegemite and cheese one."

"You hate Vegemite," I express with a smile.

"I do but for some weird reason, you love that shit and it felt like the right analogy to use."

"Look at you, using big words in the correct context."

"Focus, Tater Tot, focus. What was I saying? Ohh, yeah, right, you will get through this. You're a Summers. You're tough and you have me by your side. No questions asked."

"I miss him so much, Kain," I tearfully whisper. "How … how do I go on without him?"

"One day at a time, Tater Tot, one day at a time."

"Thanks." I sniff, wiping my nose on the shoulder of my shirt.

"That's disgusting." Kain shakes his head at me.

"Could be worse, I could have waited 'til you hugged me and wiped it on you."

"What hug?"

"The hug you're about to give me because your big sister needs it."

"Lucky I love you, sis. Now, come here and give your baby brother a hug."

"Think you can come to me? My ribs are killing me."

"How long you going to milk that for?"

"As long as it gets me what I want. Now shut up and hug me and then take me home. You and I are going to play higher or lower and get shitfaced on Fireball."

"Should you mix meds with Fireball whiskey?"

"I don't give a flying fuck. I nearly died. I deserve an afternoon to let loose."

"Sounds like a plan."

He leans over and hugs me and then we do exactly as I suggested. We get drunk, reminisce about Kip, and for the few hours before I pass out, everything is okay in the world. However, the next morning, it all comes crashing back when I have to deal with life after Kip.

22

PENN

"We therefore commit this body to the ground, earth to earth, ashes to ashes, dust to dust; in sure and certain hope of the resurrection to eternal life." The minister's words float around me. The numbness I've felt the last few days intensifies and changes into something I have never felt before. This is it. This is the final goodbye for Mads and confirming my thoughts, the minister wraps up the service. "… and this concludes today's service. The family would like you to join them at The James Hotel for a celebration of life."

Sitting here, I just stare at her coffin. Inside that shiny wooden box is the love of my life. After today, she really will be gone. As per her wishes, she'll be cremated and then I have to take her to Hawaii to the Luxe Resort in Lanikai where we went on our honeymoon. She wants me to scatter her ashes on the beach there at sunset.

"You coming, bro?" Wren's soft voice causes me to pull my gaze away from the coffin and when I look around, I realize that everyone is gone and I'm the only person still sitting here.

"Fletch—"

"Is with Mom," she informs me.

Nodding, I turn my attention back to the coffin. "I ... I need a minute to say goodbye."

"Take all the time you need." She squeezes my shoulder and walks away.

When I hear the wooden doors close, I stand up and walk over to the coffin. Resting my palm on the cool wood, I suddenly get an image of Vada crying at Thomas J's funeral from *My Girl* and I'm thankful that A. Mads didn't wear glasses and B. That we had a closed casket. I don't want to remember her all pale and deathly. I want to remember her how she is in the photos adorning her casket. Smiling brightly. Sexy as sin.

"Hey, baby," I mumble. Clearing my throat, I try again, "Hey, baby, I miss you so fucking much it hurts." I shake my head. "You'd be so disappointed in me; I've acted like a spoiled little fuck this week. I snapped at Fletcher over something so silly because I was so lost in MY grief that I made it all about me. I forgot that he's grieving too. He misses you too, we all miss you. Why did you have to leave us? Why did that person's brakes fail, causing them to slam into you and for you to then roll down an embankment? Why didn't I drive you that day? Why! Why! Why! So many fucking whys." Resting my head against the wood, I run my fingers back and forth on the surface. "This is the last time you and I will physically be in the same room together, after today, you will only remain in my memory. In photos. Not a day will go by that I won't think about you. That I won't love you. You were the PB to my jelly. I will never forget you, Madeline Brookes, never."

Pressing my lips to her coffin, I stand up, turn my back, and walk away. With leaden steps, I put one foot in front of the other and slowly walk away from the love of my life and into an unknown future.

23

TATUM

TODAY IS THE DAY THAT WE LAY MY FIANCÉ TO REST.

Today is our final goodbye.

Today is going to be fucked, there are no two ways about it.

Today. Will. Be. Shit!

How do I say goodbye? We should be planning our wedding, instead, I planned his funeral, which due to the fires, was delayed a few weeks. To be honest, I'm okay with that because it means I didn't have to face the prospect of saying goodbye, but the fires are now under control—which is fantastic news—but it means I need to face the final goodbye.

The fire that took Kip burned through seventy-three percent of New South Wales. It destroyed two hundred thousand homes, countless numbers of wildlife, and twenty-two people lost their lives, Kip included. The world rallied around Australia, and they will rebuild. The Aussie spirit is hard to break. When they're down, they get back up again and fight … just like I'm trying to today, but today is going to be the hardest thing I will ever have to face.

"It's time to go, Tatum," Mom quietly says from the

doorway to my room.

Nodding, I look over to her. "Mom," I blubber, my eyes welling with tears and my heart tearing once again. "I'm not ready, I can't do this. I can't say goodbye."

"You can, Tatum," she states in that Mom tone that's stern but also caring. She walks into the room with her arms wide open.

"I can't, Mom, I can't do this," I repeat as I wrap my arms around her. "I'm not strong enough," I mumble into her shoulder.

Pulling back, she holds my upper arms in her hands and looks at me. "You listen to me, Tatum Summers, and you listen hard. You are one of the strongest people I know, and I know you can do this—"

"But—" I go to interrupt, but she halts my refute with just a raise of her eyebrows.

"You'll regret it if you don't," she says, and I know she's right. If I hide here and don't go today, I will regret it.

Nodding in agreement, I swallow back a sob and step back from her. I retighten my high ponytail before running my hands down my formal uniform. Mom and Dad bought it over with them and I'm thankful to have it. "Let's do this," I shakily say.

Mom nods and offers me her hand. I take it, holding on tightly as we walk into the living room. When I see Dad and Kain in their formal uniforms, a surge of grief slams into me and I begin to cry again. "I can't. I can't. I can't," I repeat, shaking my head vigorously from side to side. Tears pour down my cheeks and I fall to my knees. Covering my face, I break down. The three of them squat down and embrace me as I fall apart, again. Feels like that's all I do at the moment; you'd think I'd have run out of tears by now, but I seem to have an unending abundance of them.

"Come on, Tate," Dad encourages, "you can do this. Your mom, Kain, and I are right by your side."

"Dad," I whine, "I ... I don't want to say goodbye."

"I know, sweetie, but you have to. Find that inner strength I know you have. Put one foot in front of the other and walk out that door. We'll be right here to guide you."

"Dad, you're supposed to walk me down the aisle on my wedding day. Not guide me down the aisle at my fiancé's funeral."

"I know, Tater Tot, but maybe one day that will happen."

My head snaps up and I glare at him, shaking my head. "I am *never* falling in love again, Dad. Never. I don't want to have to go through this ever again."

"Never say never, Tater Tot," Kain says.

"You don't know shit, Brozart," I snap at him. "I will never fall in love again. Never ever, ever. Don't ever say that again. Kip is my one and only true love, end of story."

He holds his hands up in defeat. "Okay, fine, whatever you say but we need to go, otherwise we'll be late."

I'm okay with that, I think as I silently follow them out to Kip's truck.

The trip to the funeral home is silent. The only sound is my sniffles. Dad pulls up and I just sit here, staring up the stairs, knowing on the other side of those heavy wooden doors lies Kip, and I have to say my final goodbye.

The truck door opens and Dad's standing there, offering me his hand. Placing my hand in his, I climb out. Kip's and my captain, Dave, comes over. "Tatum, it's good to see you."

"You too, Cap. You remember my dad, Shaun, and my mom, Ginny?"

"Yes, I remember them, we met at the hospital a few weeks ago."

"Right," I reply, nodding. I don't remember much from then so I have to believe what they're saying. A silence envelops us and as much as I don't want to, I know it's time. "Shall we?" I offer. Digging deep, I find the courage to walk up the stairs and enter the building.

When I push through the doors, I stop midstep when I see a huge photo of Kip sitting on top of his coffin, he's leaning against his truck, the ocean in the background. His arms are crossed across his chest and he's smiling. He's smiling in that way that lights up any room. My eyes well with tears and I stare at the most perfect picture of him. "I—"

"You can, Tater Tot," Kain affirms from beside me. Wrapping his arm around my shoulders, he and Dad guide me down to the front chairs. Dropping into my seat, I stare at his photo. The minister begins talking and then it's time for Kain to read the eulogy. They asked me to do it but I refused. I'm having enough trouble just breathing now, there's no way I could speak.

"Kip 'no middle name' Kitson was an amazing man. So amazing that he asked my sister to marry him, and that's saying a lot because I grew up with Tate and she's a lot to handle." Those around me laugh but me, I just stare blankly at Kip's photo. "Whenever I think about Kip, I remember his bright smile. He had one for everybody he met along the way, and that's one of the things I will miss most about him. He could enter a room and smile, and the mood would suddenly shift. I have no doubt that right now, he's up there smiling down at us with the brightest smile he can give. The pain of his death is not something that will easily go away with just sincere condolences or a bunch of flowers or a shot of Fireball, but in time, it will be easier to bear. He was a supportive friend, a loyal husband-to-be, a talented fire-fighter, and an amazing person in general. He leaves us with a memory that neither time nor even his death can ever take away. I'll miss you, Kip, love you long-time, brother."

Kain comes and sits next to me and I get the sudden urge to speak. "I want to say something," I shout, interrupting the minister. The minister invites up to the front. With shaking hands, I grip the podium and look out at the room.

It's filled with his colleagues, friends, and people who I have never met before.

"Kip was my everything and the years I spent with him in my life were filled with excitement, adventure, and so much more. This Aussie showed up for life in the biggest way possible and he touched the soul of everyone he met. Kip had a rough beginning, but he made something of himself and … and he was ripped from us too soon. From the moment my eyes landed on him at the station back in Lockhart Falls, I was smitten. He swooped in and stole my heart and in the blink of an eye, he was cruelly ripped from my grasp. He saved me that day, it should be me in that coffin." I wipe at my cheeks. "It should be me in there. Kip Kitson sacrificed himself for me, and I don't know how to live with that. On one hand I'm thankful he saved me, but on the other, I fucking hate that he left me. Why did you leave me? Why, Kip, why?" Tears are pouring down my cheeks now. "I will always love you, Kip. You were the peanut butter to my honey, Kip, and I miss you so much. So fucking much. I know my dad is going to kick my ass for swearing up here." Everyone laughs at that. "But I'll take any ass kick because that's how special Kip is, was. Past tense. I will always love you, Kip. Always and forever."

Stepping down, I walk back to my seat and blankly stare toward the front. The minister wraps up the service. "We therefore commit this body to the ground, earth to earth, ashes to ashes, dust to dust; in sure and certain hope of the Resurrection to eternal life." They wheel Kip away and as everyone exits the room. I sit here and stare at the door they just took him through. I don't want him to be eternal, I want him here with me and then we can die together like Alley and Noah from *The Notebook*.

As I walk out of the funeral home, with Dad and Kain holding me up, one thing is clear. I will never love anyone again. Kip was it for me, he's the only person who can have my heart.

24

PENN

... eight months later

When I walk into the house after dropping Fletcher at school, I stop midstep when I take in the scene before me. "What's going on?" I utter, looking around the room at the group of people waiting for me. Mom, Dad, and Maddie's parents, Teri and Sandy, are sitting, waiting for me. Wren's face is smiling at me on the TV, she's FaceTiming in, and to round out the group is a lady I have never seen before and from the look on her face, she means business.

Everyone just silently stares at me as I walk farther into the room. "Someone wanna start talking?"

Everyone's eyes dart around sheepishly but it's the strange lady who talks first. "Hello, Penn, I'm Dr. Nina. Your family is concerned—"

"I'm fine," I sneer at her, then I look to everyone else and repeat, "I'm fine. Really."

"Penn, you're kidding yourself if you think you're fine. You are anything but, and we're worried about you," Wren says through the screen.

"I'm fine," I hiss again. Throwing my hands up in exasperation, I march into the kitchen. Reaching into the fridge, I grab a beer, pop the top off, and take a sip.

My sister scoffs and it echoes through the speakers. "You're so fucking fine that you're drinking a beer at nine-fifteen in the morning. You look like a fucking hobo. When was the last time you shaved? Showered? Huh?"

"What do you know? You're however many fucking miles away in Los Angeles."

"I have eyes, moron, I can see you're falling apart. You need help."

"I'm fucking fine," I growl again.

"Penn," Dad shouts, "enough is enough. You need help and Dr. Nina thinks—"

"I don't need to hear what the doctor has to say. Look, lady, I'm sure you're great at whatever you do but as I said, I'm fine."

"Penn, your family is concerned that you're not handling the death of your wife."

"How do you fucking know? You don't know a fucking thing about me. I'm doing the best I can without her, but it's fucking hard."

"Language, Penn," Dad berates me. I just give him my 'fuck you' look.

Dr. What-ever-her-name-is ignores my outburst and continues, "Your family has filled me in, and I agree with them, you're not coping. From what they've told me, you are hopping back and forth between stages one, two, and three." I go to interrupt her but she raises her hand. "Answer me this one question and if you can answer it without an ounce of hesitation, I'll grab my things and walk out that door." She points to the front door. "No questions asked."

"Shoot," I snap, taking another drink from the bottle in my hand. Dropping into the armchair, I lean back and cross my ankle over my knee. Glancing around at everyone, I notice the different looks on everyone's faces. Sadness.

Despair. Disappointment. Concern. A combination of all three.

"Are you happy?"

Three words.

Three fucking words knock me on my ass. If I wasn't sitting down, I would be now. Sitting forward, I place the beer on the coffee table in front of me, rest my elbows on my knees, and cradle my head in my hands. Since I lost Mads, not one person has asked me that question. It's all been how's Fletcher? I'm sorry for your loss. When was the last time you ate? Showered? Shaved? As I sit here and think if I am happy, I realize I'm not happy and I'm definitely not fine. I've been putting on this mask, hiding my deepest feelings and emotions, but it seems those closest to me are seeing my struggles, and then I begin to remember the questions of concern coming from them. Lifting my head, I look around the room at those nearest and dearest to me. When I see the worry in their eyes for me, it hits me that I need to make a change in my life. "Fuck," I snigger, shaking my head. "Fuck, fuck, fuckity fuck." Squeezing the back of my neck, I inhale deeply and turn my head toward the doctor and let my eyes convey everything. I see reflecting back at me that she knows I now realize, I do, in fact, need help. "You just knocked me on my ass with that question."

"So I'm guessing I'm not leaving then?"

I shake my head at her and drop my gaze. "No," I quietly whisper. "I … I need help."

"And I can do just that." She nods and walks over to me and sits down on the coffee table. "Those three words, 'I need help' are what we all wanted to hear from you today. Penn, you're grieving and that's understandable. You lost your wife suddenly, but you need to move on from that. She wouldn't want you to wallow and waste your life. Your son needs you, as does your family, but they need you happy and fine."

Looking over at everyone, I begin to shake my head. "I'm so sorry for acting like—"

"A stubborn jackass douchehole," my sister interrupts, causing me to laugh.

"Yeah, that."

"Penn, there's only enough room in my life for one stubborn jackass doucheman, and that position is already filled. I, we, we all want happy-go-lucky Penn back. I know it's probably been said, but Maddie wouldn't want you wallowing like this. She'd want you to be the best dad/mom you can be for your son and she'd want you to be happy."

"I know," I answer her with a nod, then I look over at Mom and Teri. "I really need to thank you two ladies the most. I may have been in a fog and lost, but I've seen what you guys have been doing for my son and me. You've been there for him when I haven't. I've been a shitty father, son, son-in-law, and brother. I ... I'm so sorry."

Lowering my head back down, I focus on the area rug and smile. "Mads loved this rug. As soon as she saw it, she fell in love but it was a thousand bucks, she refused to pay that much for 'something people are going to walk over.' But I saw that sparkle in her eyes so I went back the next day and bought it. She was so mad at me for spending that much money but she was so happy when she saw it, and I loved seeing her like that. I suggested we just put it down, see it in place, and then we could return it. I didn't want her to be upset over an area rug but as soon as it was down, that glint from the store was back. She was glowing. I knew we were keeping it. We made love right there and then on this thousand-dollar rug, and it just so happened to be when we conceived Fletch. Funny story, he got his name from this rug 'cause it's called The Fletcher."

"Eeeeew," Wren protests and fake gags. "I walk on that thing ... with bare feet."

"Then I probably shouldn't tell you Mads and I have also

done it on the couch, the bed in the spare room, the kitchen island—"

"Enough," Sandy states, raising his hand. "I don't need to know all the places you defiled my daughter. I want happy memories of her—"

"They're happy memories for me," I throw back at him.

"For you yes, for us"—he flicks his finger around the room—"they aren't the happy memories we want to have of Madeline. We want to remember her laughter. Her smile. Her love for us."

"I want that too … plus the ones that I won't speak of with you prudes."

"I'm not a prude," Wren grumbles, causing us all to laugh.

Swallowing, I look to the doctor. "I want to feel happy like this again but I don't want to only feel like this when I remember her. I … I want to be the old happy-go-lucky me again."

"And I can help you with that, Penn. Admitting you need help is the first step."

Nodding, I smile and for the first time since I lost Mads, it isn't forced or fake. It's genuine. She may be gone, but I still have a life to live and I intend on living ever day to the fullest. "Okay, Doc, what's the plan?"

For the next hour, we discuss my treatment plan. I have the option of staying here and doing it slowly or I could head to a grief retreat and tackle it head-on. At first, I refuse the retreat because I'm not into that mumbo-jumbo healing bullshit, but the one Dr. Nina recommends isn't full of the mumbo-jumbo crap. So, I pack a bag, hug my lil' man with a promise to call every day and come back a better daddy, and I head to The Grove Retreat in Castaway Grove.

When I first arrive at the retreat I begin to wonder if I've made a mistake coming here. Sure, the resort is stunning with its beachfront location, but it's the yoga, meditation, and holistic bullshit that concerns me, but is keeping me here, so I stay the course. I have to do it for Fletcher but most of all, I have to stay for me. And I'm so glad I do because Rebecca, my allocated therapist, tailors a package for me with less of the yoga and more of the emotional healing. She even got me to try said yoga and, even though I hate to admit it, I love it.

My time here is coming to an end and I'm so glad I stuck it out. Rather than pushing Mads's death to the side, I tackled it head-on. It still hurts that she's gone but it doesn't hurt as much and as Rebecca said, "That hurt will ease as each day passes, but her memory will live on forever." I realize that I was scared to let her go because I was scared the memory of her would too. That will only happen if I let it and because I have Fletcher, and his namesake area rug in my life, her memory will live on forever in us.

It's so beautiful here in Castaway Grove, so I decide to stay on afterward and have a mini getaway with Fletcher before I return to the real world. Mom and Dad are bringing him and we are going to stay in this great beachfront house I found on Airbnb. This little holiday is exactly what he and I need. Now that I'm not caught up in my grief, I can focus on being the best dad for him. I feel so bad I haven't been there for him, he's been grieving too, his mom died. Luckily for me, between my and Mads's parents, they took care of him. I owe them, big time.

"How are you feeling?" Rebecca asks, joining me on the back patio.

"I'm going good," I tell her with a nod, "really good. I'm ready to head back into the real world and live again. Mads would want that."

"You need to do it for you too," she reminds me.

"I am, but knowing she'd be disappointed in me gives me that extra motivation. Being here, away from Fletcher, for the last month has made me realize I have so much to live for. I want to see him grow up and thrive and I can't do that if I'm living in a blur of booze, sleeping pills, and grief."

"That's great and you do know that after you leave here, it's okay to have the odd drink?"

"I do know that, but this past month without it has really cleared my mind and your fucking yoga really is relaxing."

"Excellent," she says in that Monty Burns from *The Simpsons* kind of way. "My work here is done. But seriously, Penn, I'm proud of you. I wasn't sure this was going to be for you when you first arrived, but you shocked me. Hell, you shocked all of us."

"How so?"

"When you first arrived you were a combative, back-talking so and so. Your face when you walked into the yoga room on that first day was priceless, but you pushed on and after that first session, I knew you'd be fine. If only we'd gotten you into a Pilates class."

"Maybe next time."

"Next time?"

"Yeah, I think I need to make this a yearly thing. Cleanse the soul and all that bullshit once a year, so I can be the best I can be for Fletcher."

"I'm glad our 'bullshit' helped you."

"Seriously, Rebecca, thank you. You gave me my life back."

"Just doing my job, Penn. I hope to see you back here next year for more 'bullshit' and if you do, I'm getting you into a Pilates class."

"Yeah, we'll see about that." Then I hear the best sound. "Daaaaaaaaaaaddddddy!" When I turn around, I see my little man barreling toward me.

Standing up, I walk toward him. "Fletcher," I say just as he launches himself at me. Wrapping my arms around him, I breathe him in. "I missed you, buddy."

"I missed you too, Daddy, but Nanna gave me ice cream to ease my pain."

"Did she now?" I ask him just as he covers his mouth and looks at me wide-eyed.

"That was supposed to be a secret."

"How about I forget you told me."

"Yes, please." He nods with excitement. "Nanna says I can go to the beach."

"We can go to the beach every day we are here."

"Now?"

"First, we need to get Daddy's things from here and then go to where we will be staying, and once we've unpacked, I'll take you to the beach."

"And can we roast marshmallows on a fire?"

"We might be able to do that."

"Yesssss," he hisses, doing a fist pump in the air. Mads used to fist pump like that when she was excited, and I realize seeing him do that and thinking of her doing that, the memory didn't hurt. It reiterates that everything is going to be okay.

25

TATUM

Sitting on the beach in Castaway Grove, I stare out at the sprawling ocean before me. I've just finished my morning run along the beach and I'm huffing and puffing. Since losing Kip, I've let my fitness go. He was my workout buddy and I miss him. It's so fucking hard to move on when you feel alone and broken. A piece of me died too that day. The fact I'm no longer in shape is probably due to the unhealthy diet I was living on after his death and everyone left—burgers and fries, beer and Fireball.

A couple of weeks ago, I moved back to the States because I was so lost and alone in Australia by myself. After Kip's funeral, which I have very little recollection of because I was so emotional, I managed to convince my parents and brother that I was fine and would be okay by myself. Somehow, I pulled off an Oscar-winning performance and convinced them I was coping and getting on with my life. Five weeks after we laid Kip to rest, Mom and Dad sailed back to the US via Tahiti and Hawaii. Kain stayed with me for another month until one day, I lost my shit with him.

"I'm fine, Kain, I don't need my baby brother hovering. You're

smothering me. I just want to get back to life and I can't do that with you here every fucking minute, so please, please go home. You have a life to live and so do I. Kip would want us to keep going, so please, help me honor him and let's move on."

After my venomous spray, and faking it for a few days that I was 'fine,' he booked a flight. The following week, he jumped on a plane and went home, leaving me to grieve and wallow on my own, just how I wanted it. I had a bottle of Fireball and my memories to keep me company, and I was fine with that.

And that's what I did—I ate, slept, cried, passed out drunk, and then did it all over again the next day. There were constant reminders of what I lost everywhere I looked but being in that house, I felt closer to him and it somehow made it all okay. That's what I kept telling myself, but in actual fact, being there was hurting me. By being there, I was living in constant pain.

Two months after everyone left, I quit my job at the fire station. Falling into a deep depression, I locked myself away in the house that Kip and I called home. It was my happy place but it was also my prison. I was existing and even that's highballing it. The pain of losing Kip was just as raw as it was when I woke up in that hospital room and discovered what had happened.

A week after I quit, Dave popped in to check on me. When he saw the state of the house, and me, he went behind my back and called Dad. He filled him in on what he saw, told him I wasn't coping, and I needed help because I was withering away here in Australia and he was worried about me.

They all jumped on the next available flight and when they got here, they were shocked at what they found. They saw firsthand that I had been lying to them about how I was really doing.

When Dad, Mom, and Kain appeared on my doorstep that's when I knew I needed help ...

... the sound of *car doors slamming in the driveway causes me to roll my eyes, I'm not in the mood for visitors today. Maybe if I just lie here and ignore them, they will go away. They knock and I hold my breath and don't move, not letting on that I'm home. They knock again and then I hear the sound of a key sliding into the lock and the mechanism clicking. The door opens and I sit up quickly, squinting at the brightness shining in, and then I see Dad, Mom, and Kain.*

"Tatum," Mom breathlessly says my name, her tone laced with shock and sadness for me. Whenever they called me, I always put on a show, hiding how I was really feeling. I hated seeing pity in everyone's eyes and right now, the look they are giving me is worse than pity. It was also the look I needed to snap me out of the funk I found myself in.

"What are you doing here?" I hiss.

"We came to check on you and I'm glad we did," Dad states. "Tatum, what's going on?"

Hearing the brokenness in his voice causes something to click inside of me. I've never seen my parents look at me like this. Standing up, I look over at my parents and brother, my eyes fill with tears and I utter, "I ... I need help." Tears begin to flow down my cheeks. "I ... I can't do this anymore."

"Ohhh, my baby," Mom cries as she walks over to me. She envelops me in her arms in the Mom hug that I needed. "I'm here, baby, I've got you," she whispers into my hair as I finally let the grief I was hiding from everyone out.

With encouragement from my family, I made the decision to pack up my life in Australia and move back home. With Kip gone, there was nothing keeping me here anymore. Mom reminded me that no matter where I am, Kip's memory will be with me. The kicker was when she reminded me that Kip wouldn't want me to be alone or upset.

That brings me to now and why I'm sitting on the beach in Castaway Grove. I'm here staying with Kain for a week or so before I return to Lockhart Falls and start work at the firehouse again. I'm staying with him and his roommate, Burton, not that Burton is here much. He's always at his girlfriend, Nix's place or her bar. But I don't mind them not being here because seeing couples together and in love is a painful reminder of what I lost. Of what I will never have again. I'm never opening my heart up to love again. I wouldn't survive losing someone I loved so deeply a second time, so if I keep my heart closed off, that can never happen.

With a deep exhale, I flop back onto the sand and stare at the sky above. Kip and I used to do this when we'd head to Husky for the weekend. We'd rent a cottage across from the beach and we'd become beach bums. It was the perfect way to relax. Sitting up, I look up and down the beach and smile. *Kip would have loved it here,* I sadly think. I wonder if I will ever get over losing him? I constantly think of him when I see or do something I know he would have liked.

"Good morning," a little voice says from next to me.

Turning my head, I see a cute little kid who has green eyes eerily similar to mine. "Morning," I reply with a smile.

"I'm Fletcher," he announces, dropping down next to me.

"Tatum," I reply. Looking behind me, I search for his parents. "Where are your parents?"

"Daddy's sleeping."

"And you're out here on your own?"

He nods. "Yep, I wants to make Daddy breakfast but I need a cocnut to make smoothies."

"That's very ambitious of you."

"I'm five, I can do anything. Daddy tells me that."

"And I believe him," I nod and agree with the kid. "Want some help to find a coconut?"

"Yes, please, but Daddy says I shouldn't go off with strangers."

"Pretty sure he'd also say not to go down to the beach by yourself early in the morning, but here you are." He looks at me with confusion. "How about, I help you get a coconut and then you can go back inside so your dad doesn't get worried, besides, we know each other's names, we aren't strangers."

"Okay." He offers me his hand. "Let's go, Tatum."

"Let's do this, Fletcher." Placing my hand in his, he helps me up. Well, I push myself up and from the huge grin on his face, he thinks he did all the work. Together, we head to the coconut trees lining the beach to get him a coconut.

It didn't take long to find one, I lifted Fletcher up and he managed to get it free. With a coconut under his arm, Fletcher takes my hand in his and I walk him back along the beach. He points out where he's staying and it turns out they're staying in a house a few doors down from Kain's.

We're almost at his place when a man yells out. "Fletcher, buddy, where are you?" Then there's a muffled, "Shit. Fuck. Shit."

"That's my dad," he excitedly squeaks, but before he can reply a man jumps down from the patio onto the sand and comes into view.

"Fletch," he shouts again but he's looking down the beach, away from us. He turns his head toward us and when he sees us, he spins around and races over.

The first thing I notice is his eyes, they're a vivid blue and then I notice his lips. They're plump and ohh so kissable. His face is covered in a beard. I'm not usually a fan of facial hair but this beard is sexy as hell. Then it hits me, he's the first man I've found attractive in a long time, but that attractiveness disappears when he opens that gorgeous, kissable, beard-covered mouth of his. "Get away from my son," he growls, pulling Fletcher away from me and into his side.

"Excuse me?" I hiss, I wasn't expecting him to react like that.

"Get. Away. From. My. Son," he repeats, accentuating each word.

"We got cocnuts," Fletcher informs his dad, clearly not reading his dad's angry vibe right now.

"Why did you take my son?" his father snaps at me.

"YOUR son came to me and asked for help finding coconuts to make YOU breakfast," I snap at the sexy asshole.

"So you just waltzed off down the beach with a child who isn't yours?"

"We didn't waltz," I spit back at him. "And what kind of father lets his son wander off down the beach early in the morning?"

"That's outta line," he growls.

"No, asshole," I lower my voice to a whisper on the asshole part, "you're outta line." I sneer the last three words through clenched teeth. Looking to Fletcher, I smile. "Enjoy your cocnut, buddy."

"Thanks, Tatum." He waves excitedly at me and before I do something stupid, I turn and walk away from them. I'm only a few steps away when I hear Fletcher tell his douchedad all about getting the coconut and wanting to make him breakfast. I smile when I hear his dad praise him on a "great cocnut," but that smile falters when I hear him add, "Buddy, you can't walk off with strangers, no matter how pretty they are. She could have been a crazy psycho lady and taken you from me."

"Fucking asshole," I mumble under my breath but then I hear Fletcher inform him he knew my name; therefore, I wasn't a stranger. I would have loved to stick around and see how douchedad dealt with that, but I'm suddenly parched and craving a smoothie too, so I head back to Kain's.

Stepping up onto the deck of Kain and Burton's place, I grab the bottle of water I left for myself and untwist the cap. Taking a sip, I drop down onto the lounger and stare out at the ocean. The sound of the waves crashing into the shoreline makes me forget all about douchedad.

Leaning back, I realize this is the calmest and most clear-headed I've felt in a very long time. While I'm in such a good mood, I decide that from this moment forward, I'm going to do what Kain said and I'm going to start living again. First things first, I need to return to Lockhart Falls and get back into a routine.

Looking at my ring finger, I stare at the engagement ring he gave me and smile, not a tear in sight—progress. Kip Kitson was my everything, and he always will be. He was my person. The one I was going to marry. As I slip the ring from my left hand to my right, I know I can do this. I know it will be hard at times but I have an amazing family behind me and with their support, I can do anything I set my mind to. From this point forward, I will no longer wallow in grief. I will honor his memory by living life for the two of us and tonight, I'm going to honor him in a way I know he'll be proud of. I'm going to get rip-roaring drunk on Fireball with Kain and tomorrow, the new Tatum Summers will rise from the ashes. From tomorrow on, I will live life for me. For him. For us.

Looking to the sky, a smile graces my face because I feel lighter. Lifting my hand, I hold it over my heart and feel it beating. Then I kiss the pads of my index and middle fingers and blow the kiss up to him in heaven and whisper, "I love you, Kip."

Standing up, I brush the sand off my ass, that Kain clearly left behind 'cause he's an animal and doesn't clean up after himself, and head inside to shower. Walking into my room, my eyes land on the photo of Kip and me I have sitting on my dresser. For the first time since I lost him, when I look at it, my heart doesn't ache, it just beats, pumping life through me. Then I catch my reflection in the dresser mirror and I see the old me reflecting back at me, and that's okay, it means I'm healing. I'm moving on.

Kip and I had a love like Dani and Emmet in *I Never Planned on You* by one of my favorite authors, Stefanie Jenkins. And like Dani, I lost the man who loved me unconditionally, but unlike Dani, I won't get a second chance at love but I will get a second chance at living and I'm A-okay with that.

Kip may have gone down with the flames, but our love, it will burn forever in my heart and with his love burning inside of me, I know I can do anything I set my mind to.

26

PENN

THIS TIME HERE WITH MOM, DAD, AND FLETCHER AFTER MY STAY at the retreat was just what I needed to reset myself mentally. Sure, I had the four weeks at the retreat, but this time allowed me to find myself as Fletcher's dad again. I'd been so lost in my head as 'Maddie's widower' that I forgot to be 'Fletcher's dad.' So after the retreat, I decided to have some time away with my son … and parents because they deserved a break too. They really stepped up, looking after my son while I broke down, and me, I guess. Without the intervention, who knows where I would be today.

Our time in Castaway Grove is coming to an end, and I think I'm ready to get back to the real world. As much as hanging out at the beach all day is nice, I think I want a routine again. Plus, Fletcher needs to get back to school and I'm ready to get back to the garage. Craig has been amazing looking after the shop for me, but it's time to get back into the swing of things.

Climbing out of bed, I sleepily walk out to the kitchen and turn on the coffee machine. I'm definitely going to need to get one of these *Nespresso* machines when I get home. Amazing coffee at the push of a button, yes please.

Making Fletcher a chocolate milk, I sit the two mugs on the island counter and head down to his room to get him but when I open his door, he's not there. I check the bathroom and when I don't see him in there either, I begin to panic.

Racing into the living room, I don't find him watching television and that's when I really begin to panic. Especially when I see the slider to the patio is slightly open. Slipping my feet into my flip-flops, I race outside. "Fletcher!" I shout. "Fletcher, buddy, where are you?" I don't see him. My eyes are locked on the ocean before me and they dart side to side looking for him. "Shit. Fuck. Shit," I grumble as I jump from the patio onto the sand, bypassing the stairs. Looking down the beach to the lagoon, I don't see him or anyone. Quickly, I turn my head the other way and, thank fuck, Fletcher is standing there with a strange but very attractive woman.

Seeing them holding hands sets something off inside of me and I race over to them. "Get away from my son," I growl, reaching for Fletcher and pulling him away from this woman.

"Excuse me?" she hisses.

"Get. Away. From. My. Son," I repeat when I feel Fletcher tug on my hand. Looking down at him, I see him smiling brightly.

"We got cocnuts," Fletcher excitedly informs me. He lifts the one he has up for me to inspect, but from the corner of my eye, I see the woman and once again, the anger I felt when I saw her with him reignites.

"Why did you take my son?"

"YOUR son came to me and asked for help finding coconuts to make YOU breakfast," she sassily snaps back at me. If I wasn't so worked up over Fletcher being missing when I woke up, I'd take the time to appreciate her in her active wear, but I don't. Instead, we throw barbs back and forth at one another. The little spitfire giving me as good as I give her.

She turns her attention back to Fletcher and I feel the loss of her gaze. "Enjoy you cocnuts, buddy," she says and begins to turn to leave but stops when she hears Fletcher's voice.

"Thanks, Tatum." He waves excitedly at her and with a nod, she turns and walks away from us.

"Do you like my cocnut, Dad?" Fletcher asks, thrusting the coconut toward me.

"It's a great cocnut but, buddy," I agree as we take a seat on the stairs. "You can't walk off with strangers, no matter how pretty they are. She could have been a crazy psycho lady and taken you from me."

"She wasn't a stranger; her name was Tatum."

"She's still a stranger, buddy. Just because you know someone's name, it still makes them a stranger, especially when you are a kid."

He nods but I'm not sure he really understands, especially when he continues to tell me all about his adventure with this Tatum woman, but I'm not really listening. Waking up and discovering him not in his bed had my heart racing like it did the night my life changed, but when I saw him on the beach with that woman, I was relieved but that relief turned to anger. Why was that woman with my son? She was a sassy lil' spitfire and, thankfully, I never have to see her again.

"Dad," Fletcher asks later as we sit around the table eating breakfast that he prepared with his coconut mocktails.

"Yeah, buddy?" I reply, wiping some cream off his nose.

Picking up my coconut drink, I take a sip. "Can Tatum be my new mom?"

My drink sprays across the table when I spit it out in shock at his question. Wiping my mouth with a napkin, I look over at him. "Your mom is in heaven, buddy."

"I know but I want a mom like Nanna is your mom."

This kid is too clever for his own good. I wipe my already clean chin to bide my time as I think of how to answer him. "Buddy, your mom is in heaven and I still love her, I always will. I don't think I'll ever love someone like I love your mom.

When you get older and fall in love with the woman of your dreams, you'll understand."

"Ewwww, Dad, that's gross. I don't want girl germs."

"But you want me to get girl germs from that lady."

"Yep." He nods matter-of-factly at me.

"Why?"

"'Cause she helped me get cocnuts."

Ohh to be almost six again and see the world that way. I need to change this train of thought quickly. "So, what do you want to do for your birthday?"

"Can we go to Disneyland?"

"Not this year, buddy, Daddy's had too much time off work. I need to get back and take back the garage from Craig. He probably hates me."

"He doesn't," Dad says, coming out to join us. "Where's my coconut mocktail?" he asks Fletch, ruffling his hair as he takes a seat next to him.

"Tatum and I only got one."

"Tatum?" Dad asks her name like a question.

"The lady who helped me. I want her to be my new mom."

Dad looks to me confused. "I'm so lost right now."

"Cliffs Notes. Someone …" I look to Fletcher and scowl at him. "… got up early and went to the beach looking for coconuts. He met this Tatum lady and because he knew her name, according to him, they weren't strangers, so it was okay to explore with her. The two of them went and got coconuts. I woke in a panic and when I hit the beach, I found the two of them returning. I may have yelled at her before Fletch and I came back here. He made mocktails while I cut the coconuts and made waffles."

"And what's this about her becoming his mom?"

"That's not happening, so it's moot."

"Right," Dad says nodding, "it's too early for this shit, I need coffee."

"I'll take one since you're offering."

"I wasn't offering but since you're my favorite son, I'll make you one."

"I'm your only son," I state.

"Hence, my favorite." With that, he heads inside to get his favorite son and himself a coffee.

Standing up, I walk over to the stairs to the beach and drop down. Staring out at the ocean, I realize I'm going to miss the lull of the waves crashing into the shore when we return to Lockhart Falls. I'm not quite ready to get back to everyday life, but I know I can't vacation and hide forever. We can always come back here and I think we will. Castaway Grove is a picturesque beachfront little town. Coconut trees line the pure white sandy beach that goes as far as the eye can see. Azure blue water laps at the shoreline and farther down the beach, along the water's edge, are catamarans, jet-skis, and canoes that belong to a resort here. They allow the locals and tourists to use them. Fletcher had the best time on the jet-ski with Dad and me yesterday.

"Hey, buddy," I say, turning to face him. When he looks at me, I smile when I see him looking so happy. I haven't seen him look so carefree since before Mads died, and that's all on me.

"Yes, Dad?"

"Wanna go on the jet-skis again today?"

"Yes, please ... can I drive this time?"

A laugh escapes me. "Do you have a license?"

"No," he huffs.

"I promise, as soon as you're bigger and have a license, you can drive."

"This is bullshit," he hisses.

"Language, young man," I berate him.

"Why is it okay for you to say bullshit but I can't say bullshit?"

"Stop saying bullshit."

"Bull—"

"Fletcher," I warn.

"Well, can I say bullpoop? Or bullturd?"

"No," I growl. "No more bullshit, bullpoop, or bullturds."

"I can't wait to be big. I can drive a jet-ski and say bull ... you know what. Being a kid sucks."

"Well, being an adult sucks too. There are bills to pay, you have to go to work, do laundry, cook dinner, and lots more."

"Life is dumb then." He huffs and I laugh.

"Ohh, buddy, you're in for a rude shock if you think it's dumb now. Head on inside, brush your teeth and get changed into your swim trunks. Let's enjoy our last few days here in paradise.

27

TATUM

Standing in my childhood bedroom, I stare at my reflection and a wave of sadness washes over me. The last time I wore my LFFD uniform, Kip was alive and we were blissfully happy. It's funny how the tiniest of things can slam me into a bout of sadness, and this time it's over a uniform.

Today is my first shift back and I'm nervous, more nervous than I was on my first official day after leaving firefighter school. It's silly really, I've worked at this station and with most of this crew for three years before Kip and I headed to Australia, and I've known most of them my entire life. They all knew Kip so I know today will be filled with reminiscing and remembering him.

"You ready, Tate?" Dad shouts from downstairs, the sound of his baritone voice startles me.

"As I'll ever be," I murmur to myself. "Coming, Dad," I yell back.

Kissing the pads of my index and middle fingers, I press them to the picture of Kip and whisper, "Love you, wish me luck." Exiting my room, I meet up with Dad and the two of us head off to work together, just like we used to.

Joining Dad in the car, I smile when he hands me my travel mug. "Thanks, Dad."

"You've got this, Tatum," he tells me, bopping his finger on my nose before he starts the car.

"How did you know?"

"I'm your father, I know all your tics and right now, you're excited but anxious."

"That about sums it up." Bringing my mug to my lips, I take a sip. The warmth of the liquid envelops me. It's like one big, caffeinated, warm hug.

"I missed this," he states before backing out of the driveway.

"Missed what? Us driving to work together?"

"Seeing that look of euphoria wash over you when you take that first sip of coffee in the morning."

"There's nothing wrong with my love of coffee, at least I'm not addicted to crack." With a shrug, I sit back in my seat and watch the houses fly by as Dad heads to the firehouse.

"And if it was crack, I'd have to kick your ass. I don't care that you are nearly thirty—"

"Dad," I interrupt, "I'm nearly twenty-seven, not thirty."

"Potato. Vodka. What I'm saying is, if you ever turn to drugs, I will kick your ass."

"I promise never to turn to drugs, Dad, besides, I don't want to ruin this pearly smile …" I grin at him. "… from snorting or shooting that shit, and we both know, I'd be snorting that stuff 'cause needles and me do not mix."

"Glad you've thought your imaginary drug habit through." He smiles and shakes his head. "You ready for this?" he throws at me out of the blue as we come to a stop at a set of lights outside of The James Hotel.

"Truth?"

"Always, you know that."

"I'm excited but scared."

"Why scared?" He looks over at me, waiting for my reply.

"What if in the middle of a rescue or a fire, I'm hit with memories that cripple me? My inaction or pause might be the difference between life or death."

"Are you sure you want to come back? I need you ready because you're right, Tate, you can't pause out in the field."

"I … I don't know, Dad. I know I need to get back to life, but how will I ever know I'm ready? It's not like a Magic 8 Ball will magically give me the answers."

"If only life was that simple." He falls silent and when we pull into the parking lot at the station, he turns to face me. "Tatum, I believe in you. You suffered an unimaginable loss. If I lost your mother, I'd be a mess. But here you are, less than a year later, getting on with things. You once again uprooted your life and moved from one side of the world to the other. I hate that my fear of flying prevented me from being there sooner when you needed me the most." I go to interrupt him, but he presses his finger to my mouth. "Tate, I admire your strength and courage and for the first time in my career, I'm going to give you, my daughter, a free pass. If it gets too much, I want you to step aside. I'm positive the rest of the crew will agree. They would rather be a man down out there than for you to not have your head in the game."

"Thanks, Dad, but I can do this … I think."

"Good, and to ease you back into things, the rig needs to be washed and polished this morning. Hop to it."

"Any chance I can pull the 'Dad's the boss and I'm not coping card' right now?"

"Nope." He defiantly shakes his head. "Now get out of my car and get washing."

Climbing out of the car, Dad and I walk into the firehouse together. Before we enter, I knock his shoulder with mine. "Thank, Dad."

"Anytime, Tater Tot, anytime."

Ugh, I forgot how nit-picky Dad is when it comes to the cleaning of the rig. He's like an army drill sergeant and today, he requested we wax and polish the rigs too. From the glint in his eye as he stands with his arms crossed watching me, I'm pretty sure this is his way of 'easing me' back into the swing of things.

Climbing on top of the fire truck, I get to waxing the roof. When I'm finished, I drop to my butt to catch my breath. I'm still a little out of shape after the stellar diet I was on during my months of wallowing. I highly DO NOT recommend only eating burgers and drinking beer and Fireball. My poor liver and stomach.

Sitting here, I'm assaulted with a memory of when Kip and I got down and frisky up here one time …

… Kip and I have just arrived at the station and have completed our handover. We are working with Kain and Calvin for the next twenty-four hours. Dad runs our station using the California swing-shift method, it's a slightly different take on the traditional twenty-four-hour schedule. Each officer is on duty for twenty-four hours at a time, every other day, for five days. After five days, we are off for ninety-six hours, or four days, basically twenty-four on, twenty-four off, twenty-four on, twenty-four off, twenty-four on, ninety-six off. I'm getting used to the twenty-four-hour shifts and being in a smaller town, it generally allows for a few hours kip— pun intended—most nights.

Speaking of Kip, the Aussie man I love unconditionally and not the sleep—man, my Aussie is showing—I love working alongside him. He's amazing at what he does and it's great learning new things from him. Even though we're both trained firefighters, coming from different countries we each do things a little differ- ently. I guess this is why they set this program up, it allows us, and him, to learn new skills.

Calvin and Kain are inside working on dinner, while Kip and I finish waxing the fire truck. I'm on the side of the truck, leaning onto the roof when I feel him behind me. "Your ass looks amazing in these pants, the things I want to do to you right now," he purrs into my ear, joining me on the ladder.

Looking over my shoulder, I swallow deeply when I see the heated look he's giving me. "Ohh yeah, and what dirty sexy thoughts are you thinking?"

"I'd lift you onto the roof, I'd strip you naked, then I'd feast on your pussy before I fuck you with my fire pole." A laugh breaks free and he too chuckles. "Okay, yeah, that last part sounded way sexier in my head. Can we forget I said that?"

"How about after you feast on my pussy, I take your cock out and languidly stroke it before I suck on it and then, just before you're about to come, I push you onto your back and I ride you hard and fast?"

"Fuck, babe, I want all of that. I want it and you so fucking bad."

Pushing myself up onto the roof of the rig, I crawl forward on all fours and spin around to face him. Lifting my hand, I beckon him to me with my index finger. While he climbs up, I flip open the button on my pants and lower the fly. "Really?" he asks when he finally registers what I'm up to.

"Uhh huh," I reply with a nod as I shimmy my pants down my legs. They get stuck on my boots but it doesn't stop Kip. He pushes me to my back, leans down, and runs his nose along my panty-covered slit. Sticking his tongue out, he licks me.

"Fuck, babe, your undies are soaked." A laugh slips out of my mouth, undies is such an Aussie term.

"Say undies again," I demand.

His eyes lock with mine and he smirks. Then with his gaze locked on mine, he whispers the word, "Undies." He licks me once more. "I hope you aren't too attached to these ... undies." Before I can ask why; he tears them from my body. The material disintegrating in his fingers. Throwing the torn material over the side, he presses a hand to my stomach, holding me down, and then shoves his face between my thighs. He licks me from taint to clit, covering my mouth with my arm, I moan as he continues to devour me with his tongue. He slips a finger in and I explode, soaking his face with my arousal. I groan into my arm as wave after wave of pleasure ripples through me.

Removing his face, he looks up at me. "I do believe that now, you need to suck my dick, but I think I just want you to ride me."

"I'm happy to ride you now and suck you later … I hear there's a roomy storage closet off the kitchen that I might be able to blow you in later."

"It's a date, now, jump up and let me lie down."

Saluting him, I sit up and we swap positions. He lies down on his back and I straddle his thighs. It's kinda awkward with my pants still around my ankles but I make it work. He goes to free his cock but I stop him. "Allow me," I demand.

"Have at it, baby."

He lies back and watches intently as I free him from the confines of his pants. The tip glistens with moisture and I know I'm supposed to be riding him but the need to lick him is too strong. Leaning down, I swipe my tongue over the tip. Kip hisses at the connection and that hiss turns into a guttural grunt when I suck the head into my mouth. Swirling my tongue around, I take him deeper into my mouth.

"Fuck, babe, your mouth must be what heaven feels like."

Pulling myself off him, I stare at him. "I thought that was my pussy?"

"Maybe you should give me your pussy so I can compare the two?"

"For the sake of science, I'm happy to oblige."

Sitting up, I kick one boot off and one leg of my pants then I shuffle up his legs, lift up, and hover over him. With my eyes locked on his, ever so slowly, I slide down his shaft. "Fuuuuuuuuuuck," he draws the word out, closing his eyes as my pussy wraps itself around his shaft.

Rocking my hips, I slide back and forth on his dick. "Yes," he mewls and as if he's in my head, he lifts his hands and caresses my boobs. Sliding his hand underneath my shirt, he pulls my bra down and plays with my nipples.

"Yes," I pant, "yes, yes, yes." The word repeatedly tumbles out of my mouth as I ride Kip like a cowboy rides a bull. My pussy walls grip his shaft tightly as I increase my speed. That amazing tingly feeling begins to develop low in my belly. "I'm close," I whisper.

"Me too," he grunts.

He knows my body and he knows what I need to come. Sliding his hand down my stomach, he presses his finger to my clit and increases the pressure on it. It's just what I need. My head drops back and like a werewolf and a full moon, I cry out and give myself over to the sensation. He quickly covers my mouth, so as to not garner attention to what we're doing. With his hand muffling my sounds, I continue to moan, groan, and hiss into his palm.

Falling on top of him, I breathlessly pant into his shoulder.

"Kip. Tatum, dinner," Kain shouts from below seconds after I collapse on top of him. Kip and I both freeze at the sound of my brother's voice. "Where the fuck are you guys?" he shouts, neither of us blinks. Our eyes are wide open and we just lie here, quietly staring at one another. "Whatever," he sneers, "more for Calvin and me." He walks back into the station and shouts, "Just dish up, Calvin, I can't find them." Calvin's reply is cut off when the door closes behind him.

After a few moments, Kip and I begin to laugh. "Oh. My. God, that was close," I pant into his ear.

"So close but so fucking worth it. I love you, Tatum," he says.

My head snaps up and I stare down at him. "What did you just say?"

"That it was worth it … ohhh, and that I love you."

"You love me?"

He nods. "Yep, with all my heart and soul."

"You love me," I repeat. He nods once again. "For the record, I'd like to state that I love you too, Kip Kitson."

"I know," he nonchalantly replies.

"So cocky," I reply with an eye roll.

"Only for you, baby." He thrusts his hips up and even though he just came, I feel his cock harden inside of me again.

"We don't have time to fuck again because we now have to reclean the roof 'cause you made me come all over your face and the roof of the rig."

"Babe, I will clean this thing until I die because making you come is fast becoming a favorite hobby of mine."

"You say the nicest things to me, now, quickly fuck me again and then we have to get back to work and reclean this thing."

"Yes, ma'am." He salutes me and then fucks me again before we reclean the roof and then head inside to have dinner with Kain and Calvin.

"What you smiling at?" Calvin asks as he climbs up to join me on the roof of the rig.

"Just thinking of the times Kip and I would polish this rig."

"I remember that time you and he fucked up here," he says. My eyes widen at his words. "Yes, I fucking knew what you two dirty dogs were up to, lucky it was me and not your brother who busted you guys bumping uglies."

"How?" I ask, mortified that a colleague knew what happened up here and my mortification grows with what he tells me next.

"I was there …" He points to the last window on the second floor "… grabbing something from my bag and I looked over and, well, saw Kip going to town on you."

"Oh. My. Fucking. God, I'm so embarrassed."

"Don't be, we've all fucked up here."

"Who did you fuck up here?" I ask him.

"A gentleman never tells." He winks at me, and I shake my head.

"But you're not a gentleman so spill the deets, Calvin."

He mimes zipping his lips and climbs down. "Nope … I just came out to let you know dinner is ready. You know, it's kind of a déjà vu moment … just without the sex."

"You know, that was the first time we told each other that we loved the other?"

"No shit."

"Yes shit." I smile at the memory.

"I missed that," he says.

"Missed what?"

"Seeing you smile like that. We've all missed you, Tate, and we're happy to have you back."

"Thanks, Calvin," I tell him as I climb down to join him. "Now, wanna spill the beans on who you fucked up there?"

"Nope." He bumps my shoulder and we head inside. As I watch him walk ahead of me, I realize that coming back to work was the right thing to do.

28

PENN

"COME ON, BUDDY, WE HAVE TO GO OR YOU'LL BE LATE FOR school," I shout down the hallway to Fletch. I still can't believe that my lil' man is old enough to be going to school now. Feels like just yesterday that Mads and I brought him home from the hospital.

We've fallen into a routine since returning from Castaway Grove and life is good. It was his birthday the other week and it was rough, a really, really tough day for me. It was the first birthday without Mads by my side but I managed … just. Not that I'll ever admit it to anyone, but after everyone at the party left, I locked myself in our walk-in closet, held one of Mads's hoodies to my face, and cried. After the tears dried and the sadness was gone, I got angry. I was angry she missed his birthday. I was angry she died but most of all, I was angry because I couldn't save her. That anger caused me to hulk out and I tore the hoodie I was holding to shreds.

One minute I was crying uncontrollably, and then next, I was so angry I fell apart, in a different way. With the torn hoodie in my hands and angry tears on my cheeks, I grabbed my phone and called Rebecca. Like she promised me while I was at The Grove Retreat, she talked me off the ledge and helped me to center myself. She helped me let go of both the anger and sadness and move into acceptance and moving on.

Once I'd calmed down, she told me this will happen from time to time and to not beat myself up over it. Sometimes we just need to break down, whether it be crying or in anger, and that's okay, we're only human and emotions are hard to deal with at the best of times.

"I'm ready, Daddy," his little voice says, pulling me back from the memory of his birthday. When I look up, I shake my head. My son is definitely not ready. He's still in his pajamas, there's peanut butter all over his face, and his hair is all over the place. The only 'ready' part of him is his school shoes and socks.

"Umm, buddy, I think we need to reassess your version of ready."

He looks down at himself and giggles. "Oops."

"What have you been doing in there?" I ask, walking toward him. I offer him my hand and together we head back into his bedroom to finish getting ready. When I enter his room, I see what's in the middle of the floor in his room, I know what he was sidetracked by. "You were talking to Mom again, weren't you buddy?" He nods. "What brought this on?"

He looks up at me and I see nothing but sadness in his eyes and marring his little face. "George said Mommy didn't love me and that's why she died."

That little fuckface asshole, I internally growl as I sit on Fletch's bed. He climbs up into my lap and rests his head on my chest.

"He doesn't know what he's talking about."

"Why did she have to die, Dad?"

Million-dollar question, buddy. My immediate thought is *the world is cruel and fucked* but I can't tell a six-year-old that, so I go with the mature, grown-up option. "They say the good die young and your mom was the goodest of them all."

"Goodest isn't a word, Dad," he informs me.

"I know, buddy, but your mom, she was the absolute best. God obviously needed your mom to help some other people. Your mom was one of the few amazing people who when they die, they use their organs to help other people."

"How?" he questions.

"They cut her open and take her organs and then the doctors give them to other people."

"She was a cyborg?"

"Not quite, but special doctors removed some of her organs and gave them to other people to help them live."

"So she's a superhero, saving people."

"Yep," I proudly declare. "Your mom is the specialist and best superhero I know."

"I miss her, Daddy."

"Me too, buddy, me too, but she will always live on in our memory and our heart."

He nods and we just sit here holding each other. "All right, mister, enough of the snuggles. As much as I would love to spend the day cuddling you, you need to get to school and I have to get to the garage so I can work on Mrs. Hagen's car." He nods but neither of us makes a move to finish getting ready.

Sitting in his room, I continue to hug him and then I feel a presence next to me, it feels like Mads is here with us. There's been a few moments I've 'felt' her since she died, but I haven't told anyone about them. I don't want them thinking I'm crazy. Looking over at the photo of Mads and Fletcher on his dresser, I smile at it, and her. Each day is getting easier and I think that's because of the little boy in my arms. "I love you, Fletch."

"Love you too, Daddy, but I need to get ready now."

"Mmmhmpf," I mumble and nod but I still make no effort to move, if anything, I hold on to him tighter. My phone ringing in the other room pulls us apart. "I'll get that and you get ready, deal?"

"Deal," he states with a nod and offers me his little hand to shake. Shaking his hand, I lift him off my lap and head out to answer my phone and leave him to dress for the day.

Picking up my phone, I smile when I see Mom's name on the screen. "Morning, Mom," I say in greeting.

"Morning, Penn, just calling to remind you that this weekend, your father and I are taking Fletcher to Smithville for the maze festival."

"I remember, Mom, it's on the calendar." The Smithville Fall Maze Festival is the highlight of Smithville's year. People from states away descend on the little town and compete to get through the box hedge maze the quickest, while others race in rowboats around Smithville Lake. Before Mads died, we made a family weekend of it. When Mom first broached the weekend, I refused to even think about going but when Fletcher heard, and I saw the excitement on his face, I offered for them to take him. After a lengthy discussion, they agreed to go without me, but at every chance Mom gets, she tries to convince me to go with them.

"Are you sure you don't want to come with us? I worry about you being home alone for the weekend."

"I'll be fine, Mom, I've been on my own before, you know?"

"I know you have but this …"

"Is my first weekend at home alone since my wife died, and this is an event that we went to together as a family," I finish for her. "I'm well aware of that and as I keep saying, "I'll be fine."

"Are you—"

"Mom," I snap and interrupt her. "I. Will. Be. Fine," I enunciate each word clearly. "Thank you for your concern, but I've got this."

"I just worry about you, you're my baby boy."

"I know I'm your baby boy, you remind me of it constantly … even if I am thirty-one years old."

"But—"

"Nope, no buts, Mom. You, Dad, and Fletch are going to have a great time and I'm going to tackle a mountain of paperwork, *aaaannnd* I might even do it with no pants on."

"Penn, I don't want to hear that."

"Well, I don't want you to worry, so how about you stop worrying about me and I stop telling you that I'm going to do paperwork pantless."

"You are so cheeky. I can see where that gorgeous grandson of mine gets it from."

"His grandad," I tell her, trying to throw the focus off me.

"And I wonder where you get it from?" she deadpans and I have no comeback because she's right. I'm a chip off the old man's block. "I must run, lots to do before the weekend but just know, if you change your mind, you're more than welcome."

"Appreciate it, Mom, but I'll be fine. Have a great day."

After hanging up with Mom, I help Fletch get ready for school and then I head into the garage … with pants on.

"Tate, can you do me a favor?" Calvin asks as I walk in after my days off.

"Sure, but it'll cost ya," I reply, placing my bag into my locker.

"It always costs me something when I ask you for a favor."

"Yet you keep coming back for more," I tease. Plonking onto the sofa next to him, I lift my feet to the coffee table and sit back. "What can I help you with?"

"Can you take the ladder truck to PJ's Auto Repair? I need to finish up a report and then I can swing by and pick you up on the way to Lockhart Falls Elementary."

"Sure, no worries. I need to ask the mechanic about this tick in my Jeep anyway, so two birds, one garage."

"You're a rockstar, Summers."

"I know," I nonchalantly reply. Then I pin him down, knowing exactly what favor I want. "You know how I said it'll cost ya?" He nods. "Who did you fuck on the truck?"

"Don't worry, I'll take it in myself," he huffs.

"Wow, that secretive? Was she, or you, crap in the sack?"

"No comment." He huffs.

"Ohhh, ohhh, I know, I know … you're embarrassed about who it was with. Was it Doris from the bakery? No, she's too old. Miss Lainey from the kindergarten? No, she's dating Hank from the gas station. Or-or-or was it that cranky nurse and you're now the reason she's cranky."

"None of the above."

"Is it Hank?"

"Jesus, woman, were you dropped on your head as a baby?"

"Actually, yes, I was."

"Really?"

"Hell no, I'm just messing with you. Now please, will you tell me who you fucked on the truck?"

He shakes his head, "Not happening, Summers. I just think that sometimes, these things need to remain private."

"I will get it out of you, Calvin, mark my word."

"Mmmhmpf." He nods but, clearly, he doesn't believe me and obviously he doesn't know that when I don't know something, I will go to the ends of the earth and back to get the information. This has to be someone super juicy for him to keep his lips zipped up.

He throws me the truck keys and heads into the office to finish up the report he's behind on. This is why I always finish things on shift, before I leave. That way it's all fresh in my mind and I can effectively lock the day away in the 'done-ski' category.

Glancing at the clock, I realize that if I'm going to drop off the rig and get to the school on time, I need to get my butt into gear. Grabbing my wallet and sunglasses, I head out to the truck to drop it off at PJ's. Then realize I need coffee and when I head back inside, I find Calvin standing there with my to-go mug in one hand and his 'too hot to handle' mug in the other.

"I love you," I coo as I take the offered coffee.

"You only love me for my coffee."

"Yes, yes, I do." I take a sip and moan. "Ohh, FYI, you making me coffee isn't going to get you out of telling me who you fucked on the rig."

"Who did what now?" Dad bellows, coming over to join us.

"Your daughter thinks she's being funny, sir."

"No hanky-panky better happen on any of my rigs ... or in this station. You're here to work, not fuck." Then Dad looks to me. "I don't ever want to see your lily-white ass again."

My mouth drops open in shock, while Calvin, the asshole, cackles beside me like the bitch that he is.

"Ohhh, don't look so surprised, Tate. You and Kip used to fuck like rabbits, I'm surprised I don't have three grandbabies by now." His words shock me, not the he caught Kip and me part—that is mortifying—but it's the grandbabies reference because Kip and I will never have any kids together. I see the moment that Dad registers what he said. "Shit, Tate, I'm sorry, I didn't even think."

Shaking my head from side to side, I bite my lip to hold back the tears that are welling in my eyes. "It's fine," I utter around the sob in the back of my throat. "I ... I need to get to PJ's." Turning around, I walk out of the station and head to the rig. Dad calls out my name but I can't talk right now so I ignore him.

Climbing into the truck, I start the engine, ready to pull out. Looking over, I see Dad standing in the doorway to the station. He looks like someone ran over his kitten. Giving him a slight wave and a fake smile, I put the truck into gear and head out of the driveway. I get around the corner before I need to pull over. My vision is blurry and it's unsafe for me to be driving right now. Gripping the steering wheel, I break-down. Just when I thought I was coping, I get hit in the va-jay-jay with a reality of something that Kip and I will never have.

Tears streak down my cheeks because there will never be

mini-Kips running around. He would have been the best dad, the absolute best. "Why, Kip," I mumble, "why did you have to die?"

Looking at the clock on the dash, my eyes widen when I see the time. I'm really going to be late now. Giving myself a few deep breaths to calm down, I swipe at my face and then head over to PJ's. The garage is full and I really hope my roadside breakdown didn't put them behind.

Pulling up, I climb out and realize I left my coffee up there, my head isn't in the game since the grandbaby shock. Reaching up, I grab my to-go cup.

"You're late," a deep voice booms from behind, the timbre of it rumbling through my body.

Spinning around, I go to tell them sorry and then I see *him*; the hot angry dad from the beach the other month. "You," he hisses before I have a chance to defend myself. "Come to take more kids, have we?"

"Fuck you, asshole. I'm here to drop the rig off and get back to work." His words piss me off so I throw my keys at him. "Someone will be back to pick it up after lunch." Without saying another word, I slam the truck door and begin walking back to the station, I'm not spending a minute longer here.

Fuck him, I think as I walk down the road, hoping Calvin will see me and pick me up. No longer am I upset, I've moved into Pissedoffville, population, one sexy asshole.

30

PENN

WHY IS THIS WOMAN SO INFURIATING? AND WHY THE HELL IS SHE in Lockhart Falls? Surely, she doesn't live here. Is she stalking me and Fletcher? Does she want to kidnap my son? Is that why she followed us back here from Castaway Grove?

My mind is racing with crazy thought after crazy thought and I can't concentrate. This oil change should have only taken an hour at the most, but it's coming up to two hours now and I'm nowhere near finished, and I still have the fire truck to do as well. Maybe coming back to work wasn't the best idea I've ever had, and I'm starting to think telling Craig to take time off was a dumb idea. Trying to juggle the job and Fletcher is hard. I don't want to rely on my parents to pick up the slack. They've already done enough by moving here. I'm still amazed they uprooted their life in Nels Cove and moved here to help me, but then again, I know I'd do anything for Fletcher and that's what they did for me.

"Hello," a feminine voice calls from the driveway.

Great, an interruption, I think as I wipe the grease off my hands. I walk over to greet a possible new customer so I plaster on a fake smile and head out to meet her. "Can I help you?" I ask the woman.

"I hope so," she says, flushed in the face. She looks no older than twenty and she reminds me so much of Wren when she was younger. "I'm looking for a job."

"You want a job? At my auto repair shop?"

"Yep." She nods. "I'm new in town and I need to get out of the house. Do something with my hands. You're the only repair shop so I took a chance and am hoping you can give a girl a job."

Staring at the woman before me, I notice the grease under her nails and the overalls covered in oil stains. She really went all out on her outfit. "What's your name?"

"Josephine, but most people call me Phine. P H I N E, Phine." She's a sassy little spitfire.

"Huh, I would have picked Jo as a nickname."

"I'm not most people, PJ," she throws back at me and gives me a 'so, how about it, you gonna give me the job' look.

"How did you know I'm PJ?"

"Well, you're the only person here and right there on your shirt"—she points to my pec—"it says Penn so I took a gamble. Went with junior and not senior 'cause, well, you're old but not senior old."

"Way to make a guy feel senior old," I joke.

"Ohhh shit, I … I didn't mean to offend you, PJ."

"It's fine, Phine, I'm just messing with you." The longer I stand here with her, I wonder if she was sent to me from Mads to help with my work/life balance that's not so balanced at the moment. "I'll do you a deal, Phine. You show me what you've got with the oil change there." I point to the car I was working on. "And if you impress me, we can discuss possible employment."

"You've got yourself a deal, Penn Jr." She offers me her hand to shake.

"It's Penn, P E N N. Penn." She smirks at me and I can't help but like this girl. "So, do we have a deal?"

She nods and offers me her hand to seal the deal. I place

mine in hers and we shake. For a wee thing, she sure has a good grip. She nods excitedly and smiles at me, seeing her excitement is a breath of fresh air. I can't remember the last time I saw someone excited about an oil change. "Off you go, then." I flick my hand toward the car and garage. "Have at it," I tell her, and I stand here and watch her jump into action.

She pulls her hair up into a messy bun and makes her way over to the car. I stand here and watch her work for a few moments, impressed with what I see. Making myself a coffee, I walk back into the garage and I lean against one of the tool-boxes and watch, not in the creepy way. She's meticulous with her work and thirty-five minutes later, the oil change is done.

"So, did I impress you with my skills, P E N N, Penn?"

Nodding, I can't hide how impressed I am. "You did, you did good, kid. By the way, how old are you?"

"I'm nineteen."

"And what about your parents?"

"Dead," she replies as if I asked her about the weather.

"I'm sorry for your loss," I offer my condolences.

"Don't be. Dad was a drunk and Mom was a weak woman who didn't know how to stand up for herself and, in the end, got herself killed and left me an orphan."

"How did you end up here in Lockhart Falls?"

"A grandma I never knew I had is my only living relative. When she discovered she had a granddaughter she moved me here."

"Who's your grandma?"

"Joyce Masters."

"Granny Masters is your grandma?" I ask her, my voice laced with shock.

"You know her?"

"Ahhh, yeah," I reply with a nod, "everyone around here knows Granny Masters and now you mention it, you are just like her."

"Thanks, I think … unless you're saying that I look like a seventy-two-year-old woman who cooks the best chicken and dumplings."

"Definitely not that, but for the record, your grandma doesn't look a day older than fifty and if you can cook chicken and dumplings as good as your grandma, you're hired."

"She says her looks are because she drinks a glass of wine a day and has never smoked."

"That sounds like her."

"As for your cooking requirement, looks like I don't get the job. I can't cook toast without burning it. Hell, I'm lucky if I can boil water without burning the house down."

"I'm sure living with Granny Masters you will become a good cook soon enough, but in the meantime, Phine, how do you feel about working here part-time?" I offer her a job without even thinking, another one of my impulsive decisions. That's how Mads and I ended up here in Lockhart Falls. I saw the garage was for sale and I needed to get out of the big city, and Mads wasn't happy in her job either so we put in an offer and the previous owner accepted. Lockhart Falls has been home for just over five years now. After losing Mads, I considered moving away from here but there are too many memories and all that shit, and this is my home. Fletcher was born here and it's where he has his memories of his mom. I don't want him to ever forget her so I decided to stay.

"You've got yourself a deal, Penn."

She offers me her hand and we agree for her to come back tomorrow and sign her paperwork. Things are looking up for me and the rest of the day passes by smoothly, and I think that's because Mads is watching over me.

31

TATUM

UGH, I SERIOUSLY DON'T KNOW HOW TEACHERS DO IT. A classroom full of snotty obnoxious kids, day in and day out, is the last thing I would want to do for the rest of my life. Being a firefighter is something different every day. Sure, it's dangerous at times but so are kids, especially when they have access to scissors and glue and glitter. When I have kids, it will be a glitter-free house. Whoever created that sparkly shit needs to be shot.

Today's presentation went as well as can be expected, except for the part when some little shitfaced turd pulled an axe out of its storage compartment and was wielding it around like an axe murderer—see dangerous. If it wasn't for Calvin's quick thinking and reflexes, I'd have an axe in my back right now.

Dropping onto the sofa back at the station, I close my eyes and sigh as the comfy cushions envelop me. A smile appears on my face when I smell coffee. Cracking an eyelid open, I smile when I see Dad walking over to me with two coffees in his hands. "I love you, Daddy," I tell him as I sit up, crisscross my legs, and hold my hand out for my mug.

"You only love me for my coffee," he says, handing the mug to me.

"Not true, I also love you for ..." I drift off and pretend to think, but in all honesty, there are too many items to list in regard to the love I have for my old man.

"Smart-ass," he throws back at me with an eye roll. "Heard today was entertaining."

"Calvin promised he wouldn't say anything."

"He didn't, Principal Eden did. He called to apologize for what happened with the axe."

"Is this going to be like the time when that kid turned the fire hose on Kain, and now people are going to tease the ever-loving crap out of me 'cause I'm a 'back stabber' or some crap?"

"Maybe, but that was funny what happened to your brother," Dad chortles as he remembers the day as if it was yesterday. Kain was only just out of firefighter school and we were down at the Christmas Fair. Santa Claus had just arrived on the top of the truck and we were giving the kids a turn using the hose. We set up targets in the open field and whoever knocked it down the quickest won a prize. Tom Turner was, actually he still is, a shit of a kid. It was his turn and he didn't listen to Kain explain how to hold the hose properly. His turn was less than stellar and he lost. Just as Kain said, "Bad luck, buddy," the little shit turned toward him, smiled in that sinister way you do before doing something you shouldn't, and then he fired. It knocked Kain on his ass due to the closeness and bruised three of his ribs. Poor Kain was black and blue for weeks. Every year when Santa arrives now, that story pops up. He will never live it down and as the big sister, it's my prerogative to always bring it up. Even with Kain now living in Castaway Grove, I will totally bring it up again this year.

The alarm goes off and we all jump into action. No fire today, just a car crash involving a school bus and a log truck.

As we ride to the scene, I keep playing different scenarios over and over in my head. School bus and truck, it can't be good. There's no mention of any fatalities or serious injuries, so fingers crossed it isn't as horrendous as I'm imagining.

Pulling onto the street, I look up and my eyes widen when I see the carnage before me. The truck hit the center of the school bus, nearly ripping it into two. "Shit," I hiss as we pull up, "how is no one dead?"

We all climb out and do our thing. Dad takes charge and calls us over after he's been inside to assess the scene and by the look on his face, he already has a rescue plan in motion. "Two kids are still inside. One little girl is unconscious and another boy is trapped. He's trapped between some seats and is quite upset."

"That's understandable," I tell him, but he doesn't appreciate me interrupting him so I zip my lips and listen.

"Tate, I need you to console the trapped boy while we figure out how to get him out." I go to interrupt him but he raises his hand and stops me. "This isn't a sexist thing, you're the only one small enough to maneuver your way through the bus to get to him. It's a mess in there, how more kids aren't trapped or worse is beyond me. It's like those kids had a guardian angel watching over them."

Ohh, okay, I think, that does make sense and I should know better. Dad doesn't give a shit that I'm a woman as he's repeatedly told me. I'm good at what I do and he gives praise where it's deserved, and if I fuck up, he treats me just like one of the boys.

"Once you reach him, I need you to assess from the inside and see if you can see a way to get him out easily, but I also need you to be there for him. Right now, he's in shock. When that wears off, he could get upset in a different way and if he starts thrashing about, he might hurt himself or others."

"Got it." I nod. "What's the little boy's name?"

"Fletcher," Dad says. It immediately makes me think of

that little kid I met in Castaway Grove, and then I wonder if it's him. I really hope he's safe at school and not the Fletcher we have to rescue.

"Let's do this," I say to the team.

Dad enters behind me and bumps into me when I take in the carnage. "Holy fucking shit," I mumble.

"Language, Tatum, there are kids in here."

Nodding sheepishly at him, I take a deep breath and begin to climb over the seats that have come loose and school bags. Squeezing past the paramedic working on the unconscious girl, I nod hello but don't stop to chat. I have a kid to get to.

"Hey, Tate," Lewis greets me when I reach him.

"Hey, she going to be okay?"

"I think so, there are no visible injuries or broken bones, just the bump on her head and I dare say, probably a concussion. Until she wakes up, we won't know for sure." He looks down at his little patient and I see nothing but worry for her. Lewis was born to be a paramedic; he has that aura about him that's calming in a situation like this. "How are there not more casualties?" he states shaking his head. "It's carnage in here. Someone was definitely looking after these kids from above, that's for sure."

"I was just thinking the same thing—"

I'm interrupted when I hear a little muffled voice cry, "I want my dad."

"Poor kid has been saying that over and over," Lewis says lowly so only I can hear him. "He's coming, buddy," he shouts out, "but in the meantime, my friend, Tatum, is going to come sit with you. Is that okay?"

"Yyyyyyy ... yes," he stammers, "hhhh ... hurry."

Smiling at Lewis, I lean over the seats blocking us from the boy. Gripping the top, I gently pull myself up and pop my head over. I can't see him clearly; all I can see is a little tuft of blond hair. "Hey, buddy," I quietly murmur as I wriggle myself over a seat. He lifts his head up at the sound of my voice but he can't see me due to the debris separating us.

"I'm here," he cries, his voice wavering and then I see a little hand lift into the air.

"I see you," I tell him. "Give me a sec and I'll be right there. Lucky for you, lil' man, I didn't have that second sandwich at lunch, otherwise, I wouldn't be able to squeeze through here." I'm almost to him but he hasn't said anything, so I start asking questions to keep him occupied. "As I said, I'm Tatum but my friends call me Tate, what's your name?" I ask him.

"Fffflecter. I'm Fletcher Brookes."

"Nice to meet you, Fletcher Brookes."

"I want my dad, Tatum."

"I know, buddy," I tell him as I start to squeeze through the final gap to get to him. Dad was right, there's no way any of the guys would have gotten to Fletcher here. How the paramedic got in to attend to the little girl back there is still mind-boggling. "Your teacher is calling him now, and I'm going to do my best to get you out before he arrives. How about that?"

"Please," he cries and I see him nod. "I'm scared."

"I'll be with you in a minute, can you hang on for me 'til I get to you?"

"Yes," comes his little reply.

"No need to be scared, I'm here." Leaning down, I whisper, "And don't tell the rest of my crew, but I'm the best at LFFD so you are in good hands."

"I heard that," Calvin growls from behind me. If I could, I'd flip the bird at him but right now, I need to finish climbing over these seats to reach Fletcher. Finally, I reach the gap he's in and when I look down, he has his back to me. Crawling over the last seat, I rest my foot on the chair to stand up. It moves beneath me and it feels like the whole bus rocks. Poor Fletcher screams and I hiss, freezing where I stand hunched over, not wanting to move and make the bus rock again. "Sorry, buddy," I tell him and since I'm right above him, he turns his little head toward me and my eyes widen when before me, I see the little boy from Castaway Grove.

"I know you," he tearfully shouts with a smile, "you got a cocnut wif me."

"I did. What are you doing here in Lockhart Falls?" I ask to keep him occupied. Carefully I hop off the seat and drop down next to him. I'm genuinely curious as to why they're here. It's been bugging me since I saw his douchedad when I dropped the rig off at PJ's.

He's so relieved to see me that he jumps into my arms. The bus rocks again from the sudden movement. The sound of the metal creaking is ominous.

"Stop jumping around," Calvin shouts as Fletcher wraps his little limbs around my neck. He holds on for dear life. The bus rocks again as I shuffle into a more comfortable position. From behind me, I hear murmurs and I deduce that they're moving the little girl now.

Fletcher's body relaxes in my arms, poor kid is so relieved to have someone with him that he doesn't notice what's happening around him. I need to keep him talking so I ask again, "So, Fletcher Brookes who likes cocnuts, what are you and your dad doing here in Lockhart Falls?"

"We live here."

"It's a great place to live. Where did you live before here?"

"I was bornded here," he mumbles into my chest. Before I can ask him another question, my radio crackles to life.

"You good, Tate?" Dad asks.

"All good, Cap. I'm with Fletcher now."

"Can you see a way out?"

Before I can answer Dad, Fletcher shimmies himself around and is now snuggled in my lap, tracing his finger over the fluorescent reflective stripe on my arm. Looking around, I shake my head at what I see. Fletcher is so fucking lucky; this could have been so much worse. Leaning over, my eyes widen when I think I see a way out. "Cap," I shout into my radio, causing Fletcher to flinch in my arms. "Shhh," I whisper to him, "I've got you." Rubbing my hand over his back, I wait for Dad to reply.

"Go ahead," Dad's voice comes through loud and clear.

"On the left side of the bus, probably about a third of the way down, you'll see a seat poking out the side of the bus. If you guys can remove that seat, or cut a hole there, Fletcher and I can climb out."

"You can't go back the way you came?" he asks.

"We could shimmy that way but the bus rocked when I climbed in, wouldn't want to risk it."

"Okay, leave it with me to assess."

"Thanks, Cap."

Letting out a sigh, Fletcher lifts his head and stares up at me. "How you doing, buddy?"

"I'm scared," he says, his voice wavering.

"Wanna know a secret?" I ask and he nods. "Me too."

"You are?"

"Yep, but wanna know something?"

"What?" he asks, excitement all over his face.

"The Cap I was speaking to, he's my dad. He's the best firefighter I know, therefore we will be out of here before you know it."

He nods and snuggles back into my chest, holding on to me tightly. After a few moments, his body starts to shake, the adrenaline is wearing off and he's going into shock. Any minute now, he's going to lose it. *Please hurry, Dad,* I silently plead and as if my prayers are answered, Dad's head pops into view. He points to the seat and indicates they are coming in that way. Nodding at him, the bus starts to rock and Fletcher whimpers in my arms. I begin to think he is shaking from fear and not an adrenalin drop-off. "Tell me about the rest of your holiday?" I ask him, trying to get his little mind off what's happening right now.

And that's what we do. Fletcher and I talk about anything and everything. "You reckon when we get out of here, you can make me a coconut drink?"

"No," he exclaims matter-of-factly.

"How come?"

"There's no cocnuts in Lockhart Falls."

"What if I could find some, would you make me one then?"

Before he can answer, there's an almighty screech of metal scratching on metal, followed by brightness. When I look over, I see Dad's head pop through the hole where the seat was. "What do you say, should we get out of here?"

32

PENN

"Mr. Brookes, it's Ellen from Lockhart Falls Elementary, there's been an accident—"

"Is Fletcher okay?"

"He's fine, a little shaken up but fine."

"What happened?" I growl into the phone as I race over to the sink to wash the grease off my hands.

"A truck collided with the school bus, almost tearing it in half."

"What the fuck?" I hiss. "Was anyone hurt?"

"Almost everyone walked away, Fletcher and Louise were trapped but the LFFD got them out. Your son is currently being transported to Lockhart Falls Memorial."

"I'm leaving the garage now. Are you sure he's okay, Ellen?"

"I saw him with my own two eyes, Mr. Brookes, he's a little shaken up but he's fine. He was clinging to the fire-fighter who rescued him in the back of the ambulance. It was like a guardian angel was watching over him and Louise. It's a miracle that no one died."

Her words stop me in my tracks. What if he died like his

mom? I couldn't handle losing him too. "I'm leaving the garage now. I'll meet you at the hospital."

Hanging up from her, I tell Phine what happened, and she offers to lock up for me. Hugging her my thanks, I jump into my car and make my way to the hospital. On the way there, I pass the scene of the accident and when I see the bus, my heart stops, it literally stops. It looks like a crash scene in an action movie. Thank fuck Fletch is okay.

Receiving that phone call just now was almost as bad as when those officers arrived at my door that fateful night, but this time it has a much happier outcome.

Parking my car, I race into emergency and see Ellen as soon as I step inside. "Mr. Brookes—"

"Where's my son?" I growl. I know it's not her fault and I shouldn't be so rude, but until I see him with my own two eyes, I won't calm down.

Her eyes are wide, fear reflecting back at me, but then she blinks and schools her features. "Follow me, Mr. Brookes, and I'll take you to Fletcher."

"Thank you," I reply, my tone much calmer this time. While we wait for the nurse to unlock the door into the back of emergency, I look to Ellen sheepishly. "Sorry for yelling before, this is bringing back some memories of the night I lost my wife."

"No need to apologize, if it was my son back there, I have no doubt that I would be feeling like you are right now but I assure you, Fletcher is fine. Not a scratch on him."

"You mentioned Louise?"

"I can't discuss another student but she has regained consciousness, so that's a good sign. I swear someone was watching over those two today."

Nodding my head, I feel the same way, wondering if it was Mads looking out for her son or if it was just pure luck.

We are finally buzzed through and Ellen leads the way down the corridor. She stops outside a blue curtain, gently flapping from the air-conditioning vent above. "He's in here. As I said earlier, he's fine but he's clinging to the firefighter who rescued him."

"Thank you," I murmur but I don't make a move. I stare at the blue curtain and I'm accosted with memories of the last time I pulled a blue curtain back. One minute Mads was there, the next she was taken away for surgery and the next, she was gone.

With a shaking hand, I pull back the curtain and when I look into the room, my heart stops beating.

33

TATUM

EVER SINCE FLETCHER AND I CLIMBED OUT OF THE BUS, HE HAS clung to me like a spider monkey. He refused let the doctors assess him, so the doctor suggested I climb on the bed next to him. We did that and once he was settled, we managed to bribe him to stay next to me and let the doctor check him over. As soon as the doctor finished assessing Fletcher and before he picked up his chart to make notes, Fletcher climbed back on top of me. It felt awkward to have a kid that's not mine straddling me and clinging on to me, but every time I tried to move him, he got upset again. The nurse suggested I let him snuggle until his parents get here.

They whisk the two of us away for a scan to make sure there are no internal injuries and just after we returned to the allocated cubicle, Dad and Calvin stop in. Once again, I try to move Fletcher but like all the other times, he gets upset and doesn't calm down until he is in my arms again and I rub his back. I don't know shit about kids, but I rub his back how Mom does to me when I'm sick or upset, and it seems to work. By some freaking miracle, there was not a scratch on him. Not one. He definitely had a guardian angel watching over him today as did Louise. She regained consciousness at the scene and like Fletcher, no injuries except for the bump on her head.

Dad told me to stay where I am and to call when the parents get here and he'll come back to pick me up. After they leave, I bring up *Bluey* on my phone and Fletcher and I watch a few episodes. A wave of sadness washes over me because Kip and I used to watch this show together. Sure, it's for kids, but there's something about those little dogs that sing out to you.

Fletcher drifted off to sleep, a little snore erupts from him and I giggle. Lying back myself, I stare up at the ceiling, wondering where his mom and douchedad are. I'm surprised that they aren't here by now. But seriously, what are the odds that the coconut kid and douchedad from Castaway Grove are here in Lockhart Falls?

The curtain is pulled back and douchedad and Fletcher's teacher are there. He stops midstep and eyes me suspiciously, *yep, still a douche.* "You?" he hisses. Walking over to the bed, he stares down at a sleeping Fletcher and smiles at his son, then he snaps his murderous gaze back to me. "Why is my son sleeping on you?"

"Because I rescued him earlier and the poor little guy has been scared out of his mind. The only time he's calm is when he's attached to me."

At the mention of his son, his gaze drops to Fletcher and his expression morphs from anger to concern. Nothing but worry etched on his face, he reaches out and brushes a tendril of hair off his son's face. "Is he okay?"

Nodding, I smile. "Physically, yes. He was extremely lucky today. Someone up above was watching over him."

"What do you mean?" Douchedad asks me.

"I don't want to scare you, but the inside of the bus was a mess. Seats were ripped from the floor, there was jagged metal and debris everywhere but somehow, Fletcher was kept safe in a little pocket between two seats."

"Mads," he whispers and before I can ask who Mads is, Fletcher lifts his head off my chest. When he sees his dad standing by the bed, he jumps out of my arms. "Daaaaaad," he cries, wrapping his arms around his dad's neck, just like he has been to me. He begins to cry in his dad's arms.

"Shhhhh," he whispers, "Daddy's here now."

Sitting here, I watch the beautiful moment between father and son. He might be a douche to me, but he has nothing but unconditional love for his son.

Shuffling off the bed, I place a gentle hand on Fletcher's back. "Fletcher, I'm going to go now that your dad is here." He's too emotional right now, so relieved to see his dad that he doesn't say anything back to me. Smiling at the lil' dude, I look to his dad and we just stare at one another and then his doucheness rears its douchey head.

"You can go now," he growls.

Shaking my head, I ignore the sexy douchehole and exit the room. "Fuck you very much," I mumble to myself as I walk out of Fletcher's room. Walking away, I begin to get angry at the way he just spoke to me. Not once did he thank me for rescuing and looking after his son. Reaching into my pocket to grab my phone to call Dad, I come up empty. Then I remember, we were watching *Bluey* and it's on the bedtable. "Crapballs," I hiss as I turn around and head back to the room. However, before I enter, I stop when I hear Fletcher and douchedad having a conversation ... about me.

"CAN TATUM BE MY MOM?"

Not this again, I think. "No, buddy, she can't."

"Why?" Fletcher questions me.

"Because you already have a mommy."

"But I want Tatum to be my mommy 'cause she's here."

Anger begins to build at him pushing this. He has a mom, Mads will always be his mom and no one will ever take that role in his life. Just like she will always be my wife, no one will ever take that spot from my heart.

"Tatum will never be your mom, buddy, you need to drop this."

"But she smells nice." A snort from nearby causes us to both turn our heads and when I do, my breath hitches in my throat. Tatum is standing there and in the afternoon light beaming through the window, I get to see just how beautiful she is. Blonde hair, green eyes, killer figure, and a nice rack to boot.

"What are you doing back?" I ask, my tone harsher than I intended.

Fletcher on the other hand, excitedly shouts, "Tatum, you're back!"

Why the hell does this woman keep appearing? I don't need, or want, Fletcher getting attached to her and if she keeps popping into our life like she has been, it's going to break his little heart when I have to keep sending her away.

"I, umm, just need to get my phone." She points to the table at the end of the bed.

"Get it and go," I snap at her.

"You know, you're a real big A S S H O L E," she spells the word and I appreciate her spelling the naughty word but at the same time, I'm pissed that she's back so soon. Fletcher is seemingly attached to this woman, even after their first meeting in Castaway Grove he was enamored with her. Yes, I can admit she's gorgeous but she's no Mads. No one will ever compare to her.

"And you need to back off and leave us alone. We don't need or want you," I snap at her.

"Fine by me," she hisses. She grabs her phone and without a word, she leaves again.

"Bye, Tatum," Fletcher yells out. Then he looks to me. "Are you sure she can't be my mom?"

"I'm sure," I snap at him. He flinches at the forcefulness of my reply and immediately I feel like a shit dad but before I can apologize, the doctor returns.

"Good news, Fletcher, you can go home. Your scans are all clear. You are one very lucky little boy."

"Thank you, doctor."

"I'll draw up Fletcher's discharge papers and you'll be free to go."

"Thank you again," I offer my hand and he shakes it and then leaves. I'm so relieved that everything is okay, I never want to get a call like that again. "You ready to go, buddy?"

"Yep, can we get Donald's for dinner?" he asks me.

"I think that can be arranged," I tell him as I slip his shoes back on.

"And maybe an ice cream too?"

"Sure, buddy, anything you want."

"Yesss." He fists pumps the air, grabs my hand, and drags me out of the room.

Stopping by the nurses' desk, I sign the discharge forms and we head out to my car. Stepping out into the cool night air, I scrunch my face up when I see *her* waiting on the sidewalk. *She's still here*. I try to drag Fletcher in the opposite direction so he doesn't see her, but I think all my luck went into saving Fletcher today because he sees her. "Tatum!" he shouts. Dropping my hand, he races over to her. "We're getting Donald's for dinner and I get to have an ice cream too."

"Aren't you lucky," she says. "I take it your scan was all clear since you've been discharged?"

Fletcher just stares at her, not really understanding what she's saying. She picks up on it. "I ran into Lewis on my way out, your friend Louise is going to be okay. She has a concussion so she has to stay here overnight but like you, she had no broken bones."

"That's good to know, thanks for the update," I tell her. Ellen wouldn't tell me anything so hearing that is a relief.

Tatum smiles at me but the sound of a car pulls her attention away from us. "That's my ride," she states when a dark-colored SUV pulls up. "Stay out of trouble, little man." Without another word, she climbs into the car and I hear her say, "Hey, Dad," before the car door slams shut.

Fletcher stands on the sidewalk and waves goodbye. Tatum waves at him and glowers at me. Can't say I blame her. I have been a bit of a dick to her, but Fletcher wanting her to be his mom hurts me in a way I can't explain. Lately, I have felt anger and sadness at the most random of times. Will I ever get used to the loss of Mads? Or am I forever going to be broken?

35

TATUM

It's been three days since the bus incident and for three days straight, all I've done is think and dream about Penn-fucking-Brookes and his kissable lips. His bitable ass. His muscular forearms and because of that, I've been in a sour mood. We are not to like the sexy asshole. His looks do not make up for the fact that he's an arrogant jerkface. My nickname of douchedad is one million percent correct.

"Are you listening, Tate?" Dad growls, he's been explaining a new procedure change. It's simple but he's making it more confusing than it needs to be.

"Yes," I hiss and because I'm in a mood, I snap and tell him exactly what I think. "We aren't five, Cap. We understand this change but you keep harping on and on about it, and you're making it confusing."

"Tatum Summers—" He doesn't get the chance to finish because someone presses the buzzer in the front office.

Needing to get away, I jump up out of my seat. "I'll get that." Before he, or anyone can say anything, I'm out of here. Opening the door to the office, I look up and my mood sours further when I see who's here. "Mr. Brookes, what can I do for you?"

"I … ummm, ahhh." He reaches up and squeezes the back of his neck. His forearm muscles flex as he does, causing my stomach to do a flip. *Down girl*, I internally berate myself. We do not go gaga over this hot asshole.

"You ummm, ahhh, what?"

"I just wanted to thank you."

His words shock me, I was not expecting him to thank me. "For?" I question.

"For what you did for Fletcher. He hasn't stopped talking about you since the accident."

"I was just doing my job," I nonchalantly reply with a shrug.

"Somehow I don't think lying in a hospital bed watching *Bluey* is part of the job description."

"Every day is different when you're a firefighter. Some days we watch *Bluey* with a cute kid, other days we race into burning buildings."

"I couldn't do what you do. It takes guts to race into a burning building."

"Thank you, Mr. Brookes."

"Please, call me Penn."

"Penn," I repeat his name. "Not as much of a dick as I originally thought." The sound of my voice breaks the silence that fell over us and then my eyes widen when I realize I said that out loud.

"Excuse me?" he hisses. "Did you just call me a dick?"

"Nnnnnno," I stammer, "I said—"

"No, you called me a dick. What the fuck have I done to you?"

Now it's my turn to hiss. "Excuse me." I slam my hands down on the counter separating us and I glare over at him. "You have been a dick to me each and every time we have interacted, therefore the dick moniker fits."

"Well excuse me, Bitchifer," he throws back at me. "Excuse

me for wanting to keep my son safe from the bitch who keeps appearing everywhere we go."

"Excuse me," I snarl back at him, "the world does not revolve around you and from where I'm standing, you're a shitty dad."

"Excuse fucking me, what did you say?"

"You heard me, now, if you excuse me, I have to get back to work." Staring at him, I notice he's seething but fuck him. "Goodbye ... Dick."

With that, I turn my back on him and just as I close the door behind me, I hear him snarl, "Fucking hell, she's a psycho as well." Shaking my head, I walk back into the kitchen and make a beeline for the coffee machine. I need a caffeine hit and I need it now.

"Who was that Tate?" Dad asks.

"Just some dick, I took care of it." A chuckle slips out when I say that.

"You okay after the other day?" He bumps my shoulder, joining me near the coffee machine.

"Yeah, I'm all good."

"Is that kid, Frank, okay?"

"Fletcher, Dad, his name is Fletcher and when I left the hospital, he was fine. His douchedad arrived and I got out of there, didn't want to intrude." *Or punch douchedad in his smarmy gorgeous face.*

"Douchedad? Do I even want to know?"

"Probably not." I chuckle with a shrug. "Hopefully I never have to see him again."

Those are famous last words because later that night, I wake up with my fingers someplace they shouldn't be, breathless and panting after the most erotic dream I have ever had ... about douchedad.

36

TATUM

I'M PRESSED UP AGAINST THE WALL, MY LEGS WRAPPED AROUND HIS waist, his dick hammers in and out of me. "Yes," *I groan, throwing my head back in complete and utter ecstasy.* "Don't stop ... ever."

"Not a chance in hell, Summers," *he replies before slamming his lips to mine.*

His tongue thrusts in and out of my mouth in sync with his dick in my vagina. Every nerve ending in my body is alight. I've never been this turned on before. That sensation low in my belly starts to simmer. "I'm close," *I pant into his mouth.*

Using his thighs to hold me up, he continues to relentlessly pound into me. Sliding his hand between us, he presses down on my clit ...

Douchedad's name, "Penn," passes through my lips as I wake up mid-orgasm, with my fingers inside me. I'm too far gone to stop so I continue to pleasure myself as I ride out my self-induced orgasm ... again. This is the third night in a row I've had this sexy dream, but it's the first time I've said *his* name while I climax.

Climbing out of bed, I trudge out to the kitchen for a glass of water.

Why am I dreaming sexy thoughts about him? I hate him,

well, hate is probably not the right word. I don't know the douche well enough to hate him, but I know that I can't stand him … and yet I can't stop thinking about him.

Placing the empty glass in the sink, I turn around to head back to bed but when I look at the clock on the wall in the hallway, I realize I have to get up in twenty minutes. So I turn on the kitchen light, squinting when the brightness blinds me, and head over to my coffee machine.

"Good morning, my beautiful friend," I greet my *Nespresso* machine, my most prized possession in the entire world. I love it so much that if this place caught fire, I would one hundred percent guarantee you that I'd grab it on my way out.

Giving it a little tap, I smile as I grab a caramel crème brûlée pod and pop it in. This morning I'm in a sweet mood, Kip got me addicted to this flavor and whenever I have one, I always think of him. "Morning, you hunk of spunk," I whisper, looking up to heaven.

With my mug of caffeine goodness in hand, I head out to the balcony of my apartment and watch the sunrise. The golden rays of the morning sun peek through the clouds and I smile. It feels like Kip smiling down at me from above.

Today is going to be a good day, I can feel it … but I was wrong, so very wrong.

"WE NEED TO HURRY, FLETCH, WE ARE SO LATE, SO, SO LATE," I shout as I race into Fletcher's room to hurry him along. There must have been a blackout last night because my alarm didn't go off, and by the time I cracked my eyelids open, the sun was shining high above and I have five missed calls from Phine.

With my phone pressed between my ear and shoulder, I call Phine back while trying to get a very tired, unhelpful, and not happy Fletcher ready for school.

"What up, boss man?" Phine says by way of greeting.

"I'm running late—"

"No shit," she hisses, interrupting me, "but don't worry, I'm an amazing employee and opened up for you. I told Mrs. Flannigan that you were running late and her car might be back late this afternoon. She was okay with that but Mr. Daniels, well, he was a right royal cu—"

"What have I told you about that word?"

"Ladies don't say cunt and I'm a lady so I shouldn't say cunt."

"Phine," I warn her, and no doubt she's rolling her eyes at me right now. "Are you rolling your eyes at me?"

"How did you know? Do you have cameras here?"

"I'm a dad, I know what all my kids are doing."

"I'm not your kid."

"Kid. Employee, same thing," I tell her. "I'll be there in thirty minutes, max."

"See you in an hour, boss man."

Before I can berate her for her sass, she's hung up and I look over to see Fletcher has his shoes on the wrong feet. "Good job, buddy, but they're on the wrong way around."

"God dammit," he hisses, kicking his shoes off.

"Language, young man."

"Sorry, Dad," he sheepishly apologizes before dropping down to put his shoes on but this time, the little legend gets it right.

"Good job, buddy, now let's get this show on the road."

Buckling him into his seat, I back out of the driveway and haul ass to his school. After dropping him off, I swing by the local café in town and grab two coffees and two muffins. With my "I'm sorry I'm late" treats in hand, I head to the garage.

Pulling up out front of my shop, I smile when I see a car up on the hoist, two more in the parking lot, and my pet project sitting in the end engine bay. I was so lucky this place didn't go bust when I was a mess after Mads died. I think she was up there, watching over it while I was breaking down and grieving.

I'm doing much better now, but some days I wake up and when I open my eyes, I expect to see her lying next to me. The moment I see her vacant side, my heart skips a beat, and it all comes crashing back to me. A few months ago, seeing that would send me into a spiral but now, now I take a deep breath, remember the good times with her, and then I get out of bed and get on with my day. Those moments are becoming fewer and fewer, but I don't think there will ever be a day that I don't think about her or miss her.

"Morning, boss man," Phine greets me when I walk into the office.

"I'm so sorry I'm late. The alarm didn't go off but I do come bearing treats." I lift the coffee tray and muffins.

"Dude, it's fine, besides you're the boss. You can do whatever the hell you want, but I am glad you're here."

"Why's that?" I ask, handing her the coffee and muffin.

She takes a sip. "That T-Bird there." She nods toward my baby in the corner. "There's something wrong with it but for the life of me, I can't figure out what."

A laugh breaks free and I can't not tease her and see where she's going to go with this. "What do you mean something's wrong?"

"Well, when I started it, it took some cranking and pumping her but it finally caught and started. After a few seconds, I noticed condensation on the passenger side of the hood. I immediately shut it off, opened the hood, and saw the whole right side of the engine compartment was soaked with gas, including puddles in all the intake low areas. Fuel had pissed out everywhere but when I took a look, I couldn't see a leak anywhere and it's pissing me off."

My eyes widen when I realize that she tried to start it and no longer do I want to tease her. "Okay, first things first, promise me you will never try and start that car again."

"Okay, but why?"

"Apart from that being a pet project of mine, there's no need for you to worry about Toni but because I know you and you will hound me for answers … the fuel leak is stumping me too. I can't figure out why but after some online searching, I'm now thinking it has dried-out gaskets in the carb, or a sticking float."

"Awesome, so I nearly caused an engine fire that could have burned the garage down, and you suck just as much as me when it comes to that engine leak."

"We don't suck. Toni just needs some pampering, but why did you need to start it?"

"Well, I was going to move it so we can use all three bays, make things run more smoothly here."

"Good thinking but Toni isn't going anywhere, not 'til I get that leak fixed."

"Toni?" she questions.

"Toni T-Bird, she's my baby girl."

"What is it with men naming their cars?"

"It's not just men, Mads introduced me to the naming of cars. When she and I first met, she had the sweetest cherry-red Mustang named Molly."

"You guys are fucking weird."

"Says the weird one."

She sticks her tongue out at me. "Okay, since you are all over this, what's the plan for today, little lady?"

Over our "I'm sorry I'm late" treats, we discuss the rest of the day and possible causes regarding Toni's fuel leak. Phine really is an amazing mechanic and I'm so lucky she came into my life when she did.

We are just wrapping up for the day when right out the front of the shop, a Jeep is rear-ended, causing the Jeep to slam into the bus stop across the street. Meanwhile, the hillbilly truck that hit it, veers into the gutter.

From where I'm standing in the garage, I feel the impact jolt through my body and I freeze. Standing here as I stare at the crumpled car, a sense of déjà vu crashes into me, this accident is similar to how Mads died. I know I need to go over and help but I'm unable to move. What if I look in that car and I see what happened to Mads? All I can picture right now is my beautiful Mads trapped in her car. Once again, I'm thrust headfirst into my grief. Even though Mads isn't in that car, I feel like I'm back at square one. I'm back at that fateful day and just like the first time, I'm numb.

38

TATUM

"Ugh," I groan, my body aches everywhere. Lifting my hand to my pulsating head, I feel wetness. When I open my eyes, I see I'm in my car and my fingers are stained red and something is trickling into my eye. Swiping the blood away, I apply pressure to my head and it slightly eases the pain.

Leaning into the steering wheel, I mentally take note of my body. Nothing feels wrong, except for my head and I can wriggle my toes, so there's that.

"Are you okay?" a voice says from beside me. I scrunch my eyes closed at the shrillness of the voice. It grates through my brain.

"I'm okay," I groan, "but I think I have a concussion." Looking out the window, I see a young woman in coveralls standing there, fear etched all over her face.

"Boss man, call 9-1-1," she shouts, but this time it doesn't grate through my head. "What's your name?"

"Tatum. My name is Tatum."

"Hi, Tatum, I'm Josephine but everyone calls me Phine. What do you say I get you out of there?"

"I would very much like that, but how's the other driver?"

"He's okay, he staggered out of his car and is sitting on the curb drinking a beer."

"The asshole is drunk?"

"Off his rocker," she confirms. "Look, I know we should wait for the paramedics, but I can smell gasoline and I'd hate for you to go boom."

"I would hate to go boom too, Phine. I'm a firefighter and from my limited medical training, nothing is broken, so I'm happy for you to get me out of my car."

She steps up to my door and tries to open it, but it won't budge. She puts all her might into it but it won't budge. "Boss man," she shouts over her shoulder, "come help me get this door open." Her face furrows in confusion. "Give me a sec." Before I can reply, she's gone.

Turning my head, I try to see where she ducked off too but from the angle of my car, I can't see where she went. Pushing on the door from inside, I try to open it but it's wedged tight. I'm going to have to climb out the window, or wait for the Jaws of Life to get here, and I refuse to have Calvin be my knight in shining armor.

A shadow appears and when I look up, my breath hitches because for a moment, I swear Kip is standing there. However, when they come closer, I realize it's *him*. Great, douchedad is my rescuer.

"Hey," I tell him, "so, I'm, umm, gonna have to climb out. This door won't be opening by itself and I refuse to allow my colleague to Jaws of Life me out. That's something I'd never live down." He chuckles and for the first time since I met him, I don't see douchedad. I see someone who is concerned and fearful right now. "Are you okay?"

"Not really, but don't worry about me, we need to get you out. That gasoline smell is getting stronger." He drops down out of sight. "Looks like your gas line has ruptured in the accident. Let's get you out before it goes boom."

"I'd very much like that." Reaching down, I try to unclick

my seat belt but like the door, it won't budge. Unlike my door, this has been sticking for weeks now so I can't even blame the accident. "It's stuck," I tell him, "I can't get out."

Just as I say this, a fire erupts under the hood. Smoke billows out the sides and I'm trapped, unable to get out. "Get me out. Get me out," I chant and when I look to douchedad, I see him running away from me and I start to panic again. "Help," I cry out, "Heeeeeeeelp."

Douchedad and Phine come back with a fire extinguisher and, within seconds, the fire is doused and my nerves start to settle. His eyes land on mine through the front windshield and I see pain in them, but as quick as our gaze connects, it's gone again. He says something to Phine and then he walks over to me. "You good?"

"Define good?" I reply with a shrug. "'Cause hanging out, trapped in a car, while the engine is on fire wasn't quite what I had in mind for this evening. I was thinking more along the lines of a hot bubble bath, my Kindle, and a bottle of wine since I have four days off."

"I'm sure that can commence after a detour via the hospital."

"Wine and concussions don't mix well … so I've heard."

He laughs and it's a deep belly chuckle. Seeing him so carefree and relaxed is the complete opposite to his usual douchey demeanor and it's surprising me. "Well, how about we get you out of there?"

"Yes, fucking please, but my belt's stuck."

"Probably jammed when that drunk guy slammed into your ass."

"Yeah, that."

He gives me a look that indicates he doesn't believe me but he doesn't question it further. "Be right back." He returns moments later with a pen knife in his hand. "May I?" he asks, showing me the knife.

Nodding, I intently watch as he reaches inside the car and

begins to cut the belt strap. Once it's cut in half, he pulls at it and I'm one step closer to freedom. Wriggling around, I wince when I push myself up. "Ugh," I grunt. "I think I have a few bruised ribs."

"Here, let me help." Carefully, he slides his hand under my armpits, reaches behind me, and starts to pull. My face scrunches in pain and I contort my body to climb out the window. Douchedad loses his balance and the two of us fall to the road. I land on top of him, my head colliding with his chin. Lifting my head, I stare down into his vivid blue eyes and he stares up into mine.

Lifting his hand, he brushes a tendril of hair behind my ear and gently runs his finger over the gash in my forehead. I flinch at the contact. He goes to pull his hand back but I reach up and cover his hand with mine. He slides it down and cups my cheek, running the pad of his thumb along my jawline. It's a strangely erotic moment, especially when I feel his dick starting to harden between us.

He's clearly embarrassed and in the blink of an eye, he lifts me off of him, placing me on my back, staring up at the afternoon sky. He jumps up and races away from me, leaving me alone on the road, staring up at the cloudless afternoon sky.

The paramedics arrive and I'm quickly lifted onto a stretcher and loaded into the back of an ambulance. The other driver is uninjured but he's taken away in handcuffs after being charged with a DUI.

Once secured in the back of the ambulance, I'm on my way to the hospital. Just before the doors close and shocking the ever-loving shit out of me, douchedad climbs in with me. He takes my hand in his and silently we head to the hospital.

39

PENN

Sitting in the waiting room, I stare down at the linoleum floor completely confused. Tatum and I shared a moment back there, and I don't know how I feel about it. She's the first woman to capture my attention since Mads but seeing her trapped in that car, it brought back so many memories. Was Mads scared like Tatum was? Or was she already unconscious when her rescuers got there? These are questions I never thought to ask and now, I keep wondering what she felt at the end.

"Penn," a nurse shouts as she comes into the waiting room.

"That's me," I say, jumping up to walk over to her.

"Your girlfriend is back from X-ray. You can go on back now."

Before I get to tell her that she's not my girlfriend, she already has her back to me and is walking away. Guess it's not really important, so I hop up and follow her. She escorts me to a curtained cubicle and when I stare at the blue curtain, I'm once again taken back to that fateful night.

"You can come in," a soft voice says. "I don't bite."

Gripping the edge of the curtain, I pull it aside and step in.

Tatum is sitting on the edge of the bed, her legs swinging back and forth in a hospital gown. "Shouldn't you be lying down?"

"I'm fine," she states and to prove her point, she hops off the bed but stumbles and begins to fall. Reaching out, I catch her before she collapses into a heap on the floor. Helping her back into bed, I shake my head. "Fine ... my ass," I mumble, earning myself a scowl. "Can I get you anything?"

"I'd kill for a coffee," she says.

"Really? I thought you'd ask for my phone to call your fiancé or something."

"Fiancé?" She scrunches her face up in confusion and it's quite cute.

"The man, or woman, you're going to marry," I point to her ring finger.

"Ohhh, umm, he ... he died. I haven't taken it off yet. Well, I did but I put it back because I'm just not ready yet. It's weird, I know but ..."

"I get it, I really do," I tell her. Holding up my left hand, I show her my wedding ring. "I know the feeling. I lost my wife earlier this year and I can't bring myself to take mine off either."

"I'm sorry for your loss," she whispers, then she lifts her head, shaking it. "Shit, I'm sorry I said that. I hate when people say that to me."

"Me too." I drop into a chair by her bed. "I despise when people say that but then again, what do you say?"

"Anything but sorry." We both laugh at her reply. "But seriously, why are they sorry? It's not like they killed them or anything and saying sorry won't bring them back."

"It's one of life's mysteries."

A silence falls over us and for the first time since meeting Tatum, I don't want to strangle her. Maybe I misjudged her and she's not the child-stealing bad guy I've made her out to be in my head. Before I can ponder that thought again, my phone rings. "Excuse me," I tell her. Standing up, I walk out to take the call and to be honest, I'm thankful for a little space. "Hey, Mom."

"Penn, are you okay? I saw what happened out the front of the shop when I came to drop Fletcher home. I saw the garage all locked up and no sign of you or Phine. Please tell me you two are okay?"

"We're fine, Mom, I'm at the hospital—"

"What happened? Are you okay? Why didn't you call me?"

"Mom, I'm fine. I'm here with Tatum."

"Who's Tatum? Are you seeing someone? Why didn't you tell me? Why are you keeping secrets from me?" Once again, Mom with her fifty million questions in a situation causes me to smile.

"Mom, I'm not seeing anyone. She was in the car that was rear-ended, I'm just making sure she's okay."

"Ohh, well, is she? Do you need me to bring you anything? What do you need?"

"If you could come get me that would be great. I rode in the ambulance with her so I don't have my car."

"Of course, I'll head back to our place and drop Fletcher off with Dad and be right there."

"Think you can pick up a coffee for Tatum on your way over? That's what she asked for."

"Of course, I'll be there soon."

After hanging up with Mom, I walk back into her room, but I stop midstep when my eyes land on her. She's standing up and has her back to me. She's in nothing but a skimpy G-string that leaves nothing to the imagination but it highlights her sexy as hell ass. Her back is bare and she's pulling on her clothes when she hears me behind her. She looks over her shoulder and when she realizes it's me, she hisses, "Shit," and drops her shirt, maybe a dress, whatever article of clothing it is. I have no clue because my eyes are glued to her ass. "I umm, ahh, thought you'd be longer."

"No, no, it's fine, I probably should have knocked."

"On a curtain?"

"Well, ummm, shit." Gripping the back of my neck, I take a step backward, "I'll ummm, ahhh, give you a moment." Stepping back out into the corridor, I run my hands over my face and I'm accosted with the vision of her sexy as hell ass.

"Penn?" she shouts my name like a question.

"Yeah?" I call out from the safety behind the curtain.

"Can you bend down and get my dress? I just tried and I got dizzy and nearly passed out."

"Sure," I sing out and step back in. She has her arms covering her boobs, but she still has her back and ass to me. Dropping to my knees, I pick up her dress. When I lift my head, I come face-to-face with her ass and up close it's even finer than I expected. "Hhhhhh … here," I stammer, offering the dress to her.

"Thanks," she whispers. When she takes the item from me, our fingers brush and a spark jolts through me. My eyes widen and when I look up, I see her staring down at me. Her eyes just as wide as mine.

Turning back away from me, she slips the dress over her head and I'm sad to see her ass is now covered. I'm still crouched beside her like a creeper when she turns to face me. She stares down at me and lifts her hand, cupping my cheek in a caring way. Silently we stare at each other, the moment is heated but my phone begins to ring, and we snap apart. She removes her hand from my cheek and drops to the edge of the bed as I pull my phone out and answer it. "Hello?"

"I'm in the waiting room, Penn," Mom says.

"Be right there," I tell her and hang up without saying anything else to her. "That was my mom, I have to go."

"Ohh, okay." Before she can say anything, I stand up and walk out.

What the hell was that? I think as I walk down the corridor and out into the emergency waiting room. Mom sees me and immediately walks over to me. "Are you okay? Is that girl okay?"

"I'm fine, Mom, and so is Tatum. She just wants a coffee, let me give this, or them, since there are three to her."

"Well, I didn't know what she wanted so I got an espresso, a latte, and one of those fru-fru salted caramel macchiato things."

"You always go above and beyond, Samantha Brookes."

"That's me." She offers me the coffee tray. "I'll wait here while you go deliver them to your girlfriend," she teases.

"She's not my girlfriend, I'm married, remember?" And to reiterate my point, I lift my left hand and wriggle my ring finger, the gold of my wedding band shining in the light.

"Widower, Penn. You're a widower."

"I prefer the term married." Before we can get into a debate over my title, I turn back around and head back to Tatum to deliver her coffee.

40

TATUM

"WHAT THE FUCK WAS THAT, SUMMERS?" I QUIETLY BERATE myself when Penn leaves my room. Why did I reach out and cup his cheek like that? That was very intimate, and apart from wanting to junk punch douchedad, that should be the only reason I want to touch him. But why, right now, do I want him to throw me up against the wall and kiss me?

"Knock knock," he sings out, pushing the curtain aside and walking in with a tray of coffees.

"I know I said I'd kill for coffee, but three? That's overkill, don't you think?" *How sweet, he got me three*, I think as my gaze flicks between the tray of coffees and his face.

"Clearly, you haven't met my mom. She doesn't do anything by halves but she didn't know what you liked so she grabbed a variety of them for you. We have an espresso, a latte, and a salted caramel macchi—"

"That one," I shout. "Salted caramel macchiatos are the best coffees around."

"Looks like we need to agree to disagree there. Coffee shouldn't be sweet. It should be punchy and put hairs on your chest." At the mention of chest, I notice he drops his gaze to mine, and I'm not ashamed to admit it but I push my arms inward slightly, giving the girls a slight uplift. My boobs aren't huge but they're enough to make men go gaga, and going by the look on Penn's face right now, he likes what he sees.

Needing to get the focus off my boobs, I turn it back to coffee. "Okay, Mr. 'Coffee Shouldn't Be Sweet,' how do you take your coffee?" Before he can answer, I hold my hand up. "Let me guess, you're a boring espresso kind of guy."

"Eeerngggh, wrong, I'm a piccolo latte kind of guy and—"

I interrupt him, "Did you just eeerngggh me like the dudes from *Grown Ups* do to each other?"

"Yeah, why?"

"You just don't seem like an eeerngggh kind of guy … especially since you drink piccolo lattes." I was not expecting him to say that coffee type and the more I think about it, the more I giggle. And then I snort in an unladylike way. "Sorry," I say, once I've composed myself. Through my tears of laughter, I add, "I just didn't expect you to say that. Big bad Penn likes a piccolo latte. Isn't one of those gone in like two sips?"

"Yep," he nonchalantly replies. "Gives me the caffeine hit I need and doesn't go cold."

"Fair point." I nod, even if he's wrong. Hot or cold, coffee is everything. "Now, gimme my coffee, this girl needs a hit." I reach out for my coffee. He picks up one of the paper cups and passes it to me. Like with my dress before, there's a spark when our fingers brush.

"You want another hit? After the massive one you took a few hours ago?" he teases me.

"Hardy har har, Mister. I meant caffeine hit and after THAT hit, I think I deserve all the caffeine and Fireball whiskey I want."

"Fireball girl, never would have picked that."

"What did you pick for me?" I ask him, taking a sip of my coffee and closing my eyes to enjoy the warmth filtering through my body.

"To be honest, I'm not sure. You don't seem like a girlie girl, so I can't see you as a daiquiri girl." I nod at his observation. "Beer is too boring for someone like you." My eyebrows raise at that assessment 'cause he's wrong, I love me an ice-cold beer on a hot summer day. "Wine, maybe on occasion." Again I nod. "I was thinking tequila 'cause you can either shoot it or leisurely sip on it with a margarita."

"Very astute observations there. Some correct, some not so correct."

But before I can tell him what I like to drink, Mom comes barreling into my room. She throws her arms around me. "Tatum Prudence Summers, do not ever do that to me again! I'm over getting calls informing me that you're in the hospital."

"I'm fine, Mom," I tell her. "And that's happened like three times."

"And one of those times I was on the other side of the world," she snaps back at me and holds me tighter. Eventually, she pulls back and grips my cheeks, looking me over. "Fine, my ass, there's a bandage on your head. Concussion?"

"Mom," I growl the word forcefully. "I'm fine. The doctors are going to let me go home if I stay with you and Dad tonight."

"Good," Mom states matter-of-factly. "Dad's in the cafeteria getting you a coffee."

Holding my cup of joy up, I smile. "Already taken care of."

"Where did you get that from? Did you go down to the cafeteria by yourself? Ta—"

"No, Mom, I've been in this bed the whole time. Penn got it for me."

"Who's Penn? And when did you start dating again?"

A scoff from behind her causes us both to look over at him. Why the fuck did he just scoff? Am I that repulsive he doesn't want to date me? Not that I want to date him, he is douchedad after all. Him being nice for one afternoon doesn't make up for his previous doucheness.

"I'm the coffee bringer, but not the boyfriend and on that note, I'm going to go. Glad you're okay, Tatum Prudence Summers," he repeats my full name with a hint of sarcasm. "I'll see you around."

Before Mom or I can say anything, he leaves.

"That was weird," I mumble.

"What was weird?" Mom asks, sitting on the edge of my bed, taking my hand in hers.

"It's nothing," I tell her, shaking my head and then regretting it as a wave of nausea washes over me from the concussion. "Thanks for coming to get me."

"I will always be here for you, no matter what. When you become a mom, you'll understand what I mean. There's nothing I wouldn't do for you or Kain."

"Thanks, Mom, but seriously, I'm fine. My car, however, I think she'll be a write-off."

"Your car we can replace but you, there's only one Tatum Summers and she's irreplaceable."

"Mooom," I whine, "don't make me cry, that hurts my head."

She pulls me in for another hug and for some reason, I believe her. Everything is going to be okay. Then I start to think about Penn. He was so different this afternoon. After hearing he lost his wife, we have that commonality, losing the one you love. I can't see myself ever falling in love again, but maybe he and I could be friends.

41

PENN

For the past week and a half, I have not stopped thinking about Tatum Prudence Summers and her ass, or Mads. There may have also been a super sexy dream that involved all three of us. Hey, I'm a man, give me a break. I woke up, covered in cum, something I haven't done since I was a teenager.

It's funny, the two of them would have been great friends. They are so similar but also so different. It's far too soon to be thinking about moving on, but I'm lonely. Maybe Tatum and I could be friends? I don't have a lot of friends. That's something Mads always pointed out, but when you are married to your best friend, all other friends pale in comparison.

Pushing the thought aside, I head into the kitchen to make dinner for Fletcher and me. He's in the living room watching *Bluey* … for the millionth time. Opening the fridge, I scowl when I see it's empty. Then I remember, I was supposed to stop at the store on my way home. Now, I'm going to have to take Fletcher to the store with me, which means two things. One, the shopping trip will be more expensive, and two, it will be full of crap we don't need 'cause Fletcher will want and neeeeeed this.

Heading back into the living room, I lean on the back of the sofa. "Come on, buddy, we have to go to the store. Daddy forgot to get stuff for dinner." But my phone rings and I smile when I see Wren's face on the screen.

"Hey, hey, baby sister."

"Hey, hey, big brother. How's that cute as fuck nephew of mine?"

"Cute as …" She laughs at my reply. "What's up?"

"Nothing, just calling for a chat."

"Why do you sound like your dog just died."

"Because Stefan is going to die … by my hands. I swear, Jaxson hates me and that's why he dumped this douche client on me."

"Or he dumped him on you because you're the best at what you do … ohhh, and Mom has a feeling about you two."

"Mom and her feelings but I swear, this time she couldn't be more wrong."

"Mmmhmpf," I tell her, rolling my eyes. "You and I both know; Mom is never wrong."

"This time she is wrong with a capital W R O N G and twenty million exclamation marks at the end, actually make that twenty million and one," Wren states matter-of-factly, and I can imagine my sister crossing her arms and scowling right now. "I would rather glue my vagina closed with super-glue than ever, E V E R, let Doucheman and his dick near me." I swear I hear her mumble 'again' but I miss it because Fletcher turns up *Bluey* and glares at me for interrupting his show.

Heading into the kitchen, I jump up onto the counter and swing my legs. "Did you just say again?"

"NO!" she hisses. "Why would you even put that thought into the atmosphere. My vagina and his cock, will never meet."

"Again," I can't help but add.

"Ugh, you are just as annoying as him."

"Yet you still love me, Wren."

"Not right now I don't, but forget about me. How you doing?"

"I'm actually doing okay." And for once, I mean it.

"That's so great to hear. I was worried about you for a while there."

"To be honest, I was too, but Fletch and I are finding a new norm and slowly getting there. Don't get me wrong, there are some days when it hits me like a linebacker, but those days are few and far between now. I don't think I'll ever get over her loss, but each day is getting easier."

"Good, 'cause I'd hate to have to come there and kick your ass."

"I'd like to see you try."

"Daaaaaaaaaaaaaaaad," Fletcher shouts, "we can go. *Bluey* is done."

"Where you guys off to?" Wren asks.

"You'll be so jealous, Fletch and I are off to the store to get stuff for dinner."

"Totes NOT jealous," she says with a laugh. Wren despises grocery shopping with a fiery passion, and I guarantee you if home delivery groceries weren't already invented, she would have invented it. "Why don't you just online shop? No pants, or a bra, is needed and you can do it drinking a beer."

"I don't want to think about you pantless or braless."

"I'm both right now," she teases but knowing my sister, it's not a tease at all.

"I'm hanging up now, love your face."

"Me and my pantless and bralessness love you too, bro. Give that nephew a squeeze from his favorite aunty."

Groaning, she laughs and we disconnect. I know I should write a list but looking at the time, we are going to be out much later than I want to be, so we're going to wing it. And since it's late, as a surprise for Fletch, I might grab takeout on the way home.

"You ready, lil' man?" I ask, jumping off the counter.

"Yep." He nods.

Oh. My. God. I swear every person in Lockhart Falls is in the supermarket tonight, there are people everywhere. So as not to lose Fletch, I lift him into the shopping cart and give him my phone to play on … and to stop him whining about being bored. Wren and her grocery delivery fascination may be on to something, but I will never admit that to her.

Pushing the cart around the corner, I bang into another cart and when I look up ready to unleash my wrath, no words come out when I see who I crashed into. Open-mouthed, I stare at the woman before me. *She really is gorgeous*, I think as I continue to mutely stare at her.

"Tatum," Fletcher excitedly screeches, jumping up and smiling at her when he sees her.

"Fletcher, my man, how you doin'?"

"Dad's letting me play on his phone."

"Lucky you." She looks up at me and smiles. "Hi," she sheepishly says, brushing a tendril of long blonde hair over her ear.

"Hi," I reply like the loser I feel. This woman causes me to become a bumbling fool. "What are you doing here?"

"Flying a helicopter," she nonchalantly replies, causing me to laugh.

"No, you're not," Fletch disagrees, "you're buying food."

The two of us laugh but our moment is interrupted when a guy walks up to her. "Let's go, Tater Tot." Before she can reply, he takes the cart from her and walks toward the cashier.

"Guess I better go," she says. "Later, guys."

"Bye, Tatum," Fletcher sings out with a wave while I just stare at her, unsure of how I feel right now. Seeing her with that guy caused my heart to drop and turned me into a mute statue. She furrows her brows at my non reply, then shakes her head and catches up to the guy she was with. Watching the two of them in line for the cashier, my blood simmers. Why does the fact she's with another man rub me the wrong way so much?

___

42

TATUM

TODAY WAS TOUGH BUT I GOT THROUGH IT AND I'M HAPPY TO have my four days off now. This last shift has dragged by so slowly because due to the concussion from my little bingle almost two weeks ago, I've been confined to desk work. I hate desk work with a fiery—pun intended—passion.

The station house is also spotless, I cleaned inside from top to bottom, and I even polished our wall of heroes' plaques. Lockhart Falls Fire Department is lucky in that we have only ever lost three firefighters in the line of duty, Kip included. Today, on the one-year anniversary of his death, we unveiled his plaque. Normally a fire fighter who died in action elsewhere wouldn't get one in a station that they aren't a member of but Kip meant a lot to everyone here so Dad made an exception and we honored him with a plaque.

Kain surprised us with a visit for the unveiling, but I also think that since Mom and Dad are heading away tomorrow, they called him in, wondering if I would break down after the memorial today. Surprising myself, and I think everyone, I didn't lose it.

Well, not publicly anyway.

After Kain and I get home, it hits me when I see the photo

of Kip and me on my dresser. Not wanting to break down in front of Kain, I sing out that I'm going to have a shower. I step into my walk-in closet, pull on Kip's Bauckle Bay Fire Station hoodie, and I let it all out. Hugging my knees to my chest, I cry and I cry.

Knowing me too well, my brother appears in the doorway. "Tater Tot," he says in that tone of voice I hate and comes over to me. He drops down beside me and takes my hand. "I was wondering when you'd crack, but thanks for winning me a fifth of Fireball from the 'rents."

"You bet on me with Mom and Dad?"

"Yep," he states matter-of-factly. "I'm officially a part of Bet Club."

"Sorry to break it to you, bro, but I've been a member for a few years now, but I think you need to share your win with me … since I'M the reason you won."

"I think that can be arranged, sis, but first, you need to let it go." He raises his hand. "And yes, I'm aware I just Elsaed you but you need to let the anger and sadness all out. No more faking that you're okay. Mom, Dad, and I know you, you're struggling. You put on this front for everyone, but we know you, Tater Tot, we know you." Processing his words, I nod. Taking his hand in mine, I sit here next to my brother, so lucky to have him in my life.

"Thanks, Kain," I mumble. I really am lucky to have him as a brother, but I want to junk punch him when he opens his mouth next.

"Now, you need to go have a shower 'cause you stink. Then we need to hit the grocery store because all you have in your fridge is sour milk and some moldy kale."

"I do not stink," I snap at him, "but I will have a shower and then we can go to the store."

"Really?" His voice is laced with shock. "I was expecting a fight or something."

"I'm too tired to fight but you're right, life's too short to fight or be upset or sad and angry. The time has come for me to get over my grief and for me to get on with things. Sure, sometimes I may sit on the sofa and cry for twelve hours but as long as I get back up, that's the main thing, right?"

"You really cry for twelve hours?"

Nodding, I wipe my nose on his sleeve. The look of utter disgust on his face is priceless, but I just smile up at my baby brother and lower my head to rest on his shoulder. "I haven't done that in a while, but yeah, in the past I have. When I was locked in my grief in Australia after you guys left, I think I cried for three days straight."

"I still kick myself for not hanging around. I knew you were struggling but you were so convincing that you were okay. That's my biggest regret and I know when I reunite with Kip, he's going to kick my ass for letting you down."

"You didn't let me down, Kain, if anything, I let you all down."

"What if we agree to disagree?"

"Deal." I nod. "Thanks, Kain."

"Anytime, sis, now, can we move on to the shower part 'cause my ass is starting to hurt from hiding out here, and I'm hungry."

Nodding again, I smile. "Deal."

"And you stink," he cheekily adds before jumping up before I can punch him.

Thirty minutes later, Kain and I pull into the parking lot at the store. It's super busy tonight, which is weird for midweek. Kain grabs the cart and we head inside. "Can you make me a parma?"

"Of course, but only 'cause you called it a parmA and not a parmI."

"I'm not Mom," he refutes, throwing a tray of chicken into the cart. Kain bumps into Mrs. Hayes, his best friend Burton's mom. Taking the cart from him, I continue on, grabbing the ingredients for our dinner. I really should have written a list because looking at my cart, it looks like the shopping cart of a seven-year-old.

Turning the corner to head into the cereal aisle, I crash into someone. Expecting to be yelled at, I'm pleasantly surprised when I see who I hit. Penn and I just stare at one another, neither of us says anything. We continue to stare until the stare off is broken when his son shouts my name, "Tatum."

"Fletcher, my man, how you doin'?" I ask the kid who always seems to bring a smile to my face.

"Dad's letting me play on his phone," he excitedly tells me, waving the device in my face.

"Lucky you." Turning my attention back to Penn, I smile and sheepishly say, "Hi." I feel like a giddy teenager around him.

"Hi," he replies back, and it seems like he's a giddy teenager too. "What are you doing here?"

"Flying a helicopter," I quickly say, causing him to laugh.

Fletcher scrunches his little face up in confusion. "No, you're not, you're buying food."

The two of us laugh, reaching out I fluff his hair. "Nothing gets past you, does it?" He shakes his head, beaming.

Kain comes up behind me, his arms loaded with who knows what. He drops the items into the cart. "Let's go, Tater Tot." He takes the cart from me and heads toward the cashier.

"Guess I better go." With a wave I say, "Later, guys."

Fletcher yells, "Bye, Tatum!" He waves excitedly at me. Penn, on the other hand, just stares at me. He doesn't utter a word, so I turn away from them and make my way over to Kain.

"Who's that?" he asks as we wait in line for the cashier.

"I rescued the kid from a bus accident and when I had my car accident it was outside Penn's auto shop."

"He likes you," Kain states, causing me to scoff. Douchedad does not like me, I don't think he has ever said one nice word to me. Well, there was that time he said thank you but that was because of Fletcher, he didn't say it out of the goodness of his heart. And he did bring me coffee, but I was just in an accident so again, he was being the obligatory nice.

"He can barely tolerate me," I snap at Kain, "and the feeling is mutual. His nickname is douchedad."

"Keep telling yourself that, sis, he likes you ... and I think deep down, you like him."

"No," I growl, "I do not."

Kain looks at me and I just know from the stoic expression on his face, he's about to impart some brotherly wisdom. "You know, it's okay if you do like him, Tater Tot, but most of all, it's okay to move on."

Anger builds at him saying this. Kip is, was, whatever, the only one for me, it's not okay to move on. It will never be okay to move on, I can never move on from his love. "Drop it, Brozart," I hiss, and the overwhelming urge to flee hits me. Needing a moment to myself, I tell him, "I'm going to get more shit paper." Before Kain can say anything, I storm away from him toward the toilet paper aisle ... making sure to go the long way around so I don't accidentally run into *him*.

How can Kain be so blasé about all of this? *It's okay to move on*. Pfffft, what the fuck does he know? He's never been in love as deeply as Kip and me. He's never felt the loss of having the one person who was your whole world be ripped way in a moment. He doesn't know shit; therefore, he needs to keep his *it's okay to move on* mouth shut.

My heart is racing, and I need a moment so I press myself against the back wall of the store. I can't tell if it's because there's a small part of me that knows Kain is right. That I do kinda sorta like Penn or because the thought of moving on from Kip makes my heart hurt. Closing my eyes, I take a deep breath and when I look up, I come face-to-face with Penn. He looks just like I look now. Confused. Scared. Unsure, and probably everything in between those emotions. It looks like he's going to come over, but he turns the corner and heads down the next aisle, giving me a view of his muscular jean-clad ass. *No, Tatum, do not look at the sexy ass*, I internally berate myself as I continue to stare.

Losing sight of him, my heart rate begins to return to normal. Pushing off the wall, I grab the toilet paper and head back to the front, but all I can think about is what Kain said, *it's okay to move on*. I know it is. Kip will always be in my heart, but is Kain right? Is it time for me to move on?

43

TATUM

After my 'time for me to move on?' moment/meltdown in the toilet paper aisle at the store last week, and my 'I need to get over it' chat with Kain, I tried but it didn't work and I've been an ogre ever since. I'm in a pissy, snappy, snarky mood, just call me Shrek, just without the green skin or ogre looks. So much so, Kain is going to go back to Castaway Grove early. My antics have pushed him away and, just now, he slammed the door to the guest room to pack. Just before the door slammed shut, he sniggered, "If I want to be reamed out by a chick, I'm going home to do it with Thalia 'cause at least I get make-up sex."

His words really hit home as to how much of an asshole I'm being because I wasn't even aware he finally manned up and asked her out on a date, let alone dating her. After their first run-in over an unattended beach bonfire, I never thought he'd get the girl. She's either a moron or my brother is actually sweet. I'm leaning to the latter, even if he's wrong about me moving on … or me liking douchedad.

Heading to my room, I flop down onto the bed and stare up at the ceiling. I hate feeling like this. I hate when you don't know exactly what the problem is but anything and everything pisses you off. I'm ninety-nine percent sure I'm pissed at Kain because there's some truth to his words, but how? How do I just move on? Is moving on not betraying Kip's memory?

Deciding to go for a run to clear my head, I jump up and change into my running gear. Slipping my AirPods in, I bring up my running playlist and with "Wonderwall" by Oasis blasting in my ears, I set off to hopefully clear my mind and get some clarity.

Running past the park in the center of town, between songs I hear a little voice call out my name and when I look up, I see Fletcher running toward me. Stopping, I remove one earbud. "Hey, buddy," I pant, still jogging on the spot. "Where's your dad?"

"At work, I'm with my nanna. She's getting me a cupcake from the bakery."

"Yum, chocolate?"

He shakes his head. "Nope, nilla. It was my mom's favorite."

"She has good taste," I tell him, his little smile widening at my praise of cupcake choice.

"Do you think they have nilla cupcakes in heaven?"

"Yeah, I do," I assure him with a smile. "They also have Fireball whiskey and burgers."

"I wish I could visit my mommy there."

"I wish you could too. One day you'll see her again."

"But who will look after Daddy if I go? Would you?"

"I guess, I could check in on him."

He beams at me. "I asked him if you can be my mom but he got mad, said I already have a mom."

"I ... umm, shit—"

"You said the 's' word," he whispers, his little eyes wide open. He looks over his shoulder. "Nanna didn't hear so I won't tell. She puts soap on your tongue if you swears."

"Fletcher Sanford Brookes," an older lady growls as she

comes racing over to him. "What have I told you about running off?"

"Sorry, Nanna, but I saw Tatum and wanted to say hello."

She lifts her gaze to me. I offer a smile, hoping to ease the situation but no, it does nothing to ease it. "You think it's okay to talk to random kids?"

Wow, I think, *I see where Penn gets his doucheness from.* "Excuse me?" My hackles raise at the audacity of the woman. "Fletcher is not a random kid to me, he's … he's my friend."

"She is, Nanna," he tells her, grabbing her hand. "She's the lady I asked to be my new mom." My eyes widen at his words, I can only imagine what she's going to say now. *You're the random whore chasing after a widow blah fucking blah.*

"You're Tatum?" she asks. "The Tatum?" Her tone is less filled with anger now, and the expression on her face softens. She's no longer scowling at me but it's definitely not a smile.

"Yes, I'm Tatum," I reply. Then shocking the ever-loving shit out of me, she smiles and throws her arms around me, hugging and squeezing me tightly. "Thank you for making him smile."

I'm a little confused but I pat her back and utter, "You're welcome." Not sure what else to say.

She pulls back and cups my cheek. "Thank you," she repeats again and then just like that, she takes Fletcher's hand and the two of them are walking away from me. Staring after them, I'm really fucking confused. Just before they turn the corner, Fletcher waves at me. Waving back, I turn around and head home. I'm going to have a hot bubble bath and try to soak my worries away.

Stepping through the front door, I find a note on the kitchen counter from Kain.

Tater Tot
Thanks for having me, even if you were an ungracious host at times.
I will always love you, but you need to stop wallowing.
Sorry if I'm harsh, but I only want the best for you and deep down, you know he does too.
Peace out, Brozart xo

With a sigh, I pick up my phone and shoot off a text to Kain.

TATUM

> Sorry for being a raging bitch while you were here.

His reply comes in while I'm grabbing a bottle of water from the fridge.

BROZART

> It's OK, I'm used to your bitchiness, Tater Tot, but you were next level this time … I presumed it was 'cause it was Kip's anniversary and the plaque thing, but I think it's more. Maybe that guy???

> I just feel …

> Feel what?

> Like I'm betraying him. Like…

My phone immediately rings in my hand. "Hey," I sheepishly answer.

"You are not betraying him by wanting to be happy," he says without even a hello.

"But—"

"Nope, no buts, Tater Tot. He would want you to be happy. You know that. I know that, hell, the postman even knows that." This causes me to laugh. "Kip wouldn't want you being a Snappy McSnapperson at everyone. Don't let his death engulf you. I want my happy-go-lucky sister back. Yes, it sucks that he's gone but you're not the only one who misses him. I lost my best friend too. I think—" He pauses and I can tell from his breathing what else he has to say is deep, and I hate that we're doing this over the phone.

"Just spit it out, dude, I can hear you thinking from here."

"At least if I do this over the phone, you can't junk punch me." This causes me to snort and smirk. "There's this place at home, The Grove Retreat, I think you should check it out."

"A retreat?"

"It's a place that helps people deal with grief. To help them move on and with the anniversary of his death and then his upcoming birthday, I'm concerned that it's going to be too much for you and, Tate, I think subconsciously that date is playing on your mind too. You may feel like you've dealt with his loss, but you haven't. You're masking it and I wish I'd said something sooner because it's eating away at you." He lowers his voice and adds, "I'm scared I'm going to lose you too. I lost my best friend. I don't want to lose my sister too."

"I miss him so much," I cry into the phone. "I thought I was okay but then whatever this thing is with Penn is happening, and now; I'm all confused. I'm lost, Kain, so, so lost. I put on a brave front for everyone else but it's getting harder and harder to fake it. Considering you just called me out on my bullshit, I don't think I'm faking it very well anymore. I … I need help, Kain."

"I know, Tater Tot, and I will support you anyway I can. You're my big sister and I want to be there for you, you just need to let me in."

Just as he says this, there's a knock at the door. "Hang on, someone's at the door, give me a sec." Walking over to the door, I open it to see him standing there.

"You gonna let me in?"

Nodding my head, Kain wraps his arms around me, and I fall apart, but while I'm in his arms I make a decision. I'm going to rise up from the ashes that are my life, and I'm going to be me again.

44

PENN

IT'S A YEAR AGO TODAY THAT I LOST MADS. A YEAR LATER, AND I love and miss her just as much. Will the hurt of losing her ever go away? It feels like just yesterday I woke to that fateful knocking on our front door. A lot has happened in the last twelve months.

"Daddy," a little voice says from beside me. Rolling over in bed, I stare at my little man beside me. Morning snuggles before we start our day have become a thing this past few weeks.

"What's up, buddy?"

"Will I ever get a new mom?"

Shit, not this again, I think, and today of all days. Really fate? "I ... I don't know, buddy."

"Jeff Jefferson just got one and now I'm the only one without a mom. I know you said Nanna and Nanna B are like moms, but I want a real mom. I ..." His little lip begins to wobble, and his eyes fill with tears. "I want a mom, a real one."

"Buddy," I coo, pulling him into my chest. "Your mom is a real mom, she's just watching over you from heaven."

"But I want to have ice cream with her and have her read to me again. I miss her reading to me."

"I can read to you," I tell him, running my fingers soothingly through his hair, just like Mads used to absentmindedly do to me.

"But you don't do the voices like she did, she was the bestest at that." A smile appears when I think about leaning against the doorframe and watching Mads in bed with Fletch reading him a story.

"She was the best at everything."

"Yep." Then he asks me the billion-dollar question, "Why did she have to die?"

"I will never understand why she did. They say the good die young and your mom was a super good one."

He sits up straight, grips my cheeks, and stares intently at me. "But I'm good, Dad. I don't want to die."

My eyes widen. *Shit! Shit! Shit! How am I going to fix this and then it hits me.* "Did you make your bed yesterday morning?"

"No." He shakes his head. When I nod, he lets go of my cheek and then sits crisscross applesauce next to me. Tracing over the tattoos on my forearm, I watch his finger skim over the lines. Everyone thought I'd lost my mind the day I came home with the outline done. I told them I was heading to the garage to get some paperwork done but instead, I stopped in at Falls Ink. I'd been thinking about doing this for a while. Last week, I found a doodle of Mads's in amongst some paperwork and ever since, I've thought about nothing but that picture. I took it in and showed, Paz. Told him what I wanted and BOOM. He created a design that I love, and now I have a sleeve tattoo dedicated to Mads.

"Well, a super good person would make their bed every single day, so I think you're disqualified from dying young." I bop him on the nose and smile.

"What's disqualified mean?"

"It means you are out of the race. You can't win."

He nods. "And you swears, especially when you are working on the T-bird, you won't be dying for an infinity billion years?"

"Something like that." Shaking my head, I can't help but smile at my little man. Yes, today is going to be tough but he and I, we will get through this together. "Want to do something really bad?" I ask him. He looks blankly at me so I just go for it. "Wanna have pancakes and ice cream for breakfast?"

"Can we?" His little eyes open wide.

"Yep." I nod. "Why not?"

"You're the best dad." He throws his arms around my shoulders. "Love you," he whispers.

"Love you too, buddy." Wrapping my arms around him, I hug him back and I swear I feel another set of arms around us too. Mads is here. Occasionally, over the last twelve months, I've "felt" her at different times. I really do believe she is watching over us. I just hope she's happy with how I'm raising our son.

45

TATUM

… six months later

ONCE AGAIN, I'M SITTING IN THE SAND ON THE BEACH IN Castaway Grove harboring a hangover. As I sit here alone, I stare out at the ocean and it hits me, I'm okay. It's all going to be okay.

It's
All
Going
To
Be
Okay

The reason I know I'm going to be okay is the difference between then me and six months later me—I'm no longer drowning in my grief.

Kain was right, I needed help. What I was doing was not living. I was existing and I was barely managing that. The retreat was just the place to help me revitalize my soul and learn to live with the loss of Kip and not be consumed with my grief. The amazing ladies there helped me to reset my mind. They gave me the tools to move on without guilt. I never realized just how much I was in denial over Kip's death. But the biggest revelation for me was that it's okay to keep living. Just because he's gone, it doesn't mean I have to stop living too. If anything, I should be living life to the fullest for the both of us. I think I said that at some point in the last twelve months, but it was a hollow statement. Now? I mean it. I'm going to grab life by the balls and I'm going to live.

After I left the retreat with a new mindset, I returned to Lockhart Falls and life was good. Great, in fact—well—apart from douchedad being a douche whenever I see him. Fletcher, on the other hand, I have all the time in the world for that kid. He's a breath of 'I'm almost seven' fresh air.

For the next week, I'm here in Castaway Grove on vacation, visiting Kain and Thalia because Dad demanded I take leave. I hadn't had a break since I returned from the retreat, and they were worried I was going to fall apart if I didn't take some time off and relax. I'd kinda thrown myself into work when I got back and if I'm honest, I'm thankful for the forced break. And since my brother lives in the beachside town of Castaway Grove, I can get a free beach holiday and see him. It also gives me time to get to know Kain's lovely girlfriend, Thalia. FYI, she isn't a moron, she makes my brother sweet and it's so fun teasing him for being in love. Thalia is perfect for Kain and I'm so happy he found her.

Yesterday was Kip's birthday. It was tough but I got through it with the help of Kain, Fireball, and what I'd learned at The Retreat. If only they reminded me that Fireball hangovers suck donkey dick.

Flopping back into the sand, I stare up at the clear blue sky. There's not a cloud in sight. Closing my eyes, the sound of the waves crashing into the shore is lulling me into a sleepy state. I know I should get up and go lie on Kain's deck, but for the first time since I woke up, my stomach isn't doing somersaults and I don't want to jinx that, so I just lie here. I can almost feel Kip here with me. I smile to myself when I think about Kip and me. We used to head down to Bauckle Beach before the sun would rise and we'd lie there together, staring at the sky above, and we'd tell stories about our future together. "I'm going to be okay," I whisper. "I love you, Kip."

Sleep overcomes me and I drift off … only to be woken sometime later when a ball smacks me in the back of the head. In my sleep, I'd rolled to my side and curled into a ball. "Fuck," I hiss, rubbing my skull.

"You said a swears," a little voice states from beside me.

Cracking my eyes open, I roll onto my back and squint at the brightness. A shadow appears above me, and then the screeching of my name vibrates through my head before a little body slams into me. "Tatum," he screeches my name again and from his straddled position on my chest, he smiles down at me.

"Fletcher, what are you doing here?"

"Having a vacation with my dad."

"Where's your—"

Before I can finish my sentence, a deep voice shouts, "Fletcher?"

That answers that, I think and no doubt earning myself another mouthful from douchedad when he joins us.

"Here, Dad," Fletcher sings out, waving excitedly. "I found Tatum." Then he reaches down and grips my cheeks. "What choo doing here?"

"Visiting my baby brother," I tell him.

"I want a baby brother but first, I need to get another mom."

Nodding my head, I don't know what to say. It's not like you can just go to Walmart and grab one in aisle five or anything like that, but before I can say anything, I feel a presence behind me. Leaning my head back, I see Penn looming over me.

"I see you found my son … again."

"Actually, he found me with a ball to the back of the head. I was asleep on the beach."

"Why were you asleep on the beach? Don't you have a perfectly good bed in a house around here?"

"I do, but I was up to watch the sunrise with a killer hangover."

"Hungover? Midweek?" he sneers, and his tone pisses me off.

"What I do midweek isn't any of your ducking concern." Lifting Fletcher off of me, I stand up and glare at Penn. "You don't know anything about my life. If I want to day drink midweek on what would have been my dead fiancé's birthday, I will do exactly that, and I won't feel one iota of guilt. Now, if you excuse me, I have … to wash my hair." Looking at Fletcher, I smile. "Catch ya round, Fletch."

Before either of them can say anything, I turn my back on them and march up the beach to Kain's place. Fletcher yells out goodbye, and even though his dad is a dick, I won't take that anger out on a kid so I wave over my shoulder and continue on to Kain's place.

Stomping across the deck, I slam the slider behind me when I step inside. Leaning against the door, I close my eyes, and take a deep breath. "He's such a fucking asshole."

"Who's an asshole?" Thalia asks and when I hear her voice, I screech in fright. Opening my eyes, I cover my chest, trying to calm my rapidly beating heart. "Shit, Tatum, I'm so sorry, I didn't mean to scare you."

"No, you're fine," I honestly tell her. "I just wasn't expecting anyone to be up yet."

"Wanna talk about the fucking asshole?"

"No," I growl. "He doesn't warrant any words."

"You sure about that? You look a little flushed."

"Not flushed over *him,* but I think I am little sunburnt." Walking into the kitchen, I grab a bottle of water from the fridge and take a sip. "I fell asleep on the beach, and well, now I'm a lobster but luckily for me, after a hot shower and some after sun gel, I'll be golden brown come tonight."

"Been there. Done that but at least you weren't naked and burned your flaps." I'd just taken a sip of water when she says this and I proceed to spray water everywhere.

"Come again?" I question, wiping at my chin. She looks at me sheepishly as I grab a cloth and wipe up the mess I made. "Oh. My. God," I singsong. "You ... you really did that?" She nods again. "You really aren't joking, are you?"

"Nope, I'm not," she confirms with a shudder shrug. "I'd like to say it was one of my friends but alas, no, it was me."

"Details now, please?" She nods but then I hold up my hand. "As long as it doesn't involve my brother naked then I reeeally do want to know."

"This was pre-Kain."

"Okay, proceed." I jump up onto the counter and eagerly await this story.

"As you know, I live next door." She nods toward her beachfront bungalow. "Well, I'm not a fan of tan lines. I have a private balcony off my bedroom and it's the perfect hidden spot to tan while naked. I'd just trimmed the lady garden, and it was a gorgeous day, so I made myself a pitcher of margaritas and headed out to tan. I proceeded to drink the pitcher by myself and drifted off to sleep, well, passed out. I woke when it was dark and when I closed my legs and stood up, I nearly passed out from the burn. My pink bits were, well, umm ..."

"Pinker?" I offer.

"Less pink and more slutty fiery red. My whole front was lobster red."

"Nips included?" I ask and she nods. "Holy fucking shit, that must have sucked."

"Major donkey dick. I now have a snatch patch so I never have to suffer flap burn again."

Shaking my head, I groan. "My lady parts are tingling—"

"Eeeeew," Kain protests after entering the kitchen at the

wrong moment. "I don't want to know about your lady tingles, and I'd hedge a bet and say my girlfriend doesn't either."

"She started it," I defend myself. "And for the record, we are referring to tingling in pain, not pleasure."

He covers his ears, "la-la-la-la-la-la-la-la-la-la, I don't want to know why you two are talking about tingly bits together, pleasurable or painful." Then he looks to Thalia with concern all over his face. "Are you leaving me for a girl? I can't go through what Burton did, please tell me you don't want my sister."

"Sorry, I'm not into tacos. Well, Mexican tacos I am, but not the lady taco. Sorry, Tatum."

"No need to be, Thalia, and for the record, I feel the same way. No lady taco for me, but now I really want tacos for dinner tonight … Mexican ones … and maybe a pitcher of margaritas."

"Sans flap burn?" Thalia asks, causing me to laugh at the horrified expression on Kain's face right now.

"Do I even want to know?" he asks.

"Nope," we answer in unison.

Shaking my head, I jump off the counter and head upstairs to shower. The water feels like a thousand knives hitting my burnt skin as I step under the spray but it'll be worth it for the tan later today. As I wash my body, I'm thankful my flaps are not burned to a crisp and then I realize, I'm excited for margaritas and tacos, Mexican ones, not lady ones, later tonight.

46

PENN

"Can we invite Tatum over for dinner?" Fletcher asks me
the following day as he changes from his swim trunks into a
pair of shorts and a T-shirt. He and I have just returned from
spending the morning on the beach. We built sandcastles,
swam, played Frisbee, and swam some more. My son is the
epitome of a water child. It was the perfect morning, but I
kept looking around for Tatum so I could apologize for the
way I acted yesterday. I was out of line in so many different
ways. She's a grown woman. She can day drink midweek if
she wants. And she's more than entitled to day drink
midweek on her fiancé's birthday. When she said that, I felt
like a right royal dick. On Mads's anniversary, her birthday,
our wedding anniversary and all the other special occasion
we had together, I would have loved to have locked myself
away and done just that, but I had Fletch to look after so I had
to do the mature thing. I waited 'til he went to bed before I sat
in our walk-in closet, hugging a sweater of hers, and drinking
red wine from the bottle.

"If we run into her again, we can."

"Thanks, Dad, you're the best." He kisses me on the cheek

and then runs into the living room and switches on *Bluey*, while I head into the kitchen to get us some lunch.

With sandwiches in hand, I join Fletch on the sofa and together we watch multiple episodes of his favorite television show and devour our lunch. Not to brag, but I make a mean ham and cheese sandwich, pretty sure Fletcher and I could live on them.

At some point, I drift off to sleep and I'm woken by a finger pressing into my cheek and a whispered, "Dad."

Cracking my eyelids open, I see two massive eyes staring at me and my lil' man's gorgeous grin. "Hey, buddy," I say, ruffling his hair. "Sorry, I fell asleep."

"It's okay. Can we go for another swim?" I'm surprised, and impressed, he didn't just go off on his own.

"Sure, go grab your trunks and we can head down to the lagoon." I stand up and stretch. I'm too old to be falling asleep on the sofa, even if it is a comfy one.

"Yes," he declares and does a little fist pump, reminding me so much of me at his age. He turns and heads off to get changed but comes back a few seconds later. "Can we have burgers and fries for dinner too?"

"Sure, why not."

"Yessssssss," he adds a few extra s's and another fist pump. "You're the bestest dad." He flies back over to me and throws his arms around my waist and hugs me tightly. Then he pushes himself off me and races to his bedroom.

Returning a few moments later, he's all set. Me, on the other hand, I'm still packing the beach bag. Luckily for the impatient kid who's currently tapping his foot and eyeing me in that 'hurry up' kind of way, I'm already in my board shorts. It's the only attire to wear on a daily basis while at the beach.

With the bag finally packed, Fletcher takes my hand, and we head off for our afternoon at the beach. Like this morning, we have a blast together. I'm sitting on our towel watching Fletcher chase some seagulls when the hairs on the back of my neck prickle. Looking toward the shoreline, I smile when I see Tatum walking in the wet sand. She looks so beautiful with the afternoon sun radiating around her. She's wearing a yellow sundress, aviators on her eyes, a beach bag is slung over her shoulder, and her flip-flops are dangling between her fingers.

She looks over to me and freezes midstep. Her carefree look disappears when she registers it's me and it's replaced with disgust. It's totally deserved after the way I treated her yesterday, and to be honest, it cuts me deeply. Standing up, I walk over to her, keeping my eye on Fletch as I do. "Hi," I say when I reach her.

"Hi," she hesitantly replies.

"I'm sorry," I spit out before she can say anything.

My apology surprises her. "What?"

"I'm sorry, Tatum. I was rude yesterday and what I said was completely out of line. You're a beautiful, grown woman who can drink midweek if she wants too, and you definitely can drink midweek on occasions like that. I know I would have loved to have drunk myself into a stupor on Mads's birthday if I could have."

"You think I'm beautiful?" she asks me.

Nodding, I take the moment to appraise her body up close. "Stunning, actually."

A silence falls between us and we just stand here, staring at one another. My heart is beating loudly and it feels as if it's going to burst out of my chest, but our moment is interrupted when Fletcher screeches Tatum's name. He comes barreling over to us. "Hi, Tatum."

"Hey, buddy, how you doin'?" she asks him. She might despise me but the affection she shows for my son warms my heart.

"We're having burgers and fries for dinner, can you come?" he asks her, then he looks to me, takes my hand, and squeezes and pulls in excitement. "Please, Dad, can she? Can Tatum have burgers and fries with us?"

She looks to me and I nod. "You're more than welcome to join us. If you like."

She looks hesitant but then Fletcher begs again in the way he's mastered where you cannot answer anything but yes, and she nods. "Sure, I'd love to."

"Yesss," he hisses, fist-pumping the air and before we can say anything else, he runs off to chase some seagulls.

"Do you want to join me?" I flick my thumb to our stuff. "Or did you want to meet up later for dinner?"

"I'll, umm, join you." She seems so unsure. "If that's okay?"

Nodding, I step aside and usher her over to our spot. She drops her bag and flip-flops in the sand. Then she grabs the hem of her sundress and lifts it over her head, revealing the skimpiest and sexiest midnight blue, itsy bitsy, teeny tiny bikini.

"Fuck," I hiss under my breath as she plonks herself down on our beach towel and leans back on her hands. She tilts her face to the afternoon sun and soaks up the rays. I thought she was gorgeous before, but she's ... I have no words for how fucking beautiful she is right now. My cock agrees because I'm currently sporting a semi. Readjusting myself, I join her. "Drink?"

She lifts her head, looks over at me, and shakes it side to side. "I'm good, thanks."

Reaching into the cooler bag, I pull out a soda can and crack it open. It must be a little on the gassy side because it sprays soda everywhere, soaking Tatum and myself in the sugary liquid. She squeals and once again I hiss, "Fuck," dropping the can into the sand. "Shit, Tatum, I'm so sorry."

As if the moment couldn't get more embarrassing, a seagull flies over and decides to take a shit at that precise moment, and a drop of bird shit lands on my shoulder and slides down my bare chest.

Dropping my gaze, I watch as the white runny liquid slides down. Looking up, I notice Tatum intently staring at me. I don't know if she's staring at the shit, my chest, my tats, or all of the above, but whatever the case, I like having her attention on me.

"Shit," she whispers and when she realizes what she just mumbled, she raises her gaze to mine and we both begin to laugh. "Oh. My. God," she cries through her laughter, "we really are a pair, aren't we?"

"Yep," I reply with a nod. Standing up, I offer her my hand. "Shall we take a dip and clean up?"

Her eyes flick from my hand to my face, back and forth several times. Indecision is written all over her face. Just when I think she's going to refuse my hand, she takes her sunglasses off and pops them on top of her bag. She then reaches up and places her hand in mine. Pulling her into a standing position, I tug her a little harder than intended and she stumbles into me. My hand slides around her waist to steady her and her palm lands square in the bird shit. I expect her to scream and hiss about her hand being in shit, but she just leaves it there and stares up at me.

This close, I notice her eyes are an unusual shade of green. We just stand here, holding one another, and staring, but the moment is broken when Fletcher joins us. "What you doing?"

"We're about to take a dip, wanna come?" she asks him, removing her hand from my chest. She steps back, placing some distance between us. Immediately, I mourn the loss but considering we are on a public beach, it's probably for the best because I was moments away from lifting her up and wrapping her legs around me as I kissed the life out of her.

She offers Fletcher her hand and at the last minute, I register which hand it is just as Fletcher screeches, "Eeeeew, what's on your hand?"

"Bird poop," she nonchalantly replies.

Fletch scrunches his face up and shakes his head. "Gross." He pulls his hand free and shakes it vigorously, trying to get the bird poop off.

"Last one in is a rotten egg," Tatum says before turning away from us and racing toward the water. Fletch giggles in delight and chases after her.

Putting my hands on my hips, I stand here and watch the two of them together. They race toward the water without a care in the world. Fletch looks back at me. "Come on, Dad," he shouts, beckoning me to them with his little hand.

Nodding and smiling, I take off after them. By the time I reach the water's edge, they are knee-deep and splashing each other. Both of them giggling and frolicking about. Racing over to them, I swoop Tatum into my arms and keep running. She screeches my name and laughs, slapping at my hands to put her down. When we are out a little deeper, I launch her into the air. She squeals and lands in the water with a splash.

Breaking the surface, she pushes her golden locks off her face and glares at me. Meanwhile, Fletcher is giggling his little head off behind us. Seeing him so happy melts my heart, and then I notice his eyes widen. Suddenly, there's a wet dripping weight on my back. Her arms are around my neck and her legs around my waist. "It's on, dude," she whispers into my ear.

"Mmmhmpf," I reply. Before she can do anything, I fall backward, taking both of us under the surface. She coughs and splutters and for a moment I feel bad. That is until she kicks her leg out and takes me down—ninja style.

Pushing myself back up, I begin to splash her and throw back at her, "Ohhh, it's on now."

Fletcher joins us and the three of us splash each other and laugh as an epic water battle begins. This is the most fun I've had in a very long time, the same goes for Fletcher. As I take a massive splash to the face from my son, I realize I don't feel guilty for having fun.

47

TATUM

IF YOU'D TOLD ME YESTERDAY THAT TODAY I WOULD BE HAVING A water fight with Fletcher and his douchedad, I would have told you to put down the crack pipe, but here I am, having fun with douchedad and his son. I'm splashing around with two relative strangers, but it feels like I know these people on a much deeper level.

Our water fight comes to an end and without saying a word, Penn and I silently walk back to our things. Pulling out my towel, I wrap it around me before sliding my sunglasses back on. Standing here, I watch Penn run the towel over this body. If I were in a cartoon, there'd be drool leaking from the corner of my lips, steam would be coming off my body, and there'd be hearts in place of my eyes.

Penn is hot.

There's no other way to put it. Tattoos. Beard. Abs on abs. He's the complete package and after spending this time with him, he's not the douchedad I've made him out to be. "You're not the douchedad I thought you were," I tell him, shocking both of us with my honest words.

"Well, you're not the child-stealing harpy I thought you were."

"Child-stealing harpy, really?"

He shrugs at me. "What can I say, I misjudged you, Tatum …."

He pauses and his brows furrow as he tries to remember my last name. "Summers, Tatum Summers," I tell him and nod in that 'hello' kind of way. "That sounded so Bond-like."

"You're hotter than Bond," he states. His words cause my cheeks to darken and for my heart to pitter patter.

"I get more of a *Fast and Furious* rebel vibe than a law-abiding … ish … secret agent one from you."

He nods at my assessment and we just stand here and stare at one another. "Daaaaaaaaaad," Fletcher shouts as he joins us, breaking our stare off. "Can we have dinner now? I'm starving."

"I guess so." Penn looks to me. "You don't mind having an early dinner, do you?"

"No, that's fine." I shake my head. "I'm kinda hungry too." I tack on with a smile. "Come on, lil' man, let's get changed and then if it's okay with your dad, I'll take you to this place that has THE best beer battered fries."

"Beer battered fries?"

Nodding, I smile. "You will never have fries any other way after you have these. My brother's girlfriend's friend owns this bar—" *Shit, we can't take a kid to a bar.* "Ummm, can Fletcher go to a bar?"

"I'm nearly seven," he proudly declares.

Nodding, I open and close my mouth, not wanting to upset him but Penn saves the day. "I know the place and I don't think we're dressed for a place like that today. How about we go to the usual place and get it takeout? Then we can have it at home on the deck. We can try yours another time?"

Nodding, we both then look to Fletcher. "Fine," he reluctantly agrees, "but I want to try the beer ones before we go."

"Well," I offer, "I know the owner ... kinda. Sorta. Why don't I see if I can get a special order of them?"

"Really?"

"Mmmhmpf," I reply with a nod. "You and your dad can head home, you shower, and then I will bring everything by."

"Are you sure?" Penn asks me.

Nodding, I smile. "I'm sure and ever since I mentioned these fries, I can't stop thinking about them."

"That good, hey?"

"Yep, better than sex good."

"What's sex?" Fletcher asks, my eyes widen in shock at his question.

"I ... ummm ... ahhh, look, a crab." I point to the sand, and we see the little crab scurry across the sand.

"Crab," Fletcher excitedly squeals, forgetting all about sex and focusing on the crab.

"Nice save there," Penn says, bumping my shoulder. "But if I know my son, later tonight he will ask that question again."

"Well, let's hope he asks the question when I'm not there." But no such luck for me. He asks the question again after dinner ... when Penn is not around, and I have to explain sex to an almost seven-year-old. An almost seven-year-old who asks waaaaay too many questions and is too smart for his own good. My explanation that grown-ups use sex to make each other feel happy led to "How do they do that?" And my favorite of the night, "Can I have sex with you?" *No, a big fucking hell no ... but I wouldn't mind having sex with your dad.*

Just as I've finished my not so eloquent explanation about sex and the billion and one follow-up questions, Penn returns. "You handled that well," he tells me, passing me another beer. Bringing the bottle to my lips, I chug half of it back, needing a buzz to relax me after the sex inquisition, and not the fun naked sweaty kind.

"How does a six-year-old fire off so many questions like

that? I felt like I was in the fast minute thingy on *Who Wants to be a Millionaire?*"

"That was nothing. Some days it's a million questions before 7:00 a.m."

"You deserve a trophy or something. That's hardcore, man. I can't function without a gallon of coffee in my system at the best of times, I'd be the shittiest, grouchiest mom ever."

"Well, I'm the grouchiest dad ever so ..." he says with a shrug. "Coffee is life when you're a parent, so you need to have the best of the best machines. This place has THE best coffee machine in the world, so after our last stay here, I ordered one for home."

"Are you trying to seduce me with coffee?" I tease him, giving him my sweetest, most innocent look.

"I ... ummm, maybe." He pauses. "Would you like a coffee?"

Lifting the beer in my hand, I smile. "Maybe another time."

"I'd like that," he says, his expression softens and it's not something I'm used to seeing on his face. He's always stern and growly. The longer we stare at one another, the atmosphere around us changes and something passes between us. I'm not sure what's happening but I do know I like it. I like it a lot.

The moment is broken when Fletcher yells out something about poop. "And that's my cue to leave." Blood, guts, fire, and I'm good, but puke and shit, nah, I'm out.

Placing the beer bottle on the coffee table, I stand up and when I turn to leave, Penn is right there. I can smell him, he's that close. His scent envelops me and it intensifies when his hand slides around my waist and he gently tugs me into him. I can feel the outline of his dick pressing into my hip. He's not fully hard but it's hard enough to be noticeable.

Our eyes are locked on one another.

Our breathing is labored.

Our heads begin to move closer.

Our lips are millimeters apart, but Fletcher shouts out about poop again and the moment is broken.

Our lips are still hovering. "I … ummm … better go deal with that," Penn murmurs. His heated breath skates over my skin, causing goosebumps to appear.

Nodding, I swallow deeply but neither of us has moved. "I'll, umm, let myself out. Thanks again for inviting me to dinner." I turn away from him and walk around the couch. Opening the slider to the deck, I let myself out. Looking over my shoulder, I murmur, "Good night, Penn," just as I close the slider.

Taking a few steps, I look back over my shoulder and smile when I see Penn still standing there, grinning to himself. I didn't imagine what just happened. I didn't imagine an almost kiss, and I definitely didn't imagine his impressive half-mast dick pressing into me. With a little pep in my step, I race across the deck, jump down onto the beach, and jog the few doors up to Kain's place. He and Burton are sitting around the firepit and giggles are coming from farther away, so I guess Thalia and Nix are inside getting more drinks.

Walking over to Kain, I take the bottle of beer from his hand, and chug is back. "Rough night?" he asks. Nodding, I continue to drink his beer. When it's finished, I place the empty bottle back in his hand just as I hear Burton uncap another one. Looking over at him, he must see the desperation on my face because without a word, he offers it to me. "Thank you," I whisper before I proceed to drink that one too.

"You okay, Tater Tot?" Kain asks me just as I finish killing beer number two.

Before I can answer, Thalia and Nix return with a pitcher of something and with Nix being here, I know it will be strong and just what I need. "Please tell me there's enough for me?"

"Umm, yeah, I'll grab another glass," Thalia replies with a smile. She places the pitcher and her glass down and skips back inside.

"Tate," Kain says, reaching out to take my hand. "Are you okay?"

"I … ummm … I … I don't know."

"Did something happen?"

"Kinda. Sorta. I'm not sure."

"Wanna talk about it?" Nix offers, but I shake my head. "Wanna drink about it?" Nodding, she smiles and proceeds to fill the two glasses and then hands me one. Taking a sip, I squint 'cause that shit is sweet, sickly sweet. Thalia joins us and the girl clearly knows me well because she returns with a bottle of Fireball and apple juice to make me an apple pie on the rocks. The only other way to drink Fireball when you aren't shooting it.

"You're the best," I tell her as she goes about mixing me a drink, a nonsweet sickly drink.

She holds out the tumbler to me but doesn't let it go. "I'll give this to you, but you need to share with us what's wrong because by the look on your brother's face, he's ready to pummel someone because he thinks they hurt you."

Shaking my head, I smile. "No, it's nothing like that. It's just, I … I think I like Penn."

"Aww, Tater Tot likes a boy," Kain teases me, earning himself a smack in the stomach from Thalia and she hisses, "Leave your sister alone."

If I wasn't lost in my head, I'd tease him for getting in trouble but I'm all messed up at being okay and liking Penn and almost kissing him. Who gets messed up from being okay from an almost kiss with a super-hot guy?

"Why are you freaking out?" Thalia asks, breaking the silence and handing me my drink.

"That's the thing," I tell them shaking my head, "I'm NOT freaking out."

"And that's bad?" she questions me, confusion written all over her face, and I don't blame her because I'm confused as hell over not freaking out.

Shaking my head, I take a sip and scrunch my face up. This is more Fireball and less apple juice, but I'm relishing the burn right now. Taking another swig, I drop down into a vacant chair and start to process everything from tonight.

"Tate, talk to me," Kain's voice is laced with concern. He reaches over and squeezes my knee, letting me know he's there for me. Have I mentioned I have the best brother? He may be a pain in the ass occasionally, but when push comes to shove, he's there for me.

Nodding, I look over at him. "Today, I had the best afternoon with Penn and his son and then dinner was perfect. Well, it was perfect apart from the sex talk with an almost seven-year-old." That admission earns me a few eyebrow scrunches and a "What the fuck?" I don't focus on that; I continue with my story. "When I was leaving, there was a moment with Penn, an almost moment, but none the less a moment. We didn't kiss or do anything but ..."

"But what?" Thalia asks.

"I didn't freak out over said almost moment. I let myself enjoy it and ... and, I don't feel guilty."

"Why would you feel guilty?" Nix asks.

"Because of Kip."

"Because of Kip," she repeats. "And why do we care what Kip thinks?" Her eyes widen when it clicks why we would care about Kip's reaction. "Okay, I get it now, my cocktail-filled brain has finally caught up." Then she asks me for more details about Penn.

"When I first met Penn, he was an asshole. I actually first met him here when I first got back from Australia." I recount the coconut story and how much of a douche he was, and then all the other moments in Lockhart Falls too.

"This is all very romance novelesque, if you ask me,"

Thalia says. "The single dad and the hot firefighter chick find love again after their first loves are ripped from their lives. It's a beautiful love story. Now, when do you think this thing started to change between the two of you?"

"This afternoon definitely saw our relationship change. But now that I look back at all our interactions, I think this thing with Penn has been building for a while now, but previously I always ran from it feeling like I was betraying Kip somehow by moving on and being happy, but tonight that feeling of betrayal didn't hit me."

"Then why didn't you kiss him?" Kain asks me the million-dollar question.

"It wasn't the right moment 'cause Fletcher needed to poop."

"You got kissblocked by a poop," Burton chortles, earning himself a smack in the stomach from Nix.

"So make it the right moment," Kain suggests as if it's the easiest thing in the world.

"How?"

"Make him a parma, that will have him begging at your knees for more than just a smooch," Kain nonchalantly says as if food is the way to win a man over.

"You really think fried chicken covered in tomato sauce and ham and cheese, will earn me a kiss and maybe more?"

A chorus of "Yes," echoes around me.

Shaking my head in confusion, I lean back in my chair and wonder if it's that simple. Will fried chicken covered in tomato sauce and ham and cheese win me the guy?

48

PENN

Kissblocked by my son due to a shit, a fucking brown turd stopped me from kissing Tatum last night. That thought races through my head for the millionth time tonight as I lie here in bed and stare at the ceiling. Sleep is eluding me because I keep wondering what would have happened. What would have happened if that shit decided to hold on a little longer? Would we have kissed? Would she have stayed the night?

Growling in frustration, I climb out of bed and decide to start my day.

Checking on Fletch, I smile at my son. He's sound asleep sprawled diagonally across the queen-sized bed. Leaning against the doorframe, I watch him for a few moments. Pushing off the frame, I pull his door closed so as not to wake him.

Entering the kitchen, I head over to the coffee machine. "Good morning, beautiful," I whisper as I turn it on and remove the water compartment to fill it up. Popping a pod into the slot, I place my cup underneath the spout and watch as she produces my cup of liquid gold.

With my steaming mug in hand, I head outside to watch the sunrise. Walking to the stairs, I drop down and stare out at the ocean. There is nothing more relaxing than watching the waves crash into the shoreline with the sky behind them changing from the darkness of night into the brightness of the day.

"Morning," a soft voice coos and when I look up, I see Tatum walking toward me. Her blonde locks are twisted up into a messy bun thing on top of her head. She's wearing purple satin sleep shorts and a matching tank and she has a mug in her hand, which I'm guessing is coffee. She looks absolutely stunning.

"Morning," I murmur in reply as she joins me sitting on the stairs. "What are you doing up so early?"

"Couldn't sleep," she tells me, taking a sip from her mug which definitely is coffee, the scent giving away her drink of choice. Then I begin to wonder if she couldn't sleep for the same reason I couldn't sleep. "You?"

"Couldn't sleep either, my mind was racing."

"Wanna talk about it? Kip always said, 'a problem shared is a problem halved' and most of the time he was right."

"When was he wrong about the sharing thing?"

"When I was pissed off at him for leaving the toilet seat up in the middle of the night and I'd get a wet ass. That would just rehash my problem and then I'd be mega pissed again."

"Nothing worse than a wet ass in the middle of the night."

"No one wants a wet ass anytime."

We fall silent after that and comfortably in silence we sit and watch the sunrise. "I had a great time yesterday," she says, breaking the silence.

"Really? Even with the sex talk and poopgate?"

"Even with those," she says matter-of-factly, bumping my shoulder. "The company was pretty great. I can't remember the last time I had an afternoon and evening like that."

"I had a great time too," I reply. "And you were right, beer battered fries are the best invention ever."

"Wait 'til you try my parma, that shits all over beer battered fries."

"Are you inviting me to dinner, Ms. Summers?"

"Maybe I am, Mr. Brookes."

We turn our heads to face one another. Reaching over, I take her mug from her hands and place it on the deck next to mine. Cupping her cheek with my palm, I stare into her eyes. She reaches up and cups my cheek too, running the pad of her thumb over my bottom lip.

This is it, I think, this is the moment I kiss her.

Leaning forward, she shimmies closer. Our lips are millimeters apart, again. I can feel her heated breath on my lips. We are just about to make contact when from behind us, a little voice squeals, "Tatum, you're here."

The sound of his voice pulls us apart when we hear footsteps padding across the decking. Fletch doesn't see our coffee mugs behind us and he kicks one over. It crashes into the other and it breaks, causing Tatum to shriek from the mess. "My ass is wet," she cries out, jumping up quickly. My eyes drop to her ass and I like what I see, even with brown liquid dripping down her legs. The material of her sleep shorts is sticking to her skin, showcasing the tautness of her cheeks. The sudden urge to bite her ass slams into me as she pulls at the material.

"I'm sorry," Fletcher begins to cry. "I ... I, it was an accident."

"It's okay, buddy," Tatum reassures him. "The main question is, are you okay? You didn't cut or burn yourself?"

Her worrying about Fletch warms my heart.

"I'm fine but you're all wet," Fletch tells her, pointing to her leg.

"I'm fine, nothing a shower won't fix," she tells him, ruffling his hair.

Once again, my eyes are locked on her lower half. She

notices me staring and raises her eyebrows at me in a 'you're busted' kind of way. "You right there staring at my A S S?"

All I can do is shrug. "I'm attracted to your A S S," I tell her, throwing a wink her way.

Her cheeks—on her face—turn pink and the over-whelming urge to grab them and kiss her hits me hard. "I better get home and cleaned up," she says. She turns and walks down the steps and then she turns around. "My place. 6:00 p.m. I'm cooking parma." And with that, she spins around and heads back to her place.

Standing here, I watch her walk away, my eyes glued to her ass, wondering if I will ever get to kiss her because once again, I was kissblocked by my son.

49

TATUM

"IT'S JUST DINNER," I MUMBLE TO MYSELF FOR THE MILLIONTH time today. I'm a nervous Nelly right now. Actually, I've been one all day, ever since I left Penn's place this morning after inviting him and Fletch to dinner. I can't remember the last time I was this nervous over a guy, or in general. I kinda feel like fifteen-year-old me before I went on my first date with Sean McMasters. And like back then, Kain is teasing me. Every time he walks into the room he starts singing "Tatum and Penn, sitting on the beach, K I S S I N G," or he makes smoochy sounds. He's an immature dickhead at times but to be honest, it's helping with my nerves—not that I'm going to tell him that.

The salad is ready. The parmas are in the oven. The wine and juice boxes are chilling, and I've just baked a batch of peanut butter chocolate chip cookies as well because I'm procrastabaking. I've just placed the last cookie on the cooling rack when Kain asks a question that has me freaking out even more, "What if one of them is allergic to peanuts? Your bomb-diggity-bomb cookies are gonna kill them."

"Shit! Fuck! Shit!" Dropping onto one of the island stools, I lower my head to the cool countertop and gently bang my head against the granite. "What if I kill them with peanuts? I'm too pretty for jail and orange really isn't my color."

"I agree, you are too pretty for jail but for the record, I think you'd look great in orange and there will be no killing. No allergies here," a deep voice says from the deck doorway.

My head snaps up and I spin on the chair toward the door. When my eyes land on Penn's, my mouth drops open and I'm pretty sure drool begins to drip down my chin. He's wearing a plain white tee and dark cargo shorts. His tee sticks to him like glue and it highlights his muscular chest and shows off the amazing ink on his arms.

"Cool tats, man," Kain exclaims, walking over to greet Penn. "I'm Kain, the younger brother." He offers his hand to Penn.

"I'm Penn, the …" He doesn't finish that, and I don't know if I'm relieved or hurt he didn't refer to himself as my boyfriend, or whatever the hell I am to him. He shakes Kain's hand and the two of them stare one another down while shaking hands, but the sound of a little voice breaks the pissing contest between Penn and Kain.

"I'm Fletcher, the kid." Kain drops his gaze to Fletch, who has his hand out for a handshake too. Kain takes his offered hand and the two of them shake.

"Good grip there, Fletch."

"Thanks. I'm seven you know."

"Not yet you're not," Penn tells him, his voice stern but playful.

"So, technically, that makes you six," Kain confirms. "How about we refer to you as 'Fletcher, who is almost seven.' How does that sound?"

"I like it." He smiles. Then he looks to Penn. "Can I watch *Bluey* now?"

"*Bluey*?" Kain repeats the show's title with a glint in his eye. "I love *Bluey*. How about I watch it with you while your dad and Tater Tot finish up dinner?"

"You're—"

"Not staying for dinner, I know, but I have time to kill before I meet up with Thalia and the gang at The Grove Bar. So for now, I'm gonna hang with 'Fletcher, who is almost seven' and watch some *Bluey* and you two can do whatever it is that old people do."

Flipping him the bird, I shake my head and turn to the fridge. Reaching in, I grab the bottle of wine and two juice boxes. Popping the wine on the counter, I head over to Kain and Fletcher and hand them their juice boxes. "Thank you," I whisper into Kain's ear.

"You can name your firstborn after me," he teases, earning himself a slap up the back of the head before I make my way back to the kitchen. When I get there, Penn hands me a glass of wine and outstretches his hand to me. Placing my hand in his, he walks us out to the deck and over to the lounger by the firepit.

Sitting next to him, my nerves ramp up. It feels like there's a swarm of bees in my stomach. Their wings fluttering and buzzing ready for takeoff, but the buzzing and fluttering stops when he rests his hand on my knee. His touch instantly calms me.

"To a great evening," I say in a toast and raise my glass.

"To a great evening," he repeats and taps his glass to mine.

We both take a sip, our eyes locked on each other over the rim of our glasses. Deciding the third times a charm, I lean over and place my glass on the deck. Taking Penn's from him, I place his next to mine and turn back to face him. He lifts his hand and palms my cheek, running this thumb along my jawline. My skin tingles from his touch.

"I really want to kiss you," he murmurs, "but I'm worried I'm going to be kissblocked by my son … again."

"That's not going to happen," I tell him and when I see his face deflate, my eyes widen. "Shit," I hiss. "What I meant was, no to the kissblocking. We will kiss tonight, Penn, that's inevitable."

He nods and runs the pad of his thumb over my bottom lip, my lip thrumming at his touch. Like a moth to a flame, our heads start to move. Our eyes dart between each other's lips and eyes, we're millimeters apart, the air around us is filled with desire. Just as our lips are about to make contact, it happens. No interruptions. His lips press against mine; a spark ignites and it's pure bliss. Lust infiltrates the air, enveloping around the two of us as we kiss. His tongue seeks access to mine and I willingly open. Sliding my arms around his neck, I shuffle closer, our lips never breaking contact. Penn obviously wants more because one minute I'm sitting next to him, and the next, I'm in his lap so I'm straddling him. He lifts me up as if I weigh nothing, and not once do our lips separate. He slides one hand up my back and into my hair. Gently gripping, he tugs on the stands, a little moan slips out, but it's swallowed by our kiss. His other hand rests on my hip, anchoring me to him. I'm ever so thankful to be wearing a sundress right now because my skin is heated and my blood is simmering, the cool breeze around us feels amazing on my skin.

Eventually, I break the connection and pull back. I stare down into his blue eyes feeling content and carefree. "Totally worth the wait," he breathlessly utters as we continue to stare at one another. I've never seen eyes like his before. The need to kiss him again overwhelms me so I do exactly that. Gripping his cheeks in my palms, I kiss him again. Our first kiss was soft and sensual but this one, it's frenzied and heated.

He breaks the kiss this time, both of us panting. "Tatum, you need to stop."

My heart drops at those words and I see the moment he realizes what I'm thinking, he shakes his head. "No, it's not that, not one bit. I'd love nothing more than to keep kissing you all night long but Fletch ..." As soon as he utters his son's name, I nod. "… has already kissblocked us twice now. He will not cockblock me too because, Tatum, when that time comes, there will be no interruptions. It will be just the two of us and we will not come up for air until I've had my fill of you. Two kisses and I'm addicted."

Fuck me, what's a girl gonna say to that? Biting my bottom lip, I nod. "I … I want that too but, Penn, I … I don't think I'm ready for that step just yet. Physically, I'd jump you right now, but mentally, it's too soon. You'd be my first since Kip, and I'm just …"

He reaches up and cups my cheek. "You'll be my first since Mads too. We can take it slow, actually, I think I'd prefer that. I worked myself up all day thinking that I HAD to fuck you tonight." He pauses. "Shit, this is all coming out wrong."

"Penn," I whisper, "I understand, and I think we're on the same page. Stop worrying that pretty little head of yours."

"You think I'm pretty?" he playfully asks.

"So, so pretty," I tell him.

"Well, since we're stating truths, you, Tatum Summers, are more than pretty. You are fucking stunning and I will wait for you. I will wait 'til you're ready because you're so, so special and you will definitely be worth the wait."

Holy fucking swoon, Batman. "You might be douchedad." He looks confused at that. "I'll explain that later but you're my douchedad, and I'll wait for you too. I know people say life's too short to wait but waiting for that perfect moment with you will be totally worth it, and I have a feeling, Penn Brookes, you will be worth the wait."

50

PENN

W ITH OUR HEARTFELT CONFESSIONS OUT OF THE WAY, I LEAN forward and kiss her again, but the moment is broken when the timer on the oven goes off.

"I'll get it," Kain yells out from inside, followed by a meek little, "I'll help too."

"Guess, we should head inside so I can get dinner sorted," Tatum murmurs but she makes no moves to hop off me.

"Guess we should," I say in agreement but like her, I don't make a move. We just sit here, staring at one another. The only sound is the errant beating of my heart and the waves crashing into the shore.

"But it can wait for a sec, I need to say something," she says.

"Sounds ominous, should I be worried?"

She shakes her head. "Please be gentle with me, Penn. Right now, I feel great and happy, but there's also a niggling in the back of my mind that it's too soon and I'm betraying Kip by moving on. Even though I know he'd want me to be happy and he wouldn't want me to mourn him forever. I know it's okay to be happy, but it's also okay to be sad. I'll always have my memories of him but there's also room to make new memories. I want to feel again but please, don't give up when I'm having a bad day."

"I met this woman, Rebecca, and that sounds like advice she would give."

"Would that be Rebecca from the retreat down the road?"

"Umm, yeah, how did you know?"

"I stayed there recently."

What a small world that we ended up at the same place. I thought she was only here for her brother, but it seems we have a lot more in common after all. Who would have thought two people dealing with grief would find each other?

"You know, I'd just left there when we first met," I admit.

"When you were a douche to me?"

"Huh?" I ask her, confused.

"The morning we first met, Fletcher and I had gotten coconuts. You accused me of trying to steal him, you spoke to me like an arrogant jerk and you acted like a douche, hence your monicker, douchedad, but I don't think that fits anymore. I'm thinking … hmmm … maybe deliciousdad."

"Or we could just stick with Penn," I suggest, "you know, my name."

"I could, buuuuut." She shrugs at me and I can't help but laugh.

"And yes, I agree, I was a douche back then, but I was grieving and still dealing."

"Excuses, excuses," she teases, "but you know what will make up for it?"

"What?"

"This." Before I can say or do anything, she grips my cheeks and kisses me deeply. Her body molds to mine as if we were cast from the same template. Her tongue slides into my mouth, she rubs herself against my cock and it sparks to life. "I think we're good now," she murmurs against my lips.

"I think we should kiss one more time, you know, for luck."

"I do like luck." Then she presses her lips to mine ... for luck. There's no tongue this time but having her in my arms and her lips pressed to mine feels right.

"I'm sorry, I was such a douche when we first met," I honestly tell her. "I'm in a much better headspace now and I promise, I will never intentionally hurt you."

"I know you won't because, Penn, I know how to light a fire and make it look like an accident." She winks at me and climbs off my lap. "You coming?"

"Soon," I offer. She drops her gaze to my crotch and bites her lip, trying to hold back the sexy grin of hers.

"Take your time but, Penn." She leans down, her heated breath skates over my skin and I shiver. "I can't wait to come with you." With that, she grabs our wine glasses and heads back inside, her parting words causing my cock to harden further. The thought of coming with her is so appealing right now but with my son and her brother inside, I need to get my dick under control.

Sitting here, I stare out at the ocean, shake my head, and sigh. I haven't felt this carefree and relaxed in a long time. Fletcher is happy and so am I, and it's all because of Tatum Summers. She's a breath of fresh air, she understands what I've been through. She's felt firsthand what I went through with Mads. These past few days with her have been amazing but when we get back to the real world, will that all still be there? Or is it just a holiday thing?

51

TATUM

Dinner tonight has been fantabulous in every way, even if Penn is wrong when it comes to saying parmA. He's Team ParmI … I guess he's not perfect after all. The three of us laughed and chatted and laughed some more. Penn is a great father—no longer will I be referring to him as douchedad—and Fletcher is an awesome kid.

He's currently sound asleep on the sofa. Penn has placed a blanket over him while I finish cleaning up the kitchen. I've just popped the last of the dishes into the dishwasher when Penn grabs my hand and pulls me outside.

When I look up, my mouth drops open and I stop midstep, dropping his hand to cover my mouth in awe as I take it all in. The outside fairy lights are on, the firepit is flickering, and the moon above is shining brightly. "Dance with me," he demands and outstretches his hand to me.

I'm powerless to say no to him. Words are impossible so I just nod. Something overtakes my body and I walk over to him. I have no control to stop myself, it's like something is pulling me to him. Reaching him, I place my palm in his and a spark shoots up my arm, causing my breath to hitch in my throat. Closing his grasp on my hand, he pulls me into him, wraps his arms around my waist, and holds me. Under the fairy lights we hold each other and gaze into the other's eyes. "Hang on," he whispers and pulls away, immediately I feel his loss but I stand here and watch him pull his phone from his pocket. He clicks a few buttons and then music begins to play. He places the device on the outdoor table and presses skip, he turns his attention back to me just as "Tennessee Whiskey" by Chris Stapleton begins to play. He steps into my space, slides his arm around my waist, and we begin to sway to the music.

How he knew this was one of my favorite songs, I will never know, but underneath the moonlight with Chris singing and the waves crashing into the shore in the background, we dance. Wrapped in each other's arms, we lose ourselves to the music and each other. This moment takes tonight from perfect to fucking amazing.

Resting my head on his shoulder, we continue to dance when the next song begins. Lifting my head, I stare up at him. "Thank you," I mutter.

"What are you thanking me for? I should be thanking you. You cooked an amazing parmI." I dig him in the ribs for that one. "And followed it up with cookies for Fletcher and now, now I get to dance with a pretty lady under the stars and kiss her too."

"Fairy lights," I tell him, "under the fairy lights and FYI, I'm not seeing any kisses."

"Well, I better fix that then, shouldn't I?"

Nodding, I wait for my kiss under the fairy lights. He pulls me into his body tightly and covers my mouth with his. When he finally presses his lips to mine, it becomes the best kiss we've had so far as our tongues battle it out together. A moan slips free from me. A groan emits from him, and when he slides his hands down my back to my ass to lift me up, I nearly come on the spot when my pussy rubs against the fly of his cargos.

Walking us backward, he presses me into the side of the house and uses his hips to hold me in place. Gripping my wrists, he lifts my arms up and holds my hands above my head. He continues to kiss me and begins to swivel his hips in a way that has my insides quivering. He rains kisses down my neck and chest toward my boobs. He gently bites my nipple through the material of my dress, and I hiss at the pleasurable sensation he draws from my body, "Yessssssss." Then I start to grind myself on his growing erection.

His cock is hitting me in just the right spot. His mouth on my breasts is heavenly. I wish my dress wasn't in the way but I'm not stopping him to remove it. My body hasn't felt pleasure like this in a very long time. It just isn't the same when you're doing it yourself. Penn continues to assault my chest when out of nowhere, the most amazing orgasm detonates. I throw my head back, colliding with the wall behind me, but I don't notice the pain. All I can focus on is the pleasure ricocheting through me as I continue to grind myself on him and he sucks on my nipple through my dress.

Penn lifts his head when I stop shuddering and we stare at one another, breathlessly panting. He adjusts me in his arms and I feel his erection between us, pressing into me. I want to give him pleasure like he just gave to me. "I want to make you come like you made me come."

"I don't expect you to do that."

"I know, I want to." He continues to just stare at me. "Please let me?"

He nods and lowers me to my feet. My legs are a little wobbly and I relish the chance to drop to my knees before him. Lifting my shaky hands, I make quick work of freeing his dick and my eyes widen when I see it in the flesh. I knew he was big but I wasn't expecting it to be girthy and long. Squeezing his shaft, I begin to stroke him. Flicking my wrist back and forth, I squeeze tighter on the downward stroke. The tip glistens with precum, leaning forward I swipe my tongue over the head. "Fuck," he growls from above. With that word of encouragement, I open wide and suck him into my mouth.

Bobbing my head up and down, he grips the side of my head, guiding himself in and out of my mouth. "Fuuuuuuuu-uuck," he groans and without warning, I feel the first spurt of salty cum hit the back of my throat.

Swallowing it all down, I lick him clean and lift myself back up. "Thank you," I murmur, cupping his cheek in my palm and running my thumb along his beard, the strands soft under my touch.

"Why are you thanking me? It should be me thanking you. It's been just me and my hand for so long now, I forgot how amazing a warm mouth feels."

"I felt the same way too just before. I can't remember the last time I climaxed that hard."

"You really know how to stroke a guy's ego."

"I think you know exactly how well I can stroke." Winking at him, we fall silent.

I'm not sure what we do now. I know I'm not ready to have sex with him, plus his son is asleep inside, but I don't have to worry because at that exact moment, his son calls out, "Daddy."

"Shit," Penn hisses quietly. His eyes widen because his cock is still hanging out.

"I'll go," I tell him. "You fix that." I circle my finger in the direction of his dick. "Join us when you're ready." Placing a quick kiss on his lips, I head inside to check on Fletcher. "Hey, buddy," I say as I walk over to him and sit on the edge of the coffee table. "What's up?"

"Where's my dad?"

"Outside, he'll be here in a moment."

"Okay," he sleepily mumbles. Lying back down, he does that double blink thing and just as Penn comes inside, he's asleep again. Lifting my finger to my lips, I whisper, "Shhh," and walk over to him. "He fell back asleep."

"I better get him home," Penn whispers, but the look on his face says that's not what he wants to do.

"Orrrrrr," I suggest, "we can have another wine by the firepit and you can stay a little longer."

"I think I'd like that," he replies, smiling brightly at my suggestion.

Nodding, I pour two glasses of wine. Handing him his glass, I outstretch my hand to him, we lace our fingers together, and head outside.

Snuggling together on the lounger, we silently drink our wine. Resting my head on his shoulder, I listen as he tells me about his work at the garage and life in general. At some point, I drift off to sleep and just before I fall into a deep slumber, I feel a kiss on my temple and hear Penn whisper, "Goodnight, gorgeous."

52

PENN

UGH, MY NECK, I THINK AS I LIE HERE, NOT READY TO WAKE UP yet. Keeping my eyes closed, I listen to the sound of the waves. I'll miss that when we head home later this week. Then it hits me, the waves crashing into the shore sound different. Cracking one eyelid open, I see the beach and when my sleep-addled brain catches up, I realize I'm outside. Opening the other eye, I look down and smile. Tatum has her head in my lap and she's sound asleep. She looks so peaceful.

"Stop watching me sleep," she sleepily says, "it's creepy."

"It's not creepy when I do it."

"It is," she declares and she opens her eyes and stares up at me. "Morning."

"Morning," I reply. "Sleep well?"

"Nope, this lounger is not comfy at all, but I will say, the pillow was soft."

"Are you hinting that I'm fat and soft?" I tease, and her reaction is priceless.

"Unintentionally, it would seem that I did but it's not what I meant at all. Is there anything I can do to make up for it?"

"Coffee and a kiss," I nonchalantly tell her, "but in the reverse order."

"I can do that." Sitting up, she leans over and presses a kiss to my cheek and then stands up to walk inside.

Reaching out, I grab her hand and tug, she falls into my lap. "That's not a kiss, this is a kiss." Gripping her cheeks, I press my lips to hers. She drapes her arms over my shoulders and kisses me back. Our tongues entwine. Our noses bump. It's the perfect morning kiss.

"That is indeed a kiss," she mumbles against my lips. "A very good morning kiss. Maybe we should kiss again to double-check that it was a kiss."

"I think I can manage that." Just like moments ago, we kiss again and again it's perfect.

"Daddy," a little voice says. Tatum quickly jumps off my lap and looks like a deer caught in the headlights. Chuckling, I turn to face Fletcher.

"Morning, buddy," I say to him as he shuffles over and stands next to me.

"Daddy, we didn't sleep at home."

"I know, I'm sorry. Tatum and I fell asleep out here, we just woke up."

"You slept on the beach?"

"Well, on the deck we did."

He nods. "I'm hungry."

"Me too," Tatum agrees, "how about I make us all pancakes?"

"Yay," Fletcher singsongs with a fist pump, while I shake my head.

"We better get going."

"It's no trouble." Tatum looks at me hopefully.

"As long as you're sure?"

"I am," she's beaming as she says this, "I also have coffee."

"SOLD!" I shout, causing her to laugh.

"Come on," she demands, outstretching her hand to Fletcher. "Coffee and hot chocolate and then pancakes."

Fletcher races over and takes her hand. I stand up and take her other hand and the three of us trudge inside and head to the kitchen. Fletcher and I sit on the stools and we watch Tatum float around the kitchen as she makes us breakfast. Sipping on my coffee, I realize I'm happy, but then I think of Mads and that happiness dips. Tatum notices the change in me. She walks over and rests her hand on my arm in that reassuring way, and my happiness perks up again. "It's okay to be happy, Penn."

"I know but it's weird, it always hits out of the blue."

"It does but regardless of when it hits, it's still okay."

"You sound like Rebecca."

"She's a wise woman."

"That she is." I nod in agreement. "Now, make me some pancakes, wench."

"Yeah, wench, make us pancakes," Fletcher adds, causing Tatum and me to laugh. She salutes us and heads back to the stove while I tell Fletch that we can't call people wench. Which then turns into a whole discussion over right and wrong, and he makes me apologize to Tatum for calling her a wench.

"Morning," Kain singsongs, heading to the fridge. He pulls out the orange juice and drinks direct from the bottle.

"Ugh, Kain. Gross," Tatum screeches, smacking her brother in the arm.

"What? I was thirsty."

"So use a glass." She shakes her head and turns her attention back to the stove and our pancakes.

"Morning, Fletcher, who is almost seven," Kain says, offering his fist to Fletch for a bump, then he looks to me. "Morning, Penn." His voice is all high and I guarantee if Fletcher wasn't here, he'd say something really, really inappropriate.

"Morning, Kain," I reply, offering my fist to him.

"We had a sleepover," Fletcher excitedly tells Kain, and he leans on the granite countertop and listens intently to my son as he explains what happened last night. "And now, Tatum is making pancakes for us. I love pancakes, so this is the bestest morning ever."

"A sleepover, hey?" Kain looks to his sister and raises his eyebrows suggestively.

"We fell asleep on the deck," she informs him, ignoring his suggestive taunt.

"Sure, you fell asleep on the deck." He air quotes fell. Tatum spins around and slaps him up the back of the head.

"Brozart, it's too early for your shit, but why are you here so early? Did Thalia finally wake up and dump your sorry ass?"

"Har har, sis. If you must know, I got called in early so I came home to get changed."

"Cool, go change and I'll have some pancakes ready for you in a jiffy."

"Thanks, sis." He squeezes her arm and heads to his room to get ready for work. Tatum turns back to the stove and focuses on the task at hand, cooking breakfast.

The pancakes have been devoured. Kain has just left for work and Fletch is watching *Bluey*, again. Tatum and I are still sitting at the dinner table, finishing up our coffees. Leaning back in my chair, I rest my hand on my stomach. "That was the best meal I've ever had."

"I thought my parma last night was?"

"Those banana pancakes just now were delish. I could eat them every day for the rest of my life."

"You'd soon get sick of them," she says, taking a sip of her coffee.

"Doubtful. Is there anything you can't cook?"

"Meringues. I cannot make them to save my life."

"I find that hard to believe." And I mean that. From what

I've seen so far, Tatum is amazing at everything she does. She puts her heart and soul into everything and gives one-hundred-and-ten percent. She has a heart of gold and I'm so lucky that she's giving me a chance. From the first moment I met her here on the beach, I've been horrible to her, over and over again. But somehow, she's put that all aside and is letting me in. "You're amazing, Tatum Summers."

"I know," she cheekily replies with a shoulder shrug. "But I still can't cook meringues."

She stands up and begins to clear the table. I offer to do the dishes and clean the kitchen but Tatum won't hear of it, just like she wouldn't let me help clean up after dinner last night. Last night I listened, but not this morning. I help her clear the table and while she ducks to the bathroom, I stack the dishwasher. When she comes back out, I'm wiping down the counters and the table.

"I thought I said no to helping?"

Shrugging at her, I rinse the cloth and then pull her into my arms. "Thank you," I tell her, popping a kiss on the tip of her nose.

"Why are you thanking me?"

"For the last twenty-four hours. I've had fun with you, Tatum."

"I've had fun too, Penn. You're not so douchey after all."

"Glad I could change your perspective of me, but I need to get Fletcher home." She nods but I can see she doesn't want us to leave. "Maybe we can catch up later for a swim?"

"I'd like that." She smiles as she answers.

Pressing my lips to hers, I give her a quick kiss. "Guess we better get going then?" It comes out like a question rather than a statement.

"Yep." She nods but neither of us makes a move, that is until Fletcher breaks the moment.

"Daaaaad," he sings out and races over to us, "I need to poop."

"What is it with this kid needing to poop whenever I'm with you?" This causes her to laugh.

"You better go deal with that because if he shits on Kain's sofa, shit will hit the fan."

"Come on, buddy, let's get you home so you can poop."

"Can't I poop here? I really need to go," Fletcher asks, jumping up and down on the spot.

"Nope." I shake my head. "Tatum does not need to deal with that."

"It's fine, he can use the toilet in Kain's room."

"You are evil … I like it."

"Come on," she says to Fletcher, "let's go poop."

Fletcher takes her outstretched hand and the two of them head to the bathroom … in Kain's room. My phone rings and when I pull it out, I see Teri's name on the screen and my eyes widen. "Hi, Teri. Fletch and I are five minutes away, he's just pooping."

"No rush, we can wait out on the deck for you guys to get here."

"Thanks, see you soon, Teri."

Just as I hang up, Tatum and Fletcher return. She has a funny look on her face. "That was Nanna, buddy, her and Gramps are at our place."

"Can we go now, please?"

"Sure, buddy, say goodbye to Tatum and then we can go see them."

"Bye, Tatum." He hugs her leg. "Let's go, Dad."

"Someone's excited to see his grandparents," Tatum says, ruffling his hair and then she walks over to me. "We can postpone our swim since your family is here."

"But I want to see you," I whine, upset that I won't be seeing her in her sexy bikini again.

"Let's play it by ear, family always comes first, Penn. I wouldn't want to intrude."

"You wouldn't be intruding. You'd—"

"Let's go, Dad," Fletcher says, interrupting us. He takes my hand and begins to pull me toward the door. "Bye, Tatum," he shouts.

"Patience, kid," I tell him.

"It's fine, go," Tatum tells me. "I'll pop over later."

"I'd like that."

She kisses me on the cheek and then Fletcher and I head home to meet our guests.

53

TATUM

After Penn and Fletcher left, I head to my room for a shower and to get dressed for the day. After showering, I pop on a load of laundry, make myself another coffee, grab my Kindle, and head out to the deck. Slipping my sunglasses on, I lie back and lose myself in my latest romance novel.

Someone taps my foot and I squeal in fright. Looking over the top of my Kindle, I smile when I see Penn standing there, trying to hold back a laugh. "You scared me, you asshole."

"Sorry, I called out but you were engrossed in your book."

"The couple finally got their shit together and it's finally getting steamy."

"You read mommy porn?"

"No," I snap, "I read spicy romance."

"Same thing, isn't it?"

"No! No! No! No! No! Porn has no storyline, it's all sex, sex, and more sex. Spicy romance has a plot and drama. It isn't just about penises and vaginas hugging."

"Penises and vaginas hugging, that's a new one."

We stare intently at each other and if I'm reading the look on his face correctly, he's thinking about my vagina giving his penis a hug … just like I am. Breaking the silence, I ask,

"What are you doing here? I thought you were spending time with your parents?"

"Maddie's parents. Mine arrive tomorrow, just in time for Fletcher's birthday. Teri and Sandy have taken him for ice cream."

"You didn't want ice cream?"

"Nope, I wanted to see you."

"Did you now?" He nods. "And why did you want to see me?"

"I missed you."

"You missed me? It's been like three hours. Do you have stalker tendencies I'm unaware of?"

"I only stalk you."

"Lucky me," I tease. Sitting up, I place my Kindle next to me and I beckon him over. "Kiss me, Penn," I demand.

"Yes, ma'am." He walks over to me, rests one knee on the lounger, and cups my cheeks in his palms. Leaning down, he presses his lips to mine. The kiss starts off soft, but it quickly turns heated. He gently pushes me back and when I lie back, he covers my body with his and continues to assault my mouth with his tongue. He slides his hand down and cups my boob, gently squeezing. Moaning into his mouth, it encourages him. He kisses down my neck and upper chest to my breasts. He undoes the buttons, freeing my boobs. I'm not wearing a bra today 'cause no one wants to wear one of those death traps when on vacation, and right now, I'm super happy with that decision. He tweaks my nipple and again I moan. He takes the taut tip into his mouth and sucks. "Yessssss," I hiss. He snakes his hand down my body and slips it underneath the skirt of my sundress. Gripping his hand, I pull it out from under my dress and stop him. Shaking my head. "Not out here, anyone could see."

"You had no problem blowing me out here last night."

"But it was dark last night."

"Just one little flick?" he begs and to emphasize his point, he pulls his hand free of my grasp and cups my mound, sliding his finger between my panty-covered lips.

"You don't play fair," I complain with a pout.

"Never said I did." He continues to run his finger up and down my slit. "Now, are you going to let me have my fun?" Biting my lip, I nod. The whole world can watch for all I care right now. He's worked me up to my boiling point. "I knew you'd see it my way."

With his eyes locked on mine, he pushes my panties to the side, he's just about to push his finger into me when from the beach someone giggles and shouts, "Faster, Gramps, faster."

My eyes widen when I recognize that little voice. Peaking around Penn, I see Fletcher, his gramps and nanna walking along the beach. They are focused on something in the water so thankfully they don't look this way. "Shit," I hiss, quickly pushing Penn's hand away from me. With deft fingers, I swiftly redo my buttons and then I cover my face in mortification. I lie here with wide eyes and not breathing. A few seconds later and this could have ended in disaster.

Penn just sits there, trying to hold back his laugh. Reaching up, I slap him. "Told you it was a bad idea."

"No one caught us and look, they walked right on by, no one saw a thing." He pauses and then hungrily stares at me, "Well, I did, I got to see your gorgeous tits and now … now I'm going to finish what I was about to start."

"Like hell you are." I slap at his hand and sit up. Crossing my legs, I glare at him. "What if they come back?"

"They won't be coming, you will be."

"No, I won't be because my legs are closed."

"Where's your sense of adventure?"

"My sense of adventure is just fine, thank you very much. I just don't feel like traumatizing your son or in-laws."

"But—"

"Nope, no buts." I'm suddenly in the mood to tease so I

change my train of thought. "I might be open to butt stuff in the future but right now, no butts."

His eyes widen at my change of butts and so do mine. I've never really been into butt stuff before but right now, it's all I can think about.

"That was an unexpected revelation and now, that's all I can think about. You are a devil woman."

"Call it payback for giving me a blue bean."

"Blue bean?"

"The female version of blue balls."

"Riiiiight." He nods as he processes my blue bean comment. "Well, since your legs and I'm guessing boobs are closed, can I at least kiss you again?"

"That I can oblige to, no one will be traumatized at seeing us kissing." He presses his lips to mine. Wrapping my arms around his neck, I begin to lean back and again, he cocoons my body with his as we kiss. Breaking the connection, I mumble against his lips, "I would just like to state that I'm not opposed to picking up what happened just before, but at a later and much more private time."

"Noted. Can I at least fondle over the clothes?"

"I'll allow it, now shut up and kiss me."

"You mean kiss and fondle above the clothes you?"

"Less talking, more kissing, and above the clothes fondling please."

Like teenagers on a Saturday night, we kiss and fondle one another until Penn has to leave. Walking him to the edge of the deck, we kiss each other goodbye. Then I watch him walk down the beach to his place, grinning like a content and happy carnival clown.

54

PENN

"Happy birthday to you. Happy birthday, dear Fletcher, Happy birthday to you. Hip hip, hooray," we all sing to a beaming Fletcher.

"Can I cut it now, Dad?" he excitedly asks after blowing out all the candles on top of the Bluey cake Mom got for him.

"Sure can, buddy."

Mom hands Fletcher the knife. "Remember, if you touch the bottom you have to kiss the closest girl."

"Eeeeew," he cries, "that's gross."

Everyone laughs. Leaning into Tatum, I whisper, "I love kissing you."

"You just like over the clothes fondling while kissing me."

"I much prefer under the clothes fondling while kissing, but someone has become self-conscious and is under the clothes blocking me."

"Poor baby," she teases but she ends the tease with a quick peck on the lips.

"Eeeeew, they're kissing again," Fletcher protests with a mouthful of cake.

"Again?" I question. "When have you seen us kiss before?"

"When Nanna and Gramps took me for ice cream and we were coming back."

Tate's eyes widen in worry at the thought of Fletcher seeing her boobs ... or more. "Oh. My. Fucking. God," she mumbles under her breath, causing me to snort and chuckle, earning myself a smack in the ribs. "Told you it was a bad idea," she hisses.

"We all saw," Teri snipes, her tone less than friendly. "Sandy took the focus from you to something in the water so as to not traumatize Fletcher."

Tatum's eyes widen again, her cheeks red with embarrassment. "I'll be right back." Before anyone can say anything, she's racing across the deck, down the stairs, and out onto the beach. If this was a cartoon, there'd be smoke tracks billowing behind her at the speed in which she slinked away.

"Is that the kind of woman you want around my grandson?" Teri sneers at me.

"Teri," Sandy berates her.

"No, I will not hold my tongue over this. I've been stewing on it since I saw what you were doing in broad daylight yesterday. That is no way for a parent to act. Who knows what happened after we left?" I've never seen Teri so angry before. "My Maddie would never have been so skanky like that. I don't like her." She crosses her arms and then adds, "She will not replace Maddie, I'll make sure of that."

"Excuse me?" I growl. "What did you just say?"

"You heard me, Penn. She's no Maddie. She's not Fletcher's mother."

"I'm well aware of that but you're out of line, Teri. No one will ever replace Maddie as his mom."

"Could have fooled me."

"Enough," Mom shouts. "This is not the time nor the place to discuss this. Now, let's focus on Fletcher and making his birthday special."

"That sounds great." I nod in agreement. Turning away

from an angry Teri, I look over at my son and dad. Thankfully, Fletch is unaware of what just transpired, he and Dad were eating cake and engrossed talking about the latest episode of *Bluey*. Seeing that Fletcher is occupied, I look to the beach and when I see Tatum, my heart hurts for her. Teri was out of line just now. "I'm going to check on Tatum." Before anyone can stop me, I'm crossing the deck and walking over to Tatum.

"You okay?" I ask when I join her. Sliding my arm around her shoulders, I pull her into me and press a kiss to her head.

"Not one bit, Penn. Your mother-in-law hates me and thinks I'm going to traumatize your son with my skanky ways."

"You heard that, huh?" She nods and I hate seeing her like this. "My mother-in-law's opinion is insignificant, Tatum. And as for my son, he adores you. Just like I do."

"Penn, how can you be so calm with all of this?"

"I'm not, I'm pissed she's treating you like this, but I don't care what she thinks. All that matters is how Fletcher and I feel, and right now, I feel strongly for you and I think you feel strongly for me too."

"I do." She nods. "But—"

Pressing my finger to her lips, I shush her. "No butts … yet." I wink at her and it causes her to laugh as she thinks about yesterday's conversation. "Butts and in-laws aside, all that matters, Tatum, is me, you, and Fletcher. Everyone else can fuck right off."

"But—" I raise my eyebrows at her. "Be serious for a moment." I nod. "As much as it would be great to live in a bubble of just us, we have to consider their feelings too. Seeing THAT isn't the best first impression, and I know I'll never be anything but the other woman in their eyes. I'm okay with that, Penn, really, I am, but what I'm not okay with is them hating me for something that you caused."

"This is my fault, isn't it?"

"We're both at fault, Penn. It takes two to fondle after all."

This causes me to laugh, but I hate this has happened because of something that I did. "I'll let her know it was all me."

"No," she refutes, shaking her head from side to side, "let her hate on me. Let her think of me as the sex-crazed harpy—only behind closed doors now—and you can remain the saint son-in-law I know you are not."

"That doesn't feel right or seem fair."

"Life isn't fair, Penn. You and I know firsthand that it isn't, but you wanna know a secret?"

"What?"

"I really don't care what she thinks of me, all I care is that you and Fletcher like me. Ohh, and Burton from Castaway Coffee, that guy knows how to make a good cup."

"Do I need to worry about this Burton guy?"

"Nah." She shakes her head. "Sure, he's hot and owns a coffee shop, but he's not you, and you, Penn Brookes, are fast becoming my number one."

"You really mean that, don't you?"

Nodding, she smiles at me and I feel that smile deep in my soul. "Very much so."

"For the record, Fletch has my number one spot but, Tatum, you're close behind in spot number two." Voicing what I feel aloud is scary as all hell, but I cannot live my life in fear. Shit happens, sometimes it's epically bad shit but other times, it can be amazing shit, and I think taking a risk with Tatum falls into the good shit category.

"I'm happy to lose out to him," she states matter of factly and her willingness to share my heart with my son proves just how amazing this woman is.

"Good." I nod and tap her nose. "Now, let's go have some cake."

"I like that plan," she replies with a smile that lights up

her face. "And if you're lucky later, and behind a closed door, I might let you have a fondle under the clothes."

"I like that plan," I repeat. Reaching out, I take her hand in mine and lace our fingers together. We rejoin the party and thankfully, Teri behaves and there are no more incidents ... just like there was no fondling of any sort too.

55

TATUM

THE REST OF THE PARTY WAS UNEVENTFUL, THANKFULLY, BUT TERI was curt with me whenever we interacted. I did get a compliment about my peanut butter chocolate chip cookies, but she ate non-humble pie when she realized she was praising me. She'd made such a show of how amazing they were, but when she found out I made them, her whole demeanor changed. The 'super amazing melt in your mouth' cookies suddenly became not so 'super amazing' and dry. Thankfully, Penn's mom came to my rescue and defused the situation before Teri could jam that knife in deeper.

I don't understand her hostility toward me. Does she seriously expect Penn to not move on? For him to be lonely for the rest of his life?

The final straw was when she accused me of stalking Fletcher since I 'was always there' when he needed rescuing. Not wanting to ruin Fletcher's special day and seeing the anxiety on Penn's face every time we were near each other, I said my goodbyes and headed home.

Changing into my pajamas and not caring it's only three in the afternoon, I grab my Kindle, a bottle of red wine, and I head outside to read in the afternoon sun. Pouring myself a glass, I lie back, get comfy, and start to read. Instead of picturing the characters in the novel, I kept imagining Penn and me in their places.

It was Penn's cock thrusting into me from behind, rather than Hunter's.

It was me licking chocolate from Penn's chest instead of Krista licking Hunter's chest.

After two chapters, I was one big horny harpy, just like Penn's mother-in-law thinks. It got so bad I had to go into my room and pleasure myself because I was so turned on.

I'd just returned outside when I got a text.

PENN

What you doing?

TATUM

Reading and drinking wine

We also need to get some chocolate dicks

Do I even want to ask?

Probably not but I can unequivocally say, you will enjoy what happens with the chocolate dicks

#JustSayin

I'll be sure to add them to my shopping list

Has she calmed down at all?

Nope. She and Sandy are leaving early now

I don't want them to leave because of me

It's not you, it's her and her holier than thou attitude

I hate that I'm the reason they're cutting their trip short. Fletcher will be so upset

No, he won't. He's seven. We're at the beach and Bluey can be streamed anywhere, anytime. Trust me, he'll be fine.

Kip used to say, 'never trust anyone who says trust me,' especially if it was him .... Why do I get the feeling this is the same right now?

I don't know what you are talking about **insert sweet angel face**

Sweet and angel are not how I'd describe you

How would you describe me?

Sexy. Hot. Devious

You just described yourself

Nope, that's all you, baby.

I like it when you call me baby

Well, then, baby, I have to go. Hunter is about to pull his head out of his ass and go grovel

... with a chocolate dick?

Possibly ... anything is possible with these two.

Well, enjoy your night. We'll come over tomorrow after Teri and Sandy head off

I'll be here

Dropping my phone next to me, I stare out at the ocean and sip on my wine. What am I going to do about Teri? Knowing I won't get the answer to that, I refill my glass, and

I'm just about to take a sip when my phone rings. I smile when I see Mom is wanting to FaceTime with me. I quickly swipe to answer. "Hey, hey, Mom."

"Hey, how's paradise?"

"Amazing," answer her with a smile. Flipping the camera around, I show her the view and my bottle of wine before flipping it back to me.

"You look well." She's taken that Mom tone and I find myself grinning further.

"I feel amazing, Mom. That retreat was just what I needed."

"I thought it might have something to do with a certain single dad I hear you've been hanging out with."

"Damn Kain and his big mouth."

"You know he's the biggest gossip around."

"This is true." I nod in agreement. "Even now with him living here, he gets the gossip back home before we do."

"He does have a knack for that, but enough about Gossy McGossipson, tell me all about this man who's causing my baby girl to smile brightly again."

"Mom, he's amazing ..." For the next ten minutes I tell Mom all about Penn, even going as far back as our first meeting.

"Sounds like the two of you were destined to meet."

"I know this is weird, but I feel like Kip guided us together."

"It's not silly at all. Kip will always be in your heart, Tatum."

"Just like his wife, Maddie, will always be in his."

"It's beautiful when you think about it."

"How so?"

"Two broken souls find love together. You each know what the other has been through so you understand the down days. You will happily listen to the other tell stories and there will be no animosity or jealousy about their first love."

"I never really looked at it like that, but that does make sense. I did kinda have a run-in with his mother-in-law, and I'm worried I've ruined Penn's relationship with them."

"I doubt it's quite that bad, Tatum."

"They think of me as the other woman and, technically, I am."

"But you aren't the other woman due to sinister circumstances."

"Either way, it doesn't matter. Her mom hates me, not sure I can salvage that."

"Give her time. She's grieving herself so cut her some slack."

"I never looked at it like that."

"When you become a mother, you will see the world differently. I couldn't fathom losing you, Tatum, so I can only imagine what she's going through. Just be you and, one day, she'll come around because I may be biased but you are an amazing woman, Tatum."

"Thanks, Mom, and here's hoping that you're right about Teri because I think I really like him, Mom."

"I cannot wait to meet him."

Mom and I chat for a little longer. Kain joins us and then she has to go. Kain and I order pizza for dinner and then settle on the sofa and start a *Final Destination* marathon. After the third movie, we call it a night.

Falling into bed, I dream sexy things about Penn and the next morning, I'm woken up in the most amazing way.

56

PENN

THE SUN IS JUST RISING AND I'M OUT ON THE DECK STAIRS WITH A coffee in hand, staring at the ocean. The incoming tide is mesmerizing to watch. Sleep has eluded me most of the night. I lay awake thinking about Tatum and Mads and Teri. But most of all, I keep hoping that Tatum still wants to be with me. I'm so mad at Teri for the way she behaved yesterday. The way she treated Tatum was hurtful, to both Tatum and me. Sure, we were a little careless with what we were doing on the deck, but we're both adults. Fletcher loves her and I, well, I feel strongly for her. I don't think I will ever love-love someone again because I don't ever want to feel loss like I did when I lost Mads. I wouldn't cope a second time.

"You're up early," Mom says, coming out to join me. She kisses me on the cheek and drops onto the step beside me.

"Couldn't sleep," I tell her.

"Something … or someone on your mind?"

Nodding, I chuckle. "How can she not be, Mom? Ever since the party, which—"

"Was wonderful. Spiteful words and all."

"It was, he's lucky to have such amazing people in his life.

He's had so much thrown at him but being the little trooper that he is, he's thriving."

"'Cause he has an amazing father," she states, smiling brightly. "I'm proud of you, Penn. You've been through so much, but you've managed to come through relatively unscathed, and you've found happiness again."

"She does make me happy, Mom, very, very happy."

"And as a mother, that is all I want for you. Why don't you go over and see her?"

"It's stupid a.m., Mom."

"And I bet she's wide awake like you."

"What about Fletcher?"

"I'll watch him, go and do something for you."

"What about Teri? She already thinks badly of Tatum and the whole situation."

"I'll tell her you went for a walk to clear your head."

"Thanks, Mom, but what if Tatum junk punches me 'cause I woke her up?"

"Is she worth a possible junk punch?"

"I think so." Before I can change my mind; I stand up and head toward her place. As I climb the stairs, still not one-hundred percent sure this is a good idea, I see Kain on the deck. He smiles at me and for some reason, I know I'm doing the right thing.

"You hurt her, and I'll kill you," he says by way of greeting.

"Good morning to you too, Kain. I'm well, thanks for asking."

"Morning, Penn. You hurt her, and I'll kill you," he repeats again.

"Got it … is she up?"

He shrugs. "It's your balls if she isn't."

Nodding, I walk past him and head inside. Making my way to her room, I stop and stand at her bedroom door. I just stand here and stare at the wood and before I can talk myself out of it, I lift my hand and push down on the handle and slink into her room.

Closing it behind me, I lean against the door and look over to the bed and smile when I see her lying there. She looks so peaceful, and I almost feel bad for wanting to wake her up, but after the shitshow from yesterday I need to reassure her I'm in this.

The sheet has slipped down and reveals her black cami and panties. I don't know what's hotter, that itsy bitsy bikini of hers or her pajamas. Pushing off the door, I pad over to the bed, and sit on the edge. Reaching out, I brush a tendril of hair off her forehead and gently trace my fingertip down her cheek. Her eyes flicker but she doesn't wake up. Cupping her cheek, I run the pad of my thumb over her bottom lip. Her eyes open and she blinks a few times, when she registers me sitting here, she smiles. "Morning," she huskily murmurs.

"Good morning, Sleeping Beauty," I tell her.

She lifts her head and looks at the clock. "Why are you here at stupid a.m.? Only crazy people or authors get up at stupid a.m."

"Well, I'm not an author so I guess I'm crazy."

"Lucky for you, I like your kind of crazy, but how 'bout you lie down next to me and we can sleep for a little longer."

"I'd like that." Standing up, I kick off my shoes and pull my white tee over my head and drop it to the carpet. Hopping back onto the bed next to her in my shorts, I roll to my side and face her. "Hi," I whisper and place a kiss on her nose.

"Hi," she whispers back but she one-ups me and kisses me on the lips.

She goes to move back but I reach up and cup her cheek in my palm, gently caressing her skin with my thumb. We lie here, staring at one another. Sliding my hand around the back of her head, I bring her lips to mine and kiss her again. She shimmies closer and slides her hand over my shoulder and pulls me into her. Her tongue pushes into my mouth, battling it out with mine. Rolling her to her back, I cocoon her underneath me. Nudging my leg between her thighs, I gently press it into her mound. My hand slides down her body and up under her cami. Caressing her breast, she moans into my mouth and the sound vibrates directly to my cock, it hardens instantly.

She pushes on my shoulders and sits up before me. I begin to panic that I've gone too far but when she grips the hem of her cami and removes it, my panic disappears. She drops the discarded item over the edge of the bed and lies back. I stare down at her naked chest and my mouth waters. "Your tits are perfect."

She cups her perfect tits, pushing them together and circling her nipples, causing them to stiffen. "Come have a taste then."

"With fucking pleasure." Covering her hands so we're both pressing on her tits, I lower my head and take one of her nipples into my mouth and suck, while I squeeze and tug on the other. She pulls her hand out from underneath mine and rakes her nails up the back of my head and around my neck, holding me to her chest. For the next few minutes, I move from nipple to nipple. Sucking, biting, and massaging her plump mounds.

"Please," she pants.

"Please what?" I ask around her nipple.

"Please just … anything. I … I need you, Penn."

Kissing up her neck again, I hover over her and stare down at her flushed face. My cock is harder than steel right now and pressing into her stomach. I have no doubt that when I finally sink inside her, I'm going to come in three point five seconds. "You have me, Tatum."

"No." She shakes her head. "I need you inside me."

"Are you sure?"

"Yes, fuck me, Penn. Fuck me now."

57

TATUM

"Yes, fuck me, Penn. Fuck me now," I demand. I need him inside of me like I need coffee when I first get up.

"Condom?" he asks and I'm glad that one of us is thinking clearly.

"Shit, umm, I don't have one. I wasn't planning on getting laid while I was here."

"Me neither," he says. "I can pull out?" he offers.

"Okay, plus I'm on the Pill and I can go to the pharmacy later today."

"Are you sure?"

Nodding my head, I reach up and cup his cheek. "I'm sure, Penn, now fuck me."

"Yes, ma'am."

He removes his shorts and briefs while I shimmy out of my panties. My heart is racing when my eyes land on his dick. It's beautiful in all the right ways and suddenly I'm nervous. I don't think I was this nervous before I lost my virginity when I was seventeen at homecoming.

With our eyes locked on one another, he situates himself between my thighs. He runs the tip of his shaft through my folds and I nearly combust from that. A real dick is so much better than the silicon ones I've been using these last few months. Then it happens, he pushes inside of me and if I thought the sensation moments ago was amazing, the feeling of him sliding inside is pure ecstasy. "Yesss," I hiss when he's fully inside of me.

"You feel like heaven," he growls as he begins to rock his hips, moving in and out of me.

"Yesss," I mewl again. Scrunching my eyes closed, I give myself over to the pleasure.

"Open your eyes, I want to see the moment you explode."

Opening my eyes, I gaze up into his and with my eyes locked on him. I focus on him and the pleasure beginning to simmer low in my belly. My body starts to tingle and I know I'm close. "I'm close," I pant.

"Come for me, Tatum, just let go."

His words light the fuse and a few thrusts later, I detonate. "Peeeeeeeeeeeeeeeeeeennnnnn," I screech as the orgasm of all orgasms explodes. Every nerve ending in my body comes alive as indescribable pleasure courses through me and into every crevice of my body.

Penn stiffens and with a guttural grunt, be pulls out at the very last second and comes all over my stomach. "Fuck, that was close," he breathlessly pants as he collapses onto the mattress next to me.

"Mmmhmpf," I mumble, words elude me right now. My brain is an orgasmic jumbled mess. I'm lucky to remember my name. Penn just blew my world. "That was amazing," I manage to spit out.

"So fucking amazing."

Turning my head, I smile. "When can we do that again?"

"Give me two minutes and I should be good to go?"

"Really? I thought only the men in my novels can go like the Energizer Bunny."

"I'm not just any man, Tatum."

"Ohh, I know, Penn Brookes, I know. Now, it's been two minutes."

Rolling to my side, I grip his cock in my hand and begin to pump and just like he promised, he comes back to life, and I jump on top and ride him. Penn sneaking into my room is now my most favorite way to wake up. I'm going to need a dickalarm daily.

After a third round in the shower, hand in hand, we walk down to his place to grab Fletcher and take him out for pancakes for brunch. Thankfully, when we get there, Teri and Sandy are out for their midmorning walk so I don't have to see them.

Jumping into Penn's rental car, we head into the main strip for brunch and I make a stop at the pharmacy while they head to the café and order. While I'm at the pharmacy, I grab a box of condoms, the morning-after pill, and I refill my contraceptive script while I'm here too since I'm nearly out. As much as I love Fletcher, I'm not ready to have a baby and I don't think Penn wants another baby either.

After an amazing breakfast, we head home and make plans to meet on the beach in fifteen minutes time. The boys drop me back at Kain's and I head inside to change. Grabbing my ruby-red halter bikini that I know will drive Penn wild, I slip it on. Then I grab the matching cover-up, my sunhat, sunglasses, and Kindle. I throw everything into my beach bag, along with some snacks and my water bottle, and then I head out to meet my boys. *My boys*, I kinda like saying that.

With a pep in my step, I skip down the beach, looking forward to an afternoon lazing in the sun and splashing about. I'm going to miss this when I go home. Then I begin to wonder if this thing between Penn and I is just a vacation thing, or if when we get back to the real world, will we still have that spark?

And boy oh boy do we spark. This morning proves that … multiple times.

"What you smiling at, baby?" Penn says in greeting from up on the deck when he sees me.

Looking up, I'm sure my smile widens when I take in the man before me. His chest is bare, glistening with sweat from the midday sun and low-slung black board shorts sit on his hips. My mouth—and pussy—immediately water as I ogle the man before me.

"I'm happy," I honestly tell him. "Today has been fantabulous and it's only lunchtime."

"That's a big call."

"Just calling it as I see it, now, let's hit the beach. I have a tan to work on and a book to finish."

"More chocolate dick scenes to devour?" he teases.

From behind him, Teri screeches, "What did you just say?" She pops up next to him and scowls when she sees me. "Never mind, I have an idea why you said something so crass." She follows it up with a snarky. "What are you doing here?"

Not wanting to let her get to me, I smile sweetly. "Good afternoon, Teri. Penn, Fletcher, and I are going to spend some time at the beach." Reluctantly, I add, "Would you like to join us?"

"I'm taking Fletcher for ice cream," she hisses, her eyes locked on me. If this was a superhero movie, and with this bitch being the villain, she'd be shooting laser beam daggers from her eyes at me, smiting me on the spot.

"He'll love that," I say with a smile—a fake smile—then add, "and when you guys get back, you can join us for an afternoon at the beach."

"Ohhh, ummm, we'll see. Fletcher might be tired and need a nap."

My face scrunches. "He's seven, he no longer takes a nap."

"Penn can decide what he does, not you."

Nodding and not wanting to deal with her, I take the high road. "Have fun and maybe we'll see you later." Looking to

Penn, I smile. "I'll get set up, come join me when you're ready." Before either of them can reply, I walk away.

I'm only a few steps away when I hear her huff, "Why is that woman still hanging around?"

Shocking me, Penn simply replies with a curt warning of her name only. He doesn't defend me or berate her for the way she's speaking to and about me.

Pissed off, I stomp down the beach and find a spot to lay my towel out. Pulling out my Kindle and sunscreen, I place them down, kick off my flip-flops, and pull my cover-up over my head and place it in my bag.

Dropping to my butt, I stretch my legs out and lean back on my hands. Closing my eyes, I drop my head back and stare up at the sky. The warm sun beats down on me. The boost of vitamin D seeps into my soul and melts away my anger about Teri … for a little while anyway.

58

PENN

Before I can say anything, Tatum turns away from us and heads toward the beach, and Teri heads inside like nothing happened. She calls out to Fletcher, telling him to get his shoes on because she and Grandad are taking him out for ice cream. Her statement earns a "Yeeeeeeessssssssss," that I'm sure they heard in Hawaii.

A few moments later, Fletch races outside. "Bye, Dad." He kisses me on the cheek and heads back inside to go get ice cream with his grandparents. Following him inside, I head to the kitchen for a drink. If it wasn't so early, I'd crack open a beer, so I settle for a glass of water and take a seat at the island. Mom walks into the kitchen a few moments later. "I thought you were going with them to get ice cream."

"Not feeling ice creamy today."

She nods and I can tell I'm about to get questions thrown at me. "How are you?"

"I'm fine, Mom."

"I call bullshit. I would have thought after the morning with Tatum that you'd be on cloud nine."

"I was. I am. I'm just …"

"Just what?" she asks, climbing onto the stool next to me.

"I really like Tatum, Mom."

"That's a good thing because, call it mother's instinct, but I think she likes you too." She pauses and then reaches over and squeezes my hand. "Penn, I think you've found her."

"Come again?" I question Mom, confused by that last statement.

"Tatum, she's your person. I have that feeling."

"You and your feelings," I shake my head at the look in her eyes right now.

"What can I say, when I know, I know."

"Not this time, Mom. I know usually your feelings"—I air quote feelings—"are on point but this time, it's wrong. Mom, I already found my one and she died. You don't get second chances in life and love."

"Penn—"

"No, Mom," I snap. "Mads was my one true love. Tatum and I are never going to be *that* serious. She and I both suffered a loss, and we're there for each other because we know how the other feels. She isn't my person in that sense. Do I care for her? Yes, but I'm not in love with her. I love Mads."

Mom nods at me. "I never said anything about love, Penn."

Rolling my eyes at her, I stare into the glass in my hands. "We're just friends," I reiterate but from the look on Mom's face, I know she still thinks otherwise.

"Yeah, friends who kiss and fondle in public." Shaking my head, I can't believe she brought that up. "Whatever you say, Penn. Now, I'm going to head to the store and get the ingredients for smoky chicken."

"That's Fletcher's favorite," I state.

"I know what my grandson's favorite food is." Her face morphs into that proud nana grin she gets when she talks about him. "And I know what's good for my son too." She grabs a pen and starts her shopping list. After her list is written, she looks to me and smiles. "What are your plans while you have the house to yourself?"

"I'm going to spend some time at the beach with Tatum." As soon as I tell Mom that, I know I've made a mistake because that look reappears on her face.

"Yes, and there's nothing serious going on with you two, considering you spent the morning together."

Before I can tell her it's not serious and just some fun, she's already heading out the door to the store.

Finishing my water, I head into my room and change into my board shorts. This thing with Tatum is just fun, I'm not falling in love with her. I will never fall in love with another woman again. I don't ever want to open myself up to the possibility of pain like that ever again.

59

TATUM

Knowing if I don't apply some sunscreen, I'm going to look like a lobster, again, I sit up, cross my legs, and grab my sunscreen. Squirting some of the cream into my hands, I begin to slather up my arms, chest, and stomach.

"If we weren't on a public beach, I'd demand you slide your hand underneath that fabric you call a bikini and make you pleasure yourself before I sink myself balls deep inside of you," a deep voice growls from behind me.

Looking over my shoulder, I wink at him. "If you play your cards right, maybe we can reenact that one of these days."

"That comment is locked away in the vault," he tells me and continues to stand there. He stares at me running my hands over my body, rubbing the cream in.

"Can you get out of my way? You're blocking my sun."

"I'm going in for a quick dip, you want to join me?"

"Not yet, I'm just going to sit here and unabashedly ogle your body and imagine all the dirty, dirty things I'm going to do to you with the chocolate dicks that I'm going to order for when we get back to Lockhart Falls."

"Can't believe I'm going to say this, but I can't wait for your chocolate dicks to arrive."

His comment causes me to snort in an unladylike manner and shake my head. "Go for your dip and leave me to ogle in peace."

"Yes, ma'am." He mock salutes me, turns on his heel, but before he races off, I reach up and grab his hand.

"Before you run off, any chance you can put some sunscreen on my back?"

"If it means my hands can slip and slide over your delectable body and ass, I'll cream you all day, every day." His eyes widen when he registers what he just said. "That came out dirtier than I anticipated."

"I don't mind," I tell him with a wink, "and for the record, I like you creaming me."

"Babe, you can't say shit like that to me when we are on a public beach."

Shrugging at him, I throw the sunscreen up to him, roll over onto my stomach and place my hat next to me. He drops down onto the towel and pushes my hair over my shoulder. His fingertips graze my shoulder blade and I have to hold in a moan. That ever-so-light touch sets my body ablaze.

Penn squeezes some sunscreen into his hand and begins to rub it into my skin. His hands on my body feel amazing and my clit begins to thrum, and I have to press my thighs together to ease the ache building.

He leans down and whispers into my ear, "I saw that thigh press, is my touching you like this turning you on?"

Turning my head to face him, I nod. "Very much so."

"Maybe I should do something about that."

"Not here on the beach, anyone could see."

"There's a whole ocean just over there." He flicks his thumb toward said ocean and waggles his eyebrows at me.

Rolling over to my back, I stare up at him. "I think you

missed a bit." For emphasis, I run my hands up my chest and over my breasts.

"Didn't you already rub cream there?"

"I did but *you* didn't. Better to be safe than sorry when it comes to sunscreen and sunburn."

"This is true. It's my civic duty to make sure you don't burn your tits."

"Exactly, now cream me." Now it's my turn for my eyes to widen. "I didn't mean for that to sound so dirty."

"Considering you just fondled your own tits, I call bullshit, but I will happily cream you … now with the sunscreen and later with my …"

"Jizz. Cum. Spunk. Semen, take your pick."

Shaking his head, he leans down and kisses me. Reaching up, I place my hands over his shoulders and pull him down to me. He holds his weight on his arms so as to not crush me and kisses me back. His tongue pushes into my mouth. His knees push into my pussy, hitting my clit in just the right spot. I know we're on a beach in public, but this man causes me to lose my mind. Swiveling my hips on his knee, I begin to ride him and out of nowhere the most amazing orgasm washes over me, and I moan into his kiss.

Breaking the connection, he pulls back and stares down at me. "Well, that was unexpected."

"Mmmhmpf," is all I can breathlessly manage as a reply.

"How about a swim now?" he asks me. "Maybe help a guy out with a hard problem?" That's when I notice his rock-hard cock.

"It's my civic duty to help you with that hard problem, and one I will happily oblige."

Penn hops up off me and offers me his hand. Placing my hand in his, he laces our fingers together and we head to the water so I can help him with his problem. Then he helps me with a throbbing that appeared between my thighs while I was helping him with his problem.

Once we're both problem free, we head back to our things. Penn lies down on his towel, resting on his elbows. He's an Adonis, there is no other word to describe him.

"Just so you know, when I got the morning-after pill this morning—"

Before he can reply, a curt, "I knew you were a heathen and that statement just confirms my thoughts," comes from Teri. Behind her I see Fletcher and Sandy flying a kite in the distance, thankful they're not here to hear this conversation.

"Excuse me?" I hiss, my hackles raised.

"The Pill and especially the morning-after pill violates the right to life. You should be ashamed of yourself, you … you whore. And you …" She looks to Penn, who is now standing beside me. "What would Maddie say about this? This woman is making you do reckless things and be irresponsible. I've never been more disappointed in you, and Maddie would be too. She'd be disgusted with who you are banging, and mad you're allowing this harpy around her son." She crosses her arms and shakes her head, glaring at me.

I'm waiting for Penn to speak up, to defend me. To defend us but he just stands there and blinks. Shaking my head, I look to Teri. "You have no right to but into my and Penn's relationship. What we choose to do is between us."

"It does involve me because Fletcher is my grandson. You will never replace his mother. Maddie is ten times the woman you are."

"I'm not trying to replace her," I snap back at her. The audacity of this woman causes my blood to boil. "And I'm trying to be there for Penn too."

"He has a wife," she throws at me.

"I know that. Just like I have a fiancé—"

"What?" she screeches like the evil banshee she is, garnering the attention of those around us. "You really are a whore. You have a fiancé and you're slutting it up with my son-in-law."

I'm beyond angry now and I know if I stay here, I'll say something that I'll regret, and my hand will possibly collide with her smarmy holier-than-thou face. I turn to Penn, who I notice is still just standing there, not saying anything to defend me. He's staring out to sea as if Teri and I aren't even here. His nonchalance hurts. "I'm suddenly not feeling well, I'm going back to Kain's."

"He's probably not even your brother," Teri snaps. "Just another man in your harpy harem."

Ignoring her, I grab my things, throwing them haphazardly into my bag. "I'll see you later," I snap at Penn and then storm off, angry she said those things about me and super pissed off that Penn didn't say anything in my defense.

Tears begin to well in my eyes. I knew my happiness wouldn't last, but what hurts the most is he did nothing to defend me when it came to the horrible things Teri was saying. Maybe I don't know Penn as well as I think and maybe, just maybe, he is a douche after all.

60

TATUM

I'm in a shitty, foul, snappy mood when I return to Kain's. I'm slamming cupboards and breaking things left, right, and center. Kain senses my mood and says he's going to Thalia's. Him leaving his own home because of me only adds to my antsy disposition.

Needing a stiff drink, I open the liquor cabinet looking for the Fireball and when I come up empty, I growl in frustration. "Of course we're fucking out of Fireball." Spying the tequila, I reach for it. "Tequila it is then," I murmur to the empty house.

Grabbing a shot glass, I pour a glass and shoot it back. "Blergh," I hiss as the tart liquor burns its way down my esophagus. Pouring another, I bring it to my lips but I can't do it. Out of the corner of my eye, I see the margarita mix and smile. "Finally, something is going my way."

Pulling out a fancy glass, I mix myself a margarita and when I take that first sip, I close my eyes and sigh in delight as the flavors dance on my tongue. Taking another sip, my mood begins to brighten. Chugging it back, I quickly make another one and then I grab my Kindle and head outside and lose myself in my book. Hunter finally got the girl. His brother was less douchey and everyone is happy … for now.

"If only my life was happy," I mumble to myself.

Placing my Kindle next to me, I lean back and stare up at the sky. It's clear blue, reminding me of Penn's eyes. As if he senses I'm thinking about him, he appears in my peripheral vision. Turning to face him, I scowl over at him.

"Hey," he sheepishly says.

"Hey," I reply back.

A silence envelops us and it's awkward. It's never been like this before between us and I don't like it. "What are you doing here?"

"You stormed off."

"Your monster-in-law was out of line earlier and you did nothing to defend me. You just stood there and let her run me into the ground. In case you hadn't noticed, it takes two to tango, but in her eyes, you can do no wrong."

"It's not like that at all," he replies in her defense.

"Are you fucking shitting me right now?" I shout. "She hates me."

"She doesn't hate you; she just wants what's best for me."

"And clearly, I'm not that. I know I will never replace Mads in yours or Fletcher's eyes, and I'm not trying to. I just want to be with you. I want to build something with you. Be there when you need a shoulder to cry on—"

"I don't need you to fix me, Tatum," he hisses, "I'm not broken."

That sentence pisses me off. "I'm not trying to fix you, Penn," I sneer. "I'm trying to love you in a way that's different to what you had with Mads. After Kip, I never thought I'd be open to love again. But you and Fletcher have worked your way into my heart, and I thought we might have been starting something, but I'm not going to stand by while your monster-in-law tears me apart for loving you. Maddie wouldn't want you to stand there and do nothing either."

"Don't you fucking dare bring her into this," he growls.

His voice is laced with pure venom and I have never seen him angry like this before.

"It's the truth, Penn," I snap at him. "From the little I know of her and from what you've told me, she would want you to move on. To be happy and you know it. Right now, you're hiding behind Teri and her words because you're scared, and I get that. I'm scared too, but living in fear is no way to live."

"But I still love her," he states, dropping his shoulders as if he's defeated.

"And that's okay, Penn. I still love Kip and I always will, but guess what?"

"What?" He lifts his gaze to mine and I see a broken and confused man.

"There's room for two in my heart, well, three if you include Fletcher. I think there's room in yours for me too, but you're hiding behind Teri's actions because you're scared of loving me back." He goes to interrupt me, but I'm not finished so I raise my hand in a stop motion. "As I said, I'm scared too, Penn. So fucking scared. The thought of letting someone in again is more frightening than running into a burning building, but I'm willing to try because this last week, here with you guys, has been the best week in a long time." Standing up, I grab my Kindle and empty glass before I look over at him. "You need to decide if I'm worth it. Listen to your heart, Penn, not someone else's words."

With that, I turn my back on him and walk inside, tears building in my eyes with each step I take away from him. As soon as the slider closes behind me, I draw the blinds, drop to my knees, and cry. We could have had something special but one person's words and hate have ruined that. I'm glad this happened before I got in too deep because I cannot go through another loss, it would ruin me.

61

PENN

As the slider clicks closed and I watch her close the blinds on me, I start to wonder if I just made the biggest mistake in letting her go. She's right, I should have defended her. Teri was out of line, but Teri was correct in that I'm being reckless with Tatum. I need to be a better father for Fletcher but most of all, I'm scared to open my heart again. I'm falling for her, fast—just like I did with Mads—but what I feel and have, had, with Tatum is different than what I had with Mads. I can't lose anyone again. I wouldn't survive another loss, but as I stand here and stare at the closed door, I realize I have already lost her.

Turning on my heel, I head back to the house. "Dad," Fletcher excitedly calls out when he sees me. He and Mom are sitting at the outdoor table and he's eating half a watermelon, literally. Mom has cut it in half and given him a spoon and from the looks of his face and chest, it's a juicy one.

"Hey, buddy, you got a little something on your chin." I ruffle his hair before pulling out the seat next to him. He uses the back of his arm and smears watermelon juice and seeds all over himself. "What do you say, after you finish your watermelon, we head to the water to wash off and have a quick splash before we head back for dinner?"

"Can Tatum come too?"

Shaking my head, I tell him, "Not this afternoon. I wanna spend some time with my lil' man."

"Okay, Dad." He digs back into his watermelon and leaves me to my thoughts, which are once again on Tatum.

"You okay?" Mom asks. Not wanting to get into it, I just nod.

"Finished," Fletcher declares. He lifts up the watermelon carcass and spills juice all over the table. "Oops." He giggles.

"You go for a swim with Dad and I'll clean this mess up."

"Thanks, Nanna," he says, smiling at Mom. "Let's go, Dad."

He pushes back from the table, grabs my hand, and begins to pull. Letting him think he pulled me up, I lift him onto my back and race toward the water. He giggles and it's music to my ears. I wish Mads was here to see how amazing our little man is. He's growing up so quickly. Before I know it, he'll be off to college and I'll be all alone again.

Fletcher and I have an amazing afternoon on the beach together, just the two of us. It reaffirms that all I need is Fletcher in my life. "Okay, buddy," I say when I realize the time. "Time to head home and get ready for dinner."

"Can Tatum come to dinner?" he asks just as we reach the deck.

"No!" Teri sneers.

"But—" Fletcher tries to plead his case, but Teri raises her hand at him.

"I said no. That woman is NOT coming to dinner with us."

"Teri," I berate her, "you don't get to speak to my son like that. Apologize now for being rude." My inner voice is telling me I should have said that earlier today too, but I shake that thought away as I stare at Teri, waiting for her apology.

"Sorry, Fletcher. I just want a family dinner tonight since Grandad and I have to leave tomorrow."

"Okay," Fletcher agrees and with that, he skips inside to get ready.

Stepping around Teri, she reaches out and grabs my arm. "She's not coming, right?" Teri asks me.

"No," I confirm, with a headshake. "She and I had a fight earlier."

"Good, you don't need a woman like that in your life, Penn. It's for the best to part ways from that woman. You and Fletcher will be fine on your own. Maddie will watch over the two of you and guide you when needed. That's all you need."

Standing here, I process her words and nod. Mads has been there watching over us. On several occasions, I've felt her and when Fletch was in that bus accident, everyone said it was as if someone was watching over him. Sure, Tatum was with him, but she wasn't there during the initial crash, that was all Mads. "I need to get ready," I mutter. Offering her a smile, I head inside to get ready for dinner.

We've been seated at our table and the waitress has just left with our drink order when Fletcher screeches, "Tatum!" We all turn to where Fletcher is running and see Tatum with her brother, his girlfriend, Thalia, his roommate, Burton, and his girlfriend, Nix. The rest of her group take their seats and Tatum walks toward Fletch.

Teri mumbles something under her breath. From the scowl on her face, I guess it's something untoward and going by Mom's frown, whatever Teri said was harsh. Dad hollers for the waitress to bring us water and Sandy focuses on the menu. And me? I stand up and stare at Tatum and notice that her usual spark is gone.

"Hey," I say in greeting when I reach her and Fletcher.

"Hey, Penn," she replies and like earlier, an awkward silence envelops us. "What are you doing here?"

"Having dinner. You?"

"Same." And then that awkward silence is back.

"Can you sit with us, Tatum?" Fletcher asks her, grabbing her hand and starting to pull her toward our table, but she pulls her hand free and then drops down to his height, like she often does when chatting with him.

"Thanks for the offer, buddy, but I'm here with my brother and you need to spend time with your family before they leave."

"Can we go to the rock pools again tomorrow, together?"

"Sorry, buddy, I'm heading home tomorrow," she tells him.

"You're leaving?" I ask her. "I thought you were here 'til the end of the month."

"Plans change," she murmurs, and I see the hurt etched on her face but even with sadness marring her beautiful face, she still looks stunning.

"You look beau—"

"Don't finish that sentence, Penn. You don't get to compliment me as if nothing happened earlier." She stands up shaking her head, "I … I can't do this." She turns to Fletch and plasters on a fake smile. "See ya later, Fletch." She ruffles his hair and without another word, she turns and walks away from us.

Fletcher returns to our table, leaving me standing in the middle of the restaurant feeling alone and upset. That feeling of dread once again washes over me. Tatum looks up, and across the restaurant our gazes meet. She quickly looks away and that feeling of regret and unease from seeing her upset slams into my chest. Leaving my heart aching and me wondering if there is room for her in there too. But I guess I'll never know because from the look on her face, I'm mud to her.

62

TATUM

... three weeks later

"IT'S THAT TIME OF YEAR AGAIN," MOM SINGSONGS AS SHE walks into the firehouse, earning an eye roll from me.

"Yay." I feign excitement.

"Ohhh, hush, Tatum. You put on this front but I know, deep down, you love this annual ball just as much as the rest of us."

"As I say each year, I would rather run into a burning building or rescue a cat."

"You can live in denial all you want, a mother knows."

"Let's agree to disagree, Mom. Now, hit me with your ideas for this year."

For the next three, long, painful hours, Mom and I nut out everything for this year's event. Once it's all organized, she sneaks me away for a coffee. She's up at the counter ordering when the hairs on the back of my neck stand on end and when I look up, I see Penn and Phine walk into the coffee shop.

Our eyes lock.

My heart skips every second beat.

The air is sucked from my lungs.

My mouth goes dry.

Why does he have to be so mouth-watering? And I get the irony that my mouth is currently dry, but there's a part of my body with lips that is currently moist. Very, very moist.

Sitting here, I pray he just goes to the counter but fate is a fickle bitch and he comes this way after obviously giving his order to Phine, who joins Mom in line.

"Hey," he croons when he stops before me.

"Hey," I say in return.

The two of us just stare at one another. "Can I sit?" he asks, breaking the silence.

"I … I don't think that's a good idea." However, he ignores my answer and sits down anyway. "Or you can take a seat." I huff.

"You look good."

"I know." My eyes rake over his face and I notice he looks tired, but he still looks amazing, and then I add, "So do you."

"I know," he throws back at me with that smirk that lights his face up. "But you and I both know I look like shit. I … I've missed you," he quietly murmurs the last three words. Lifting his left arm, he runs his fingers through his hair from his forehead back and then grips the back of his neck. Something I notice he does when he's anxious, but my eyes are locked on his arms and the new artwork on his tricep coming up from his elbow.

"You got a new tattoo," I say, stating the obvious.

He stretches out his arm and rolls it over, allowing me to fully see it. Flames lick up his arm from his elbow and emerging from the flames is a phoenix. Its wings wrap about his upper arm. Reaching out, I trace my finger ever so gently over the flames. "It's exquisite," I murmur.

"You're exquisite," he replies.

Shaking my head, I lift my hand from his arm and raise my palm to him in a stop motion. "Please," I plead. "Don't do this, Penn," I mumble in a hushed tone. Looking to the table, I inhale deeply.

Now it's his turn to beg, "Please, Tatum, I ..." He doesn't finish his thought, and when I lift my gaze back up, I come face-to-face with the bluest of blue eyes that I still dream about. Then the hurt of what happened crashes into me.

"*You* let me go, Penn. *You* did nothing to defend me. *You* didn't fight for me and with everything you and I have been through, you fight for the one you love, like, whatever, but you didn't. And it hurt. It hurt." Pushing my chair back, I swallow back a sob and shake my head. "I ... I have to go."

Racing out of the coffee shop, I run all the way back to the station house. Pushing through the staff door, I race through the common room and into the bunk rooms. Slamming the door behind me, it bounces back open from the force. Dropping onto the far bottom bunk, I roll over and throw myself onto the mattress. Burying my face into the pillow, I scream out in frustration.

"Tatum," Dad's voice startles me as he sits on the edge of the bed next to me. "What's wrong?" He touches my shoulder in that Dad way and it causes the dam to break and I cry into my pillow.

"Why wasn't I enough, Dad? Why?" I cry into the pillow.

"Ohh, Tater Tot." He begins to rub circles on my back, and it reminds me of when I was ten and Damon King uninvited me to his Nerf birthday party 'cause I was a girl. Dad soothed me and it included a back rub like this but eighteen years later, I don't think a rub will fix the hurt this time.

"I took a chance and tried to move on, but he threw it back in my face as if I was nothing. Why, Dad? Why?"

"He's clearly a moron, Tater Tot. Want me to make him disappear? The guys and I are back burning near the falls in the next few days, I'm sure something can accidentally happen."

"Thanks, Dad, but Fletcher needs his dad, even if he has a

douchedad for a dad."

"What can I do then? I hate seeing you upset like this."

"Nothing, Dad. There's nothing you can do, unless you can make him love me back?"

"You love him?"

Rolling to my back, I stare at the bunk above. "Yes. No. I don't know." But that's a lie, I do know. I wipe away the tears, sit up, look over to Dad, and I nod. "Yeah, Dad, I think I do." I smile through my tears and chortle, "Dad, he pisses me off like no tomorrow but when it's just he and I, everything around us ceases to exist. He's happy for me to still love Kip, and I feel the same about Mads. We understand that. Even though I'm the one who walked away, I can't stop thinking about him. These past three weeks have been rough to get through."

"Why didn't you say anything?"

"Because I'm twenty-eight years old, I should have my life together by now."

"Tatum, there's no set timeline for when you should have XYZ locked down in life. Hell, you've suffered an unimaginable loss and you managed to pull yourself out of the funk that it left you in."

"Funk? I was in more than a funk when I lost Kip, Dad."

"Funk, funking hole, call it whatever you want but, Tater Tot, you rose up and started to live. You opened your heart up again, and yes, it didn't quite pan out, but guess what?"

"What?"

"Next time you do, it will be everything you dreamed love could be."

"I've had an all-consuming love, Dad." I look to the mattress and wring my fingers together in my lap. "I don't think I'm due to get a second, second chance at love."

"Who said the first second chance is over?" My head snaps up toward the bunk room door and my breath hitches when I see *him* standing in the doorway.

63

PENN

"Penn," she whispers, "what are you doing here?" But before she can answer, the fire alarm goes off and she has to go, and I'm left standing in the empty firehouse wondering how I can make her smile again.

After watching the crew do their thing, I dejectedly make my way back to the garage with my hands in my pockets. "Coffee is in your office," Phine tells me when I enter the workshop.

"Thanks," I mutter and when I enter the office, I see Mom sitting behind my desk. She looks like the cat that got the canary. "Hey," I say in greeting, dropping onto the ratty sofa that I really need to replace.

"Don't you hey me, how did it go?"

"How did you know?" I ask, genuinely confused.

"I saw you go into the station house and that can only mean you pulled your head out of your ass and went to get your girl. My feeling that you two are meant to be is still strong."

"Well, your feelings are wrong, we didn't get to talk."

"Why not, Penn Brookes Jr.? I'm still mad you listened to that woman and not your heart. I get she's grieving the loss of her daughter; I couldn't fathom losing you or Wren, but life goes on. As harsh as that is, it's true. You deserve to be happy, both of you do, and you two together understand unimaginable loss. You understand the love you have for Mads and her fiancé—"

"Kip. Her fiancé's name was Kip."

Mom nods. "You each understand the love you had for Kip and Mads respectively. You accept they still hold a piece of your heart, alongside the pieces that now belong to each other."

"Mom, I was a douche, I don't think I'll get another chance with her. I really hurt her."

"So give her no choice but to give you a chance, and if you have to play dirty, you use Fletcher to help you. He loves her just as much as you do."

"I don't love her, Mom. It's too soon for love."

"Says the man who loved his first wife from the moment he saw her."

"That was different."

"Bullshit, Penn. Love is love. You can't help who it's with or when it comes along. It happens when it's supposed to and you two are meant to be. I fe—"

"Feel it. I know, Mom, you keep reminding me that you feel it with Tatum. After seeing her today, I want to try, but I think I blew my chance."

"Nonsense, you just need to man up and get the girl."

"I agree," I tell her, nodding my head, "but first, I need to finish Mrs. Jenkinson's car, and tonight I'll come up with a plan to win her back."

"That's my boy. I'm so proud of you, Penn."

"Thanks, Mom, I had great guidance from you and Dad."

"Just like I had great guidance from Nan and PopPop. Now, how are you going to win Tatum back?"

"That's the million-dollar question, Mom. She's not the type of girl to fall for flowers and chocolates and gifts, so whatever I do, it needs to be epic. I'm open to ideas," I tell her. "How about you and Dad come over for dinner tonight and after Fletch is in bed, we can brainstorm."

"Sounds like a plan." Mom gets this wistful look on her face. "I'm so proud of you, Penn."

"How can you be proud when I destroyed a girl's heart?"

"Love makes us do crazy things, so don't beat yourself up too much over that. It's what you do next that will define you as a man. Now, get to work and I'll see you tonight."

With that, Mom hops up, kisses me on the cheek, and leaves.

The rest of the day flies by. I've just popped the casserole into the oven and still have no clue what I'm going to do to win Tatum back. There's a knock at the door and when I open it, I expect to see Teri and Sandy, who are visiting for the weekend. Instead, I'm met with a morose-looking Mom and a feeling of dread settles in my stomach.

Reaching out, I pull her in for a hug. She wraps her arms around me tightly and hiccups on a sob. Pulling her away from me, I hold her upper arms. "What's wrong?" I ask her and then I realize Dad isn't with her and my stomach drops. "Where's Dad?"

"He's … he's fine and at home still," Mom says, pulling free from my hold. She reaches down and takes my hands and squeezes. That feeling of dread intensifies. My heart starts to race. "I was at the store, there's been an accident."

"Teri and Sandy?" I question, but she shakes her head.

"No, it's Tatum."

64

TATUM

"Tatum," Dad growls, "get your head in the game."

"Yes, Captain," I reply with a nod and then I get back to it, but my mind keeps drifting to why Penn followed me back to the station and what he meant by "Who said the first second chance is over?" Because from where I'm standing, whatever we had is over. He let me walk away and it's been three fucking weeks of silence from him.

"You good?" Calvin asks me.

"Yes. No. I don't know."

"Should you be here?" he questions, and my hackles raise that he doesn't think I can do my job.

"I'm fine," I hiss, "now let's put this bitch out."

"There's the ballbuster we know and love." He winks. "Now, as you said, let's put this bitch out."

As the owner found out, you should not start a bonfire with gasoline and you definitely should not burn old tires, plastic, rubber, or light one near propane cylinders. The owner is extremely lucky that when the propane cylinders—plural—exploded, Calvin and I weren't killed.

Calvin and I were walking around to the other side of the fire when a prickly feeling washed over me, and I stopped midstep. I called out for Calvin to stop. He turned to face me just as the first explosion went off. He was thrown off his feet and tumbled to the ground like a sack of shit. I raced over to him, but before I reached him, another explosion detonated, throwing me backward.

My head hit the ground with a thud and my eyes closed. Within the darkness of my mind, Kip appears before me. He's sitting on a beach. The sky is clear, crystal clear. Kip looks content and peaceful. He looks up and like the first time I laid eyes on him, our gaze connects and that feeling of contentment washes over me when he smiles.

"Kip," I murmur but the sound of my voice echoes in my head.

"You are just as beautiful as I remember."

"Kip," I mutter again.

"I will always love you, Tatum Prudence Summers, always and forever. Let him in. Let him love you like I love you. Love him like you love me. Live. Laugh. Love." Before I can reply, the image of him vanishes before me.

Opening my eyes, I see Dad standing above me. "Tater Tot, can you hear me?"

"Kip," I whisper his name again.

"Where's the ambulance?" Dad shouts. The shrillness of his voice echoes through my head and I close my eyes again. "Stay with me, Tatum, stay with me, baby."

"I'm fine," I tell him. "I just have a headache." Pushing myself up, I rub the back of my head and blink a few times to blink away the black-and-white spots. "How's Calvin?" I ask.

"Bloody lucky to be alive, you both are. Are you really okay?"

"I'm fine, Dad."

The paramedics arrive and do their thing before Calvin and I are loaded into the vehicles for transport to Lockhart Falls Memorial. In the explosions, Calvin was struck with debris and as a result he has burns to his face and hands, and a possible concussion from being thrown through the air. I was lucky in that I was just thrown through the air and need to be assessed for a concussion. I'm ninety-nine percent sure I'm fine, but regulations state that I need to be taken in for assessment.

"You know," I say to Calvin, "if you wanted a few days off, you just had to ask, you didn't need to get blown up."

"I'll remember that for next time but, Summers, don't make me laugh. Crinkling my face up hurts at the moment."

"I can't help it that I'm naturally funny."

"I think you hit your head hard, you're delusional."

Flipping him the bird, I chuckle to myself. Then I look over to Calvin. "Is it weird that when that all went down, I felt like someone was there. Silently warning me that something was about to happen?"

"Is that why you called out to me?"

Nodding, I bite my lip. "I ... I think Kip was watching over us because when I was knocked to the ground, he appeared before me, telling me to let him in." Calvin just stares at me and rapidly blinks like I'm a crazy person. "You think I'm crazy, don't you?"

"I don't believe in that mumbo-jumbo crap but what I do know is that man loved you to the moon and back. And I'm positive, even in death, he'll be looking out for you so if you 'felt'"—he air quotes felt—"Kip there with us, then I believe you." He looks to the heavens. "If you were there, thanks, dude, for looking out for us."

"Really? Just like that 'cause I believe, you believe?"

"Sure, why not. The universe works in mysterious ways, Tatum. No one knows what happens after death, so anything is possible. Now, I'm going to lie back and close my eyes, my face hurts."

"Now you know how we feel looking at you every day."

He flips me the bird and then closes his eyes. I watch him for a few moments and then I do the same. I'm jolted awake when we are being unloaded at the hospital. My eyes open but I quickly close them again when the fluorescent lights above blind me. Tilting my head to the side, I open my eyes again and watch as the hospital staff does their thing.

Calvin is whisked one way and I'm whisked the other. It's a slew of poking, prodding, blood work, and scans. A few hours later, I'm all cleared to leave. With my discharge papers in hand, I ask where Calvin's room is and pop in to check on him before I leave.

Due to his burns and mild concussion, he'll be in the hospital for a few days, maybe even longer. I told him I'll bring some things up for him tomorrow 'cause right now, I'm going home for a shower, a glass of wine, and my bed.

Mom, Dad, and I are walking toward the exit when I hear someone yell my name. Turning around, I see Penn standing at the information desk, demanding details on me. "Is she alive?" he growls. "At least tell me that."

"Sir," the lady behind the desk shouts, just as I say, "Penn?" He spins to face me and as soon as he sees me, he races over and wraps his arms around me.

"Thank God you're okay."

"Wwww … what are you doing here?"

"I heard you were in an accident an—"

Interrupting him, I ask, "Why are you here?" He ignores me and continues on his rant.

"And no one was telling me shit. I … I thought you were dead and … and I can't lose you. Not again, I can't go through that again. I'm sorry I was such a douchehole and pushed you away. I made a mistake. I'm so, so sorry, Tatum. So, so sorry."

"Penn," I repeat his name again because I don't know what to say right now.

He takes my hands in his and squeezes. A warmth radiates through my body at his touch and my heart begins to beat differently. "Let me in, Tatum, please. Let me love you. Live with you. Laugh with you."

"Live. Laugh. Love," I whisper. "Live. Laugh. Love," I repeat again and smile.

"Why are you smiling?"

"This is going to sound crazy but when I was knocked out from the explosion, Kip came to me. I know it sounds insane, but he told me to live, laugh, love, and then you come here and say the exact same thing. If that's not a sign that we're supposed to give this a go, then I don't know what is."

"What are you saying?"

"I want this, I want to live. Laugh. Love with you and Fletcher."

"Really?" he asks.

Nodding, I bite my lip and stare into the blue eyes I've been missing for the last three weeks. "Really, really, Penn. I want to give this a go but what about Teri? She hates me."

"She doesn't hate you and I don't care what she thinks. My happiness matters more than her feelings. Will I always love Mads? Yes, yes, I will, but there's room in my heart for you too. She's just going to have to learn to deal with that."

"Are you sure?"

"Positive, plus Mom has her feeling thing and she's never been wrong before."

"Huh?" I question, confused right now.

"That's not important, all that's important is I have you in my life." He pauses and smiles. "Fletcher is going to shit his pants when I come home with you 'cause I'm never letting you go, now that I have you."

"You want me to live with you?"

"Live. Laugh. Love. Can't do that if we don't live together."

"Well, we can." But the thought of not waking up next to Penn every morning doesn't sit well with me. "Fuck it," I throw out there, "life's too short to not take a risk, so let's live. Laugh. Love together under the one roof."

"Really?"

"Really, really," I tell him. "I love you, Penn Brookes Jr. and I cannot wait to live my life with you and Fletcher." Gripping his cheeks, I cover his mouth with mine and in the middle of the hospital foyer, I kiss Penn like my life depends on it.

He breaks the kiss and rests his forehead against mine. "I love you too, Tatum."

Penn pulls away from me and steps toward mom and dad. "I want to formally introduce myself to you both, I'm Penn Brookes and I'm hopelessly in love with your daughter."

"Ohh I like him," mom swoons, "I'm Ginny." She pulls him in for a hug and whispers something to him that causes him to smile and nod. When he's free he turns to dad and offers him his hand, Dad gives him in 'dad' look but he takes his outstretched hand and shakes it. "You can call me Shaun."

A silence envelopes the four of us but it's broken when mom looks to dad, "You owe me a spa weekend," she says, and I can't help but laugh.

"Ginny, this is one bet I'm happy to lose because look at that smile on our daughter's face."

"I promise to make her smile like this each and every day," Penn tells them, pulling me into his side and pressing a kiss to my temple.

"You better, I know how to make a body disappear in a fire."

"Kain said the same thing to me once."

"Like father like son but, Penn, you hurt her again—"

"I won't, sir. The last three weeks not seeing her was shit. I don't ever want to feel like that again."

"Good," Dad states.

With the formal introductions over and an agreement to go to dinner tomorrow night, we say our goodbyes and then he and Mom leave. Turning to face Penn, I smile. "Take me home, Penn."

"Home, I love hearing you say that, Tatum. Now let's go home so I can love you forever."

Lacing my fingers through Penn's, we exit the hospital and head toward his car and home, together.

Life is a roller coaster and the ride so far for me has been a wild one. I went from the highest of highs, happy and in love. About to marry the man of my dreams and in an instant, I was experiencing the lowest of lows and became stuck in a vortex of grief. I never thought I would smile again but one day, I met a little boy on a beach looking for cocnuts and that little boy changed my life when I met his dad. At first, I liked his son better but as time went on his dad grew on me and, once again, I opened my heart to love. The love we share is different than the love I had with Kip, but it's still love, and I love Penn, with all my heart. Just like I still love Kip. I always will but there's room in my heart for both of them. Moving on doesn't mean I've forgotten; it means I'm healing. I'm a stronger and better person for what I went through, and I now appreciate things in a different way. After the ashes settled, I rose up and took flight again. Now with Penn and Fletcher by my side, I'm going to live, laugh, and love.

EPILOGUE
TATUM

… *two years later*

"Hurry up, Penn, Fletch, we're going to be late," I shout as I stand in front of the bathroom mirror and slip my earrings in. The hairs on the back of my neck prickle and when I look up, I see Penn's reflection in the mirror. He's standing in the entrance to our en suite, leaning against the frame, looking totally fuckable in his suit.

"The only reason we're going to be late is because I'm going to have to strip you out of this sexy as hell dress and fuck you."

Spinning around to face Penn, I unabashedly eye-fuck my husband, yep, husband. Penn proposed last weekend in front of our family and friends at our baby shower—ohh, yeah, I'm eight months pregnant right now. This afternoon, Penn and I ducked down to city hall and with Fletcher as our witness, we made it official and became man and wife. He wanted me to have his last name before our little man arrives. Life's too short to not leap, so I leaped and officially became Tatum Prudence Brookes.

"As much as I'd love to fuck my husband and consummate this marriage of ours, you are going to have to wait for a few more hours because I need to get to The James Hotel and help Mom out. I already skipped out on this afternoon, to you know, get hitched. I can't leave her in the lurch again."

"But—" he whines. Walking over to him, I press my fingers to his lips.

"But nothing, dear husband of mine. You and your dick can wait a few hours and because I'm such a giving person, I'm going to let you do that thing with your tongue."

"Which thing would that be?" he asks, pulling me into his arms to stare into my eyes.

"You know which thing I'm referring to." Waggling my eyebrows, I lean up and place a quick kiss on his lips. "AAAAAAND since I'm such an amazing wife, I'll do that thing with mine that you love too."

"Tonight is going to be long … and hard." To reiterate his point, he tries to rub his long and hard dick against me, but my protruding belly is in the way, so he grabs my hand and places it over his junk.

"Yes, I'm aware my husband has a long and hard dick, but you'll be fine. Now, let's go." Giving his junk a gentle squeeze, I step around him and head into our room. Picking up my clutch from the end of the bed, I walk out to meet Fletcher, who is still in his suit from earlier this afternoon.

"You ready?" I ask him as I walk over and straighten up his tie.

"Yeah, Mom, I am."

My eyes widen at his use of Mom. "You … you just called me Mom."

"Yeah," he blurts with a shoulder shrug. "With you and Dad getting hitched that officially makes you my mom, even if you've been my mom for a few years now."

"But Mads is your mom."

"Yep, and so are you. Therefore, I have two moms."

"Fletch," I cry and do that rapid blink thing to stop myself from crying. Pulling him into my arms, I hug him tightly to me. "I love you, Fletch."

"Love you too, Mom, now let's go. Granny G will be mad if we're late. Plus, Cappy and me ..." He stops himself, his eyes wide at nearly spilling the secret he has.

"You and Cappy what?"

"Naaaarthing," he draws the word out.

"Fletcher Sanford Brookes, what are you hiding from me?"

"Ohhhh, you just got middle named," Penn chortles, joining us.

"Our son here is hiding something from us ... and it involves my dad."

"Shit, this can't be good." He looks to Fletcher. "What are you and Shaun up to?"

"It's nothing. We just ... shit—"

"Language, Fletcher," Penn berates him. "Now, what are you and Shaun hiding from us?"

"I can't tell you," he cries, and quickly adds, "but it's nothing bad. I just ... I just wanted to do something for Mom, and now because of my stupid big mouth I'm going to ruin the surprise."

"Fletch, you haven't ruined anything." Cupping his cheek, I smile. "I'm sorry I ruined your surprise, but it's technically still a surprise because I don't know anything about the specifics of said surprise."

"I guess," he dejectedly agrees.

"I promise to act super surprised if it makes you feel better."

"Not really, but what if Cappy gets mad at me?"

This causes me to laugh. "Please," I scoff, "you are the apple of his eye. There is nothing you could do that will make him mad at you."

"Really?"

"Really, really, but we really need to get going now, otherwise Granny G will be mad at me, and I'm not as cute as you, so I can't just smile and get away with it."

"I think you're pretty cute," Penn interjects.

Blowing him a kiss, I pull Fletcher in for a hug and kiss him on the head. "Love you, Fletch. Don't ever forget that."

"I love you too, Mom," he mumbles into my armpit, and hearing him call me Mom again causes the waterworks to flow.

"Dammit." I snivel. "Now I'm crying."

"Fix your beautiful face in the car 'cause if you go back in there, we will be late 'cause, well you know." He raises his eyebrows suggestively at me and with all the pregnancy hormones at the moment, I'm one-hundred-and-fifty percent wanting to take him into our bedroom to ride him for a quickie before we go.

Shaking my head, I laugh. "You need to learn self-control, dear husband of mine." *Just like I am.*

"I love hearing you call me that, wife of mine."

"Husband," I purr, "we need to go because," I step over to him and whisper, "the sooner we go, the sooner we can get back here and I can do that thing you love." Kissing him on the cheek, I step back, spin on my heel, and head toward the front door. Reaching for the handle, I look over my shoulder and see that Penn is still just standing there. "You coming?"

The sound of my voice snaps him out of his trance, and he walks down to meet us. "Let's do this."

We pull up at the hotel and Penn drops me and Fletcher off at the entrance and then goes and parks the car. While we are waiting, Mom and Dad arrive.

"Granny G, Cappy," Fletcher shouts and races over to hug Mom and Dad. I love the relationship he has with Mom and Dad. He's lucky in that he has three amazing sets of grandparents. Yes, I said three. Teri and I buried the hatchet and now, she and I have a lovely relationship. It was rocky for a while there but one day, Penn's mom pulled both of us aside when we were celebrating Penn's birthday and told us to pull our heads out of our asses. She scolded us and said that Maddie would be ashamed of both of us. That was the wake-up call we needed and, over time, the animosity started to melt away. I think when I got pregnant was when it all changed. She realized that we have to move on with our lives and I'm not trying to replace Maddie. She will always be Fletcher's mom, and I'm okay with that.

"You're glowing, Tatum," Mom says as she walks over to me. She takes my hands in hers and squeezes, then her eyes widen. "Tatum, why does the ring on your ring finger feel bigger?"

"Because it is." Pulling my hands free, I lift my left one up and show her the gorgeous wedding band sitting next to my just as gorgeous princess-cut engagement ring. "Surprise, we got married."

"But …. What? How? When?" It's not often that Ginny Summers is left speechless and this is going to sound bitchy, but her reaction has made today all the more amazing.

Smiling brightly, I tell her what transpired last night and this morning "… and then I became Mrs. Brookes."

"Ohhh, Tatum," Mom cries, "I'm so, so happy for you both."

"Why are you happy?" the man in questions asks as he joins us.

"Because you two got married." She pulls Penn in for a hug. "Welcome to the family, Penn."

"Thanks for letting me marry such an amazing woman," he tells them as he steps behind me and slides his arms around me, resting his hands on my bump.

"Well, I said yes, along with Shaun, when you asked but I wasn't there when she said 'I do' earlier." She looks to Fletcher, who just joined us with Dad. "And you, how could you keep a secret like this from me?"

"He's good at keeping secrets," Dad says, winking at

Fletcher. His little face lights up at the praise from Dad. I love the relationship that has developed between the two of them. I hope Dad has a similar one with Nugget. He walks over to me and pulls me in for a sideways hug. He kisses me on the temple and rests his hand on my bump.

Then he leans around me and looks over to Mom, grinning like the Cheshire cat. "And I'll take that bottle of Johnny Walker Blue next time we're at the liquor store."

"You two bet, again?"

"Yep," Dad proudly declares while Mom morosely grumbles, "Mmmhmpf."

Then she looks to Dad. "I think we need to stop because you're on a winning streak at the moment, and it's just not fair."

"It's what you get for betting on us," I tease her. "Now, let's get inside, I need some—"

"Nuggets," everyone singsongs at the same time. Chicken nuggets have been my craving during my pregnancy, hence the affectionate name of Nugget for our lil' man.

Sticking my tongue out at them, I lace my fingers through Penn's and offer Fletch my other hand. He looks at it but doesn't take it, he takes a deep breath. "Mom," he nervously asks, and I find myself beaming at hearing him call me Mom. "I got you something with the help of Cappy. I wanted you to know that Nugget and I love you to the moon and back." He turns and holds out a box to me.

Taking it from him, I lift the lid and cover my mouth, my eyes welling with tears. Inside is a rose gold necklace with the word 'Mom' on it.

"It's my own Carrie necklace," I tearfully blubber as I lift it out. Ever since I first saw *Sex and the City*, I've always wanted one, but I never buy myself jewelry and I'm so glad I waited because a 'Mom' one is so much better than a 'Tatum' one.

"I love it, Fletch. Thank you so much." Pulling him into me, I hug my son tightly. "I love you," I whisper, and Nugget gives an almighty kick as if to say don't forget about me. Resting my hand on my bump, I smile at my swollen belly. "And I love you too, Nugget."

Penn helps me put my necklace on and then hand in hand with my boys, we follow Mom and Dad into the hotel.

"You ladies really outdid yourself this year," Dad states as we enter the ballroom.

"I haven't been here since Mads worked here," Penn murmurs as we follow my parents.

"She was an amazing event planner. Don't tell Lauren I said that."

"Your secret is safe with me, but your dad is right, this is amazing," he says, smiling brightly at me.

"I always envisioned my wedding reception here after having the ceremony in the garden out back. Maybe we need to have a party here to celebrate our nuptials?"

"Maybe after Nugget arrives we can do that."

"Really?" I ask him, my voice high and full of excitement.

"I'd do anything for you, Mrs. Brookes."

"Why thank you, Mr. Brookes. How about you get us drinks and I'll grab some nuggets?"

"Deal." He presses a kiss to my lips and heads to the bar with Fletcher, while I go in search of my precious nuggets.

Standing at one of the high-top tables, I eat my precious nuggets when a pain in my lower back appears. "Stupid heels," I mumble to myself, rubbing the spot on my lower back, hoping to ease the pain. I'm the least girlie girl and whenever I dress up, I end up in pain, but then I look at my nuggets and all thought of back pain vanishes. Devouring the rest of my nuggets, I look up and watch as my husband saunters across the room and over to me.

"You look so fuckable standing there right now," Penn croons when he reaches me. Reaching up, he cups my cheek and my body comes alive.

"Wanna duck away for a quickie?" I offer.

"Really?" he excitedly asks.

"Really, really."

"Okay," he agrees. Offering him my hand, he takes hold and together we exit the ballroom. Finding a powder room nearby, we slip inside and I flip the lock. Leaning against the door, I wince again when that lower back twinge reappears.

"You okay, Tatum?"

"Fine," I tell him with a smile, "but if you don't fuck me in the next three point five seconds, I'm going to combust."

"Well, I suggest you turn around, lift up your dress, remove your G-string, place your hands on the door, and I will do exactly that."

Nodding, I do as he asks. The sound of his fly lowering echoes around the room and my heart rate increases as I wait. His hand rubs over my ass cheek and I feel a wetness begin to trickle down my leg, I've never been this wet before. "I need you," I pant.

"You have me," he whispers into my ear as he grips my hips and with one flick of his hips, he thrusts deep inside of me.

"Yes," I pant as more arousal drips out of me.

"You're so wet," he pants and he continues to thrust in and out of me.

That feeling builds low in my belly and back but it's more intense than usual and just as I reach my climax, there's an excessive amount of liquid that pours out of me and my eyes widen. "I ... I think my water just broke," I pant.

Penn stops mid thrust. "What did you say?"

"I think my water just broke. What I thought was pain from wearing heels was actually the start of my contract—" I don't get to finish that sentence because a pain like I've never felt before tears through my stomach. "Shit, Penn," I hiss through clenched teeth, "he's coming."

"Shit. Shit. Shit," Penn repeats as he pulls out of me and puts his now soft cock away. It's funny how quickly the impending arrival of your son can deflate a dick. "Okay, let's get you to the hospital."

"Mmmhmpf," I growl, breathing deeply.

When we are semi put together, Penn opens the door and we run into Mom. "Yes." She fist pumps. "I won. I told your father you two would bump uglies tonight."

"You can gloat later, Mom, I need to get to the hospital. Nugget is coming."

"What?" she hisses. "Now?"

"Yep. Can you—"

"We've got Fletcher. You just get to the hospital and deliver our little man safely."

Nodding, I clench my teeth and hold tightly onto Penn's hand as we exit the hotel and head to the hospital.

Three long painful hours later, Archer Kip Brookes comes screaming into the world. He has ten gorgeous fingers. Ten chunky toes, the cutest button nose, and cheeks I just want to gobble up.

My life may have been one huge loopy roller coaster but with Archer in my arms, I know that it's all been worth it. Yes, I've had the highest of highs, the lowest of lows, and everything in between. But as Eric Draven says in *The Crow* "It can't rain all the time" and that statement certainly came true for me when a little boy looking for cocnuts appeared in my life, introducing me to his douchedad, who wasn't so much of a douche after all. Just like me, he lost someone and was trapped in the rain, but together we give each other the shelter needed to survive the rain.

My entire life burned to the ground in an instant but after the ashes settled, like a phoenix, I rose up. Now with my little boy, Archer, in my life, along with his older brother, Fletcher, and my husband, Penn, by my side, I can do anything.

Am I afraid of burning again? Hell fucking yes, but if losing everything has shown me anything, it's that life goes on. Fireball whiskey is the best and love is what makes the world go around. I'm going to take life by the proverbial balls and I'm going to show the world just how strong Tatum Brookes nee Summers is, because when you knock me down, I'll get back up stronger than before and with my boys by my side, I'm unstoppable.

THE END!!!!!!!!!!

ACKNOWLEDGMENTS

Thank you for sticking with me on this journey. I'm sorry for what I did but if it makes you feel better, those scenes gutted me too. For the first time in my author career, I bawled as I was writing, so every emotion you felt, I felt it too … repeatedly … while I got those scenes perfect and throughout the editing process.

The idea for this story first came about in March 2020, but I wasn't ready, then I was invited to an anthology, and I decided to write Tatum and Kip's story. At first, it was just going to be about Kip and Tatum but then Penn and Maddie came along, and I knew Penn and Tatum needed each other so *After the Ashes* was born. I'm so glad I waited to write this story because I'm proud of it, so, so proud.

My editor, **Karen** from **Barren Acres Editing**. Thank you for once again working with me. You push me to be a better writer and I thank you for your support and guidance…even if after thirty plus books together I made you cry.

My proofreader, **Lisa** from **More Than Words Proofreading**. It's always a pleasure to work with you, thank you for going through After the Ashes with a fine tooth comb and polishing the final draft…and sorry for making you cry while you were in editor/proofer mode.

Amanda from **Amanda Walker Design & PA,** thank you for the gorgeous cover. As soon as I saw it back in 2020, I knew I had to have it for this story.

Kate Farlow from **Y'All That Graphic.** like with the original cover, as soon as I saw the pre-made, I knew I'd found the alternate cover for After the Ashes.

To the ladies of **Stupid AM Club**, thank you for getting up at stupid AM with me and smashing out the words. I could not ask for a more supportive or encouraging group of ladies and I cannot wait to get our shirts and mugs.

My beta babes, **Tara, Lana, Rhi, Margaret, Bec** and **Vi;** you ladies are amazing. Thanks for giving me your advice on making this book everything it could be. Like above, sorry for the tears but also #NotSorry

Thank you to my husband **Troy** and my munchkins, **Piper** and **Kade**. Without you guys, I wouldn't have the courage to do this. Your support and love mean the world to me and I love you all to the moon and back.

And finally, **you, my reader.** Thank you for taking a chance on me, again. I know After the Ashes is a little different, people still died but this time, I made you fall in love with those people first and the people I killed weren't the asshats from the story. This story shows that even after unimaginable loss, there is light and love at the end of the tunnel. Kip, Maddie, Penn and Tatum will always, always, hold a special place in my author heart.

Cheers,
Dana Xo

ALSO BY DL GALLIE

STAND ALONES

Antecedent

Doc Steel

Oops

Off the Books

Fractured:A driven world novel

Deck…the Balls

Secrets and Sunrises

Always in the Cards

Out of Nowhere

Love Me Like You Do

Never Let Me Go

Seven Nights

Seven Kisses

After the Ashes

PUCKING NOVELS

I Pucking Hate That I Love You

A Pucking Good Christmas

…and a few pucking more

FALLING NOVELS

These men make it hard not to fall for them

Falling for Dr. Kelly

Falling for Dr. Knight

Falling for Agent Cox

Falling for Agent Cruz

Falling:The Complete Collection

THE UNEXPECTED SERIES

When it comes to love, expect the unexpected

The Unexpected Gift

The Unexpected Letter

The Unexpected Package

The Unexpected Connection

The Unexpected series: The Complete Collection

THE CASTAWAY GROVE COLLECTION

Love has arrived in the Grove

Oasis

Unequivocal Love

Five Words

Broken Rules

…and a few more to come.

The Castaway Grove Collection, Vol 1

———

THE LIQUOR CABINET SERIES

Liquor has never been so disturbingly saucy

Malt Me (Book 1)

Tequila Healing (Book 2)

Wine Not (Book 3)

The Final Shot (Book 4)

The Liquor Cabinet: Series boxset

ABOUT THE AUTHOR

DL Gallie is from Queensland, Australia, but she's lived in many different places all over the world, including the UK and Canada. She currently resides in Central Queensland with her husband and two munchkins. She and her husband have been  together since she was sixteen, and although they drive each other crazy at times, she couldn't imagine her life without him.

Shortly after her son was born, DL began reading again. With encouragement from her husband, she picked up the pen and started writing, and now the voices in her head won't shut up.

DL enjoys listening to music, drinking white wine in the summer, red wine in the winter, and beer all year round. She's also never been known to turn down a cocktail, especially a margarita.